# PROJECT APEX

MICHAEL BRAY

*"I do not see why man should not be as cruel as nature"*
**— Adolf Hitler**

*"The last enemy that shall be destroyed is death."*
**— J.K. Rowling**

*'Multiply, vary, let the strongest live and the weakest die."*
**— Charles Darwin**

# CHAPTER ONE

CONGO BASIN
AFRICA
AUGUST 7th 1999

ELEVEN DAYS INTO HIS expedition, Richard Draven's skin was a blanket of mosquito bites. He swatted the droning insects away from his face, temporarily denying them another meal as he followed his guide deeper into the dense jungle. He was tired but excited. He knew they were getting close to their destination.

"How far is it?" he asked, wiping a forearm against his brow.

"It's just ahead sir," said his guide, Buto, who seemed just as excited. He turned and grinned, white teeth seeming incredibly bright against his dark skin.

Draven nodded, pushing aside thick branches and stepping over roots, the almost impassable terrain seemingly unwilling to give up its secrets just yet. Somewhere up ahead, a monkey chattered. Draven paused. “Is that it?" he whispered, staring into the dense tangle of trees. He wiped his forehead again, the humidity making something as simple as breathing a never ending battle.

“Could be, Mr. Richard." the guide said. He took a sip of water, then ducked, staring deep into the tangle of branches. "Follow me. Must keep quiet."

Draven nodded, sticking close to Buto as he moved off whatever track he'd been following and doubled back the way they had come, veering off into deeper foliage.

"Why are we heading back?" Draven whispered.

"We are downwind, Mr Richard, sir. The animal will smell us."

Draven glanced at his shirt, which was grubby

and sticking to his skin. "I think I'm pretty easy to smell either way."

Buto flashed a wide smile then continued on, leading Draven deeper into the jungle. Although it was the middle of the day, the sun barely penetrated the gloom. Draven had been all over the world, but this was by far the most hostile environment the twenty-four-year-old had ever encountered. Another mosquito buzzed in front of his face, and as he swatted it away he thought it was a minor miracle he hadn't contracted malaria. He watched his guide twist in and around the thick branches, then pause to take another drink from his canteen. With skin the colour of coffee and a smile which was bright and full of warmth, it seemed that even Buto was showing the first signs of fatigue. Draven wasn't surprised. This particular stretch of the jungle was uninhabited and mostly unexplored. Like much of the Congo, the sheer density of the foliage combined with the uneven ground and abundance of wild animals made it a dangerous place to explore. Draven thought he was fit, and as a keen cyclist thought that lack of stamina was the least of his worries. However, one thing he hadn't anticipated was the intensity of the heat. The temperature had risen to thirty-eight degrees, a dangerous level where it would be easy to get severe sunstroke. He knew that out here, so far away from civilisation, it could be lethal. He blinked sweat from his blue eyes, and took a mouthful of water, reminding himself it had to last. Although it was slightly warm, it was still divine. He tugged at his shirt, pulling the soaked material from his sweat slicked skin. He was sure he had lost at least twenty pounds since they first set out from camp. As the blazing sun reached its zenith, his calves screamed for mercy as they began to ascend another rise. Ahead of him, Buto stopped and held out a warning hand. Draven froze mid-stride, taking the opportunity to suck in some hot, dry air.

"Must be very quiet now," Buto said, crouching and inching forward, somehow barely making any sound as he moved amid the foliage. Draven followed, incredibly aware of his own clumsiness as he tried to replicate Buto's graceful movements and crashed through the jungle behind him.

They arrived at a clearing, the claustrophobia-inducing tree canopy opening up to allow full access to the blazing heat of the day. Just below them and downhill on the opposite side of the ridge was the reason for their journey.

"Are you sure these are the same ones, the ones you said they use in the village?" Draven whispered, knowing immediately by the excitement which surged through him that he was looking at an entirely new species of monkey.

"Yes," Buto said. “They are the same."

“Incredible.” Draven whispered as he crouched beside Buto and looked at them, the pain and toil of the trip suddenly worthwhile. He counted around twenty of them, their grey coats flecked with distinctive yellow streaks. They were small, around the same size as an average house cat and sported an unusual cranial shape, the forehead being much higher and more curved than any other species of monkey Draven had ever seen. Buto’s decision to head off track in order to avoid their scents giving them away had proved a good one, as the monkeys seemed to be oblivious to their presence. To think he had travelled almost four thousand miles from his home in London to the Congo basin on nothing more than a rumour had been causing him to question his sanity, an idea which had in one instant been vindicated as he watched the small animals frolic and play in the sun.

He had first heard about the Timika tribe from a friend, a fellow scientist called James Turner who had been to the Congo in late ninety-seven. He had gone in as a fresh faced palaeontologist on a six week expedition to study local plant life in the area and had come back six months later a changed man. When he returned, he told Draven all about a tribe he had encountered who were renowned in the area for the incredibly good health of its people. James hadn't thought too much of it at first until he had decided to hike out and pay a visit to the village. There, he had seen first-hand that the stories and rumours may have actually carried some weight.

Indeed, he was able to see for himself that the Timika had an inexplicable immunity to not just illness, but physical harm. James had expected extracting information about how this was possible to be difficult, however, the Timika were more than happy to show him what they referred to as 'the yellow magic'. James was given a demonstration, knowing that the more it unfolded, the more he was witnessing something incredible. He saw men cut themselves to the bone without feeling pain, a wound which should need stitches and hospital treatment, bleeding only for a short time before clotting and starting to heal. He saw another man put his hand into a fire, grinning as the flames ate at his flesh, the smell of it sizzling and burning repulsive. Two days later, the man's burns were already starting to heal. James was stunned, trying to comprehend what this new discovery could mean for science, and then learned that this was far from an extraordinary feat, for the Timika tribe it was a normal way of life and had been for generations. James had asked how it was possible that something so incredible could happen and was told by the Timika that it was magic granted to them by the yellow beasts of the jungle. James had neither the time nor the funding to stay and investigate any further, and so had reluctantly returned home and relayed the information to Draven, who he knew had had just begun researching the possibility of transmitting the genetic traits of animals into humans. To Draven, James's story almost sounded too perfect. Even so, it was enough to pique his curiosity to look into things further. His initial attempts to research the Timika were frustrating, each avenue of enquiry throwing up another dead end, which he acknowledged was no real surprise. This was a tribe who had remained shielded from the modern world, isolated and living within their own ecosystem as the wider world grew and prospered around them. They knew nothing of the way modern society lived, or of technology. For the Timika, existence was simplistic. Hunters went out with spears to find food for the village, and disputes were dealt with exclusively by the tribal elders in whichever way they saw fit. The less info Draven could find, the more curious he became and the more the idea that James might have discovered something truly unique ate away at him. As extreme as it seemed later in hindsight, the decision to fly out to the Congo and search for the tribe and see for himself seemed like the most natural thing in the world. Using the last of his savings, Draven scraped enough money together to make the trip, and immediately upon his arrival started asking for information at the various fishing villages scattered down the length of the Congo River.  The first two weeks proved to be a frustrating exercise in trying to gather snippets of information to point him in the right direction. It was quite by chance he met Buto, a local fisherman who not only knew of the tribe but where their village was located. Draven relayed what James had said, asking questions which Buto was all too happy to answer. He confirmed that the tribe existed and that they possessed great healing powers. Draven had asked to be taken to the village, upon which Buto had shaken is head and told him that the Timika were an incredibly private and territorial tribe and that a white man such as him, may not be welcome. He told Draven, however, that he would be willing to take him out to see the yellow beasts from which the Timika drew their powers. Ten days later, Draven was looking at them, peering down into the clearing with a grin on his face as his mind swam with possibilities.

“What would you like to do now, Mr. Richard? Buto asked.

"Can we catch one?" Draven whispered.

Buto considered the question. "Yes, but we will have to make it sleep first," he said as he quietly untied the rifle strapped to his backpack. He loaded it with a tranquillizer dart, its tail a bright red ball of fur then nestled the rifle against his shoulder and took aim. Draven held his breath and waited for the explosion of gunfire, however to his surprise, there was no such explosion. Instead, the gun fired with a pneumatic whoomph, the dart hitting the targeted monkey on the thigh. Draven watched, half excited, half guilty as the poor primate leaped into the air with a shriek then scampered into the jungle as its brethren fled, scrambling up trees and into the safety of the canopy.

"Come on Mr. Richard, “Buto said with a wide grin as he started down the slope to the clearing. "Drug acts quickly. He won’t go far."

Draven wiped sweat from his eyes, struggling to keep his balance as he followed Buto down the slope. "How long have the Timika known about the healing properties of these animals?" he asked as they escaped the blazing heat of the clearing and back under the cover of the jungle.

"Many years. My grandfather was friends with the first man to discover the magic inside this monkey."

"What happened?"

"My grandfather’s friend was hunting for food and encountered the monkeys. One was pregnant and thought my grandfather meant them harm. It bit him here." Buto pointed to the underside of his skinny forearm. "Usually, animal bites are bad. They mean infection. Very dangerous."

"I take it that didn't happen?"

"No," Buto said, shaking his head. "Instead, my father's friend grew strong. The bite healed. The people of the village were afraid. They thought my father's friend had been taken by the spirits of the forest. At night, the elders came and took him whilst he slept."

"What did they do?" Draven asked.

"They hung him," Buto said with a shrug.

"Jesus."

"Remember, Mr. Richard. The Timika have their own laws unlike the world you come from. They are very spiritual people."

"Still, it seems a little extreme."

"There is more to this tale yet," Buto said, hopping over a fallen tree branch.

"Go on," Draven said, more interested now in the rest of Buto's tale than finding the monkey.

"As I said, the Elders took my grandfather's friend into the centre of the village and hung him as a warning to their people not to toy with the yellow magic. But my grandfather's friend, he did not die.”

“Say again?”

“He hung by the neck for three days and nights, yet the life would not leave him. This angered the elders, so they cut him down and buried him alive in the shallow ground by the river. Three days later, he returned to the village after digging himself out of the dirt. Now the elders were frightened and begged my grandfather’s friend for forgiveness. It was then he told them that the monkeys were magic and had given him the power of healing."

"Magic?" Draven said as he ducked under a branch.

"What else could he say, Mr. Richard? They had tried to kill him twice. He promised to show them the monkeys and teach them how they too could become one with the gods."

"And that's how the tribe became so resistant?"

"I don’t know this word resistant," Buto said over his shoulder.

"Uh, I mean is this how they learned not to feel pain?"

"Yes."

"This is incredible. I wish I could have spoken to him myself."

"You could if the Timika would allow visitors to their village," Buto said with a grin.

"He's still alive? That's impossible."

"He lives. He is the same today as the day he was bitten."

"That can't be true. Are you saying he's not aging at all?"

"All I know is the man is alive and still healthy. He has lived with the Timika since that day he told them about the monkeys."

"Surely if this was true the village would be huge, overpopulated even."

"Not everyone in the village is deemed worthy of the magic Mr. Richard. Only those chosen by the elders are given the gift of life."

It was mind blowing, and it took Draven a moment to gather his thoughts. "If this is true, what's to stop members of the tribe going behind the back of the elders? Surely once you have the gift, or magic, or whatever it is, there is nothing anyone can do about it."

Buto stopped walking and looked Draven in the eye. "Something worse than death awaits anyone who does such a thing, Mr. Richard. Something much, much worse."

"What?" Draven said, seeing the fear in Buto's eyes.

"Not now, that is a story for another time," Buto said, shaking his head and turning away towards the trail. "Here, Mr. Richard. Your monkey is found."

The monkey lay on its side, the dart fired by Buto still embedded in its leg. It breathed with the rhythmic peace of sleep. Up close, the yellow streaks in its fur were even more evident. Draven couldn't help but stare, wondering what secrets it held.

"How long will it stay unconscious?" Draven asked as he shrugged out of his backpack.

"An hour. Two possibly. We should head back to camp before the dark comes. Lots of dangerous animals in this jungle, Mr. Richard."

Draven took a brown cloth bag out of his backpack and gently picked up the monkey and placed it inside, before tying the bag closed and attaching it to his rucksack. Buto helped him to shrug back into it and adjust to the added weight.

"Can I ask you a question, Mr. Richard?"

"Yeah, go ahead," Draven said, noting that the glimmer of fear he had first seen in Buto's eyes had grown considerably.

"Why do you want this animal?" the guide asked, his eyes bright and curious despite the fear.

"Where I come from, my job is to study if animals can help cure diseases in humans. This could be potentially huge. A breakthrough discovery."

"Is it not dangerous to take this magic into the world?" Buto asked. "Here, the Timika decide who is worthy. Out there, who is to say who can and cannot have this gift?"

Draven paused, unsure what to say. Buto had a point, and a good one, even if it wasn't a point to be considered in the middle of the Congo basin in the stifling heat of the afternoon. "I'm not thinking that far ahead yet. Right now I just want to do a preliminary study of this animal and find out the truth behind these stories of magic and eternal life."

"And what if you find them, Mr. Richard? What will you do then with such information?"

"What do you mean?" Draven asked, aware that his guide had completely changed demeanour, his tone now serious, the fear he had to that point managed to hide showing through.

"If you have this magic. If you learn to understand it. Does that not make you responsible for it?"

Draven smiled, a nervous gesture designed to put Buto at ease, even if the question was again a valid one. "All I want to do is study it, here in its own environment. I have no desire to take it from here. All I want to do is learn what I can then set it free. You have to trust me on that."

Buto was still agitated, but he managed one of those good-natured smiles which Draven had started to miss. "That's very good, Mr. Richard. You're a good man. When we get back to camp, we can have those beers we saved for after we had made this discovery, yes?"

A cold beer would be heaven, there was no doubt about it. Under the circumstances, he would settle for a slightly warm local brand just fine. "Okay Buto, that sounds good enough to me. Let's get out of here before these mosquitoes bleed me dry."

"Yes sir," Buto said, the relief in his grin evident. "Come on, this way."

Draven followed his guide, his mind swimming with questions and possibilities of the way his research could go if even half of the things he had been told were true.

# CHAPTER TWO

BAGHDAD
IRAQ
SEPTEMBER 6th 2013

THE STREETS OF BAGHDAD were filled with chatter and noise. The symphony of cars as drivers honked horns and shouted at each other was complimented by the swarming density of the population as market traders sold their goods and citizens tried to go about their business in the hope it would be a day of peace. Despite the ongoing unrest, the local populous had learned to adapt in the best way they could despite the heavy military presence and the ever-present threat of another terrorist attack. Eleven year old Akhtar Mahmood kicked his tattered football against the whitewashed wall without enthusiasm as his disabled younger brother, Youness, watched from his wheelchair, drooling and whooping from the shade.

"Do you want me to do some kick-ups?" Akhtar said to his brother as he pointed to the white Real Madrid football shirt he wore.

Youness gargled and flexed his hands, laughing as Akhtar kicked the ball into the air, showing deft skill at keeping it up with a series of knees or kicks before it could touch the ground. Across the street from the alleyway where the boys played, the American soldiers watched him, appreciative of both his skills and the distraction from the monotony of the day. Making the most of his audience, Akhtar performed some more complex tricks, ducking and catching the ball between his shoulder blades then flicking it back up into the air. Unlike many of the other citizens of Baghdad, Akhtar didn’t mind the Americans. Their presence made him and his family feel safe in a world filled with hostility and uncertainty. His father had told him that having them to protect the city was good, and could only lead to a better future for everyone.

Distracted, he lost concentration and miss kicked the ball, slicing it towards the alleyway entrance. He glanced at the soldiers as he jogged after it, scooping it up from the floor, but they had lost interest in him now and were staring down the street. Akhtar followed the direction of their gaze, watching as a beaten up red Ford rolled towards the checkpoint they were manning, leaving a plume of dust in its wake. He squinted against the sun as he watched the car come to a stop thirty feet away from the checkpoint. Akhtar could feel the change in atmosphere. The soldiers who had been calm and relaxed were now tense and readying their weapons, falling effortlessly into formation as they watched the car. One of them, an olive-skinned man with a carroty beard took a step towards the checkpoint barricade and waved the car forward. The car remained in situ, engine idling, its occupants impossible to see through the dusty windshield which was reflecting the blazing sun.

"Come forward," another of the soldiers

shouted in rough Arabic, flashing a quick glance towards his carrot bearded colleague who flicked off the safety on his weapon.

Still, the vehicle didn't move. The soldiers had seen enough. They split into two separate groups of two, one approaching the driver's side, the other towards the passenger side, all four men training their weapons on the vehicle. Akhtar watched, the football and even his brother temporarily forgotten.

"Out of the car," one of the soldiers said, first in Arabic then in English.

The car door opened, and the driver slowly exited, hands raised.

"On the ground," He ordered.

The driver - a stocky Arabic man, smiled and watched the soldiers approach him without showing the slightest hint of fear. Akhtar could feel the tension and noticed that people all around the checkpoint station had stopped what they were doing and were now watching events unfold, hoping for a peaceful resolution but expecting the worst. Some, who had seen situations like this and the usual outcome, fled, distancing themselves from the scene, abandoning purchases and vehicles alike. It was at this point, as Akhtar was about to go back to his brother and get him to safety when the driver of the car activated his suicide vest, which in turn detonated the explosives packed into the rear of the car.

Akhtar was on the ground before he even heard the explosion, thrown by the devastating concussion wave back into the relative safety of the alleyway.

Debris rained down, glass shimmering like diamonds on the ground where it had been ejected from the windows of surrounding buildings. Behind the intense ringing in his ear, Akhtar could hear the dull sound of gunfire and the crackle of flame. Even above all the carnage, he could hear the screams. He scrambled to his knees, coughing dust and smoke which hung heavy in the air. At the mouth of the alleyway, he could see the remains of the checkpoint. Of the four soldiers who had approached the car, only two now remained, hunkered down and returning fire against unseen assailants from the rooftops, the second part of what was obviously a planned attack. Akhtar saw one of the soldiers who had been watching him play football splayed out on the ground, his body terminating in a pulpy mass of entrails where his legs should have been, dead eyes staring at the ground. With ears still ringing, Akhtar turned to check on his brother, who was crying in his wheelchair, his chin slick with drool. Deciding he was safe enough towards the rear of the alley, Akhtar turned back to the gunfight happening just twenty feet away from him, mesmerised and horrified in equal measure. The violence of the situation surrounded him now, filling his nostrils with the stench of acrid smoke and charred flesh, his ears ringing from the explosion and the roar of the fire from the blackened remains of the car in the middle of the street, which billowed black smoke into the air. Another of the soldiers, the one with the carrot beard, was hit, bullets striking him in the chest and ejecting a thin mist of blood out of the back. Akhtar always thought seeing death would be like in the movies, with an exciting musical score and a hero who seemed impervious to things such as bullets or explosions. The reality, however, was proving to be quite different. The soldier who was shot simply crumpled against the sandbags he was using for cover and then failed to move again. His solitary colleague ducked for cover as another barrage of gunfire slammed into the checkpoint, kicking up great gouts from the sandbags he hid behind. He was directly across from where Akhtar cowered, and the two locked eyes, boy, and soldier. Individuals from separate worlds who were experiencing the exact same thing at the same time. The frightened soldier screamed words at Akhtar which he could neither hear nor understand amid the relentless zing of gunfire which rained down on the checkpoint. Akhtar was about to flee when his eye was caught by another soldier approaching the firefight from further down the street. He was noticeable not because of his intimidating appearance, but because he was walking towards the skirmish with absolutely no sign of fear. He was tall and broad with heavily muscled forearms. Unlike the other soldiers who were at the checkpoint, he didn't wear armour or protective clothing, just a pale mustard coloured shirt and army trousers. The shirt bore an insignia on the shoulder, a red skull on a black background with the letters P and A at either side of it in white. The man also wore what looked to be yellow paint on his arms and neck, the stripes standing out in stark contrast against his cocoa coloured skin. Without pausing, he picked up the weapon of his deceased colleague who slumped on the sandbags and walked towards the carnage. Akhtar felt his stomach tighten. He was certain the man was about to die from sheer stupidity. Seconds later, a hail of bullets tore through the soldier's body, puffing his shirt open and sending a fine cloud of claret out behind him. As impossible as it was, the soldier didn't fall, nor did he slow his pace. With absolute calm he aimed the weapon towards the rooftops and fired a single shot, hitting one of the rooftop shooters in the head, then swung the rifle to the opposite side and repeated the process, again hitting his target in the head, blood and brains spraying out of the back of his skull. The soldier didn't break stride as he walked further into the street and out of Akhtar line of sight.

The gunfire had almost died out now, and Akhtar couldn't resist scrambling to the edge of the alleyway on his hands and knees to watch what happened next. Akhtar could see him now, standing beside the roaring inferno within the blackened shell of the car. He was scanning the rooftops, seemingly unaware the skin on his arm nearest the flame was starting to blacken and burn. From Akhtar's vantage point, he could see the distended skin on the man's back where the bullets had hit him and pushed insides towards the outside, tearing away his shirt in the process. Despite all the horror and violence around him, Akhtar was infinitely more afraid of this man than the constant threats of violence which had plagued his country for as long as he could remember. Another crackle of gunfire came from one of the rooftops, the soldier staggering back as the projectiles hit their target, once in the leg, and another through the stomach, the bullet going straight through the soldier and sending a great chunk of dusty concrete up from the street just a few feet from Akhtar. In a single fluid motion and showing no physical reaction to the wounds, the soldier swung his weapon towards his assailant and fired once. Akhtar saw a figure tumble from a roof down the street, landing hard in the dust.

Silence.

The soldier tossed aside his weapon and strode towards the man he had shot, somehow able to walk despite a shaft of bone jutting out of the leg where the bullet had entered. He grabbed the prone man by the shirt where he lay moaning and started to drag him back towards the burning car.

The soldier who had been cowering behind the sandbags stood and checked on his friends, even though it was clear to see that none of them had survived the attack.

"You need some help?" the soldier said as he

approached the burning car. The wounded soldier with the insignia on his shirt didn't respond.

"What unit are you with?"

Again, the wounded soldier didn't respond. Instead, he dragged his prisoner to his feet, ignoring the pained howl as he was forced to stand on what was clearly a broken leg.

"Hey, I'm talking to you, buddy. What unit are you from?" The checkpoint soldier asked again, frowning at what should have been debilitating wounds on the man walking towards him.

"Apex team." The soldier grunted.

"You look pretty messed up there. You need some help."

"I'm fine."

"You're shot."

"It's fine."

"You don't look fine. I see an exit hole on your back I could fit my fist through, let me -"

The soldier was silenced by a single gunshot as the wounded Apex team soldier calmly unholstered the pistol on his belt and shot him in the head. He watched for a moment as the soldier fell against the sandbags, his helmet rolling off into the gutter, the back of his skull a ragged mess. Satisfied, that the intrusion was over, the Apex soldier turned back to the man who had fallen from the roof. Akhtar recognised him. His name was Abu, and always seemed to be quiet and polite. He owned a market stall selling grains and vegetables from which Akhtar would on occasion buy groceries for his mother. Abu was skinny and posed little threat, especially now with a broken leg and a bullet wound to the shoulder, which was staining his white shirt a vivid maroon colour. In contrast, the soldier's wounds which should have been infinitely worse to the point of being disabling or even fatal were now barely bleeding at all, and certainly weren't doing anything to stop him functioning normally.

"Who sent you?" the Apex soldier said in perfect Arabic to his frightened prisoner.

Abu pursed his lips and didn't answer, staring with defiance at the Apex soldier.

"Who sent you?" the soldier repeated.

"You can interrogate me all you like. I will not speak." Abu said, his voice trembling.

"I don't have any intention of interrogating you," The soldier said.

Akhtar stared in disbelief as the soldier grabbed Abu by the throat and shoved him back into the burning wreckage of the car. Abu began to scream and thrash as the flames ate his flesh, and yet the soldier didn't flinch or deviate, even as the flames did the very same thing to his own arms. He held them in the flames until Abu stopped screaming, and then dropped the hissing, foul-smelling corpse into the fire to let the flames finish the job. He stepped back from the burning wreckage, arms burned black, great cracks exposing the fleshy raw muscles beneath. Akhtar looked on as the soldier approached, whistling and unaffected by the wounds which should have killed him. The Apex soldier stopped by the entrance to the alley and looked at Akhtar, who cowered away in fear. Now that he was in close proximity, Akhtar could see the yellow markings on the soldier's skin weren't paint, but veins running under his skin. The ones on his arms were lost in the devastating burns, but the ones in the soldier's neck and face pulsed in stark relief against his skin. The soldier reached down with a blackened hand and picked up Akhtar's football and held it out to Akhtar, eyebrows raised. Too afraid to reach out for it, the young boy could do nothing but stare, wondering if he too was about to be killed. The soldier shrugged and rolled the ball into the alleyway, where it came to a stop against Akhtar's leg. There was a bloody black handprint on the leather where the ball rolled to a halt.

"Keep practising with that, boy. You have some skill." The soldier said calmly and in flawless Arabic, then walked away, soon lost into the cloud of thick smoke that had enveloped the street.

# CHAPTER THREE

## CAMP BLANDING JOINT TRAINING CENTER CLAY COUNTY, FLORIDA

SITTING ON THE EDGE of Kingsley Lake, Camp Blanding served as the primary training centre for both the Florida National Guard and the Florida Army National Guard. Located just thirty-six miles from Jacksonville, the camp was a hive of activity for recruits as they prepared for combat either in simulated situations or on one of the onsite live firing ranges. Acting as something of a revolving door for those looking to sharpen their skills, Camp Blanding often housed a mixture of both Special Forces units and regular army personnel. As was typical of the region, it was a gloriously hot day with blue skies as far as the eye could see.

Due to the lack of external stimulation between training sessions, it was often left to the personnel on site to find ways to keep themselves entertained. As a result, a five on five basketball game had started out in the yard and was now being cheered on by a good sized crowd of soldiers and staff who were enjoying a rare day off.

Thirty-six year old Steve Denton hesitated, bouncing the ball in situ as he tried to spot a teammate, his muscular body slick with sweat. Before joining the National Guard he had almost turned pro, and for as much as the opposition were putting up a good fight, it was obvious to see they lacked his level of skill, that was, with one obvious exception. Denton eyed the player in question who stood eight feet away, watching Denton with sharp eyes. Unlike the others, he seemed both tireless and in possession of the skills Denton himself lacked which stopped him stepping up into the big leagues. He was tall, his shoulders broad and tapering into a thin waistline. His hair was long for a soldier and touched the nape of his neck. The man was now shirtless, however before he had removed it, Denton had caught his name which was embroidered onto the breast pocket. J. COOK. Denton didn't recognise the insignia on the shirt - the red skull on black with the letters P and A at either side, although it didn't surprise him. So many different units were on site at any one time that it wasn’t unusual for different squads to mingle and merge. Even so, pride meant a lot especially in the army, and he wasn't prepared to lose to a rival squad, even someone who seemed to tick all the boxes skill wise. With dismay, Denton noted that Cook, whoever he was, hadn't even broken a sweat despite the intense heat as they neared the middle of the day. Denton saw his buddy, Smithson unmarked and open. He feinted to the right, then passed left, watching as Smithson duly scored to draw the teams' level. Cook looked furious. Denton tipped him a wink and a cheeky grin.

Game on motherfucker.

II

Commander James Robbins had spent the last three hours trying to chip away at the mountain of paperwork on his desk without success. He gave the stack of files and documents a sour glare as he leaned back in his office chair and rubbed his temples, trying to coax away the persistent headache which he had woken with earlier that morning. A month shy of his fortieth birthday, he felt he was too young to be spending his days behind a desk, not that he had any say in the matter. Although as physically fit as a man twenty years his junior and a skilled combat veteran who had seen action in Iraq (twice), his superiors had seen fit to promote him into a position which was strictly off the field of battle. Rumour upon rumour did the rounds that he had been pulled off active duty because of an attitude problem, something which was entirely unfounded. Sure enough, he was harsh and direct with his words, but, no more than necessary to get the job done. His father, who was also a military man had instilled a philosophy into Robbins which had stuck with him as long as he could remember.

Don't go to work to make friends, boy. Go there to do what you have to, even if it means making the tough decisions nobody else will.

The advice had been followed to the letter, and Robbins quickly ascended the ranks of the military system, enjoying the rigid, ordered lifestyle. He had never married or had children. Not because he didn't want to, but simply because he had so devoted his life to the army. He knew, of course, he wasn't well liked. His short fuse and lack of tolerance for anything other than absolute perfection made him a man who most of those below him wanted to avoid wherever possible. His eyes had a natural glare, which perfectly suited his perfectly bald head which was kept that way through choice rather than necessity. Turning his attention back to his reports, Robbins tried to focus. Try as he might, he couldn't concentrate, the words on the page may as well have been written in a foreign language for all the sense they made. He heard the dull sound of a cheer erupt from outside and cast an envious glance towards the window. He could see the basketball game in progress and decided a little fresh air might do him the world of good and at least, let them clear his head a little before he went back to his reams of paper. He found it odd that when he first envisioned a career in the military, pen pushing wasn't one of the things he expected to be spending his time doing. Tossing his pen on the desk, Robbins stood and stretched. The benefit of being his own boss meant he could make such decisions as leaving his reports until later. He reasoned he would stand a better chance of blasting through them with a clear head anyway. Besides, it was a Sunday, and even commanders deserved a little break from the daily grind sometimes.

## III

What had started out as a friendly game of basketball designed to pass a little time had become a fiercely competitive match up. The unforgiving sun baked the courtyard and the men who stood on it, their shadows pushed into long skeletal versions of themselves. Most had now dispensed with their shirts, and Denton was pleased to see others were looking as fatigued as he felt.

All apart from Cook, that was. He still looked fresh and still hadn't broken a sweat. As those around him started to tire, Denton noticed how Cook was becoming a more dominant force within the game. With the scores tied at eighteen each, it was still all to play for. Denton caught the eye of Smithson, who, like him seemed to have taken an intense dislike to Cook. Maybe, Denton thought as the ball was passed to him, it was just their own jealousy which was to blame. Sure enough, Cook had a confidence about him, and Denton supposed it could easily be confused for arrogance. Smithson moved into space as Denton dribbled the ball towards Cook. He tried the same move as earlier, the feint and pass, but on this occasion, he overthought it and telegraphed it too much. Cook stepped forward and body checked Denton, knocking him to the floor.

"Hey, watch it, man," Smithson said, abandoning his position and approaching Cook. Smithson was a big guy, well over six feet tall with huge shoulders. Cook, however, didn't seem at all intimidated by the larger man.

"My apologies, let me help you up," Cook said. His voice was soft and calm as he held a hand out to Denton, who still couldn't understand why he wasn't breathing heavy.

“Why the hell did you knock him down? Fuckin' asshole." Smithson said, getting in Cook's face. The rest of the players had formed a rough circle around them now. Some waiting to break up any fight that might occur, others hoping it would come to blows so they could watch it play out.

Denton got to his feet, wiping his grazed palms on his pants. "It's fine, Forget about it," he said, not liking the cold look in Cook's eye as he glared at Smithson. "Let's just get on with the game."

"No, this prick did that deliberately." Smithson raged.

"You, sir might be wise to watch your mouth," Cook grinned as he said it, which heightened Denton's unease.

"Sir? Are you fucking kidding me? What unit are you?" Smithson said, pushing his chest out as his confidence grew.

"Special projects. Apex Team." Cook replied, remaining calm in the presence of the physically superior man.

Denton noticed two other men wearing the same insignia on their shirts as Cook had pushed to the front of the crowd and were watching the exchange, their expressions impossible to read.

"Well, Mr 'special projects', you happen to be in my back yard. This is my base. I'm stationed here. Most of these boys have my back. Now I think you owe my friend here an apology."

Cook didn’t appear to be in any way intimidated. He looked around the crowd, locking eyes with each and every man, then returned his icy stare to Smithson.

"Is that supposed to impress me?"

"No," Smithson said with a shake of his head. "Just take it as a warning."

"You're not the only one who has people with him," Cook said, the threat in his voice clear.

"Yeah, I see that," Smithson shot back. "Way I see it; it looks like three of you and thirty or so of my boys."

"Three is enough." Cook fired back with a smile, which even despite the blazing heat, made Denton feel a wave of cold.

For as frustrated and angry as Smithson was becoming, Cook seemed perfectly cold and at ease. Denton decided he was either unafraid, crazy, or a brilliant bluffer, all of which meant trouble.

"You wanna start something little man?" Smithson said, poking a finger in Cook's chest. “I’ll fuck you and your boys up."

"Don’t do anything rash," Cook replied, calm as ever.

"Rash?” Smithson repeated, looking at the crowd with a grin. “You think you're better than me using words like that huh?"

Cook didn’t reply. He met Smithson’s gaze, unblinking, unwavering and without fear. To Smithson, the show of disrespect was like a red rag to a bull. He looked past Cook to his two squad mates.

"You got something to say?" Smithson said.

"Not to you.” One of the men replied with a smirk.

Smithson took a half step forward and was stopped by Cook, who grabbed his arm. “I wouldn’t do that.”

"Get your fucking hands off me," Smithson hissed, pulling himself free of Cook’s grip.

Denton noticed some of the other men had stepped out of the circle and were behind Smithson, the three Apex Team members now on the opposite side of a very obvious divide. Denton wanted to call them off, to tell them they were making a mistake. He looked at Cook and his men and saw nothing resembling fear or uncertainty. Since he first signed up, the army taught Denton to ignore such things as instinct and respond to orders without question. Denton had rejected that idea. He relied on and trusted his instincts without question, which made him wonder why he was more afraid for Smithson and his men than for Cook.

"I think you need to calm down a little-"

Smithson spat in Cook's face.

Cook smiled, making no effort to wipe the mucus from his cheek. “That was a mistake.”

Denton knew it was coming. There was a split second of absolute silence, then all hell broke loose.

IV

Robbins had made a quick stop at the vending machine. He really wanted a cold beer or two but decided a Pepsi would have to do it. He had already given up on doing his work for the day, and although he could get away with that easily enough, he knew he wouldn't be able to explain having booze on his breath if someone happened to smell it on his and report him to his superiors. As a result of the delay to grab a drink, he had missed the initial confrontation between Smithson and Cook. He fed the machine, took his dispensed Pepsi and headed for the yard. He pushed out of the door, leaving the air conditioned confines of the base behind for the oven like heat of the Florida day. At first glance, he thought the men were switching teams. There was what looked to be a huddle of sorts in the centre of the yard. He unscrewed the cap of his Pepsi just as the mass brawl erupted and almost thirty men attacked three.

Denton knew his instincts were right. He had witnessed death first hand in Bosnia and Syria, and so knew without question that Smithson was dead the instant Cook hit him. With frightening power and almost inhuman speed, Cook had thrown a punch. In the still air, the sound of the impact as knuckle connected with skull was sickening, second to the wet watermelon sound as the back of Smithson's skull smashed into the concrete as he crumbled to the floor. In a surreal moment in which time seemed to slow to a crawl, Denton saw a broken tooth arc through the air and skim his face as it was ejected from Smithson's mouth. Denton had seen fights, and was a huge fan of both professional boxing and Mixed Martial arts, but never had he seen anyone deliver a blow with such venom or power. Denton was about to lunge for Cook, when someone beat him to it, reigning blows on him which were easily blocked and avoided. Cook's fellow squad members waded in, swinging indiscriminately and attacking anyone who was nearby. Denton was knocked to the floor as someone barged into him trying to get towards the three men from the Apex team, which he would later think probably saved his life. All around him had become a tangle of flailing fists and kicks, shouting and grunting. Denton wasn't surprised to see that against all odds, Cook, and the Apex team were not only holding their own, they were winning.

An Asian soldier who was already bloodied unhooked his knife from his belt and waded back into the mix. From his vantage point on the ground, Denton saw it clearly. The Asian stabbed Cook in the stomach at least a dozen times, driving the blade up to the guard several times in quick succession. Cook didn't flinch. He shoved away the two soldiers he had been comfortably holding off and turned towards the Asian, delivering a vicious open palmed strike to the man's throat, crushing his windpipe. The Asian man fell, dead eyes unseeing as he landed. Denton looked up at Cook from his prone position on the ground, eyes filled with terror. Cook was smiling. He wiped the blood from his stomach. Impossibly, the wound had already stopped bleeding. The two men stared at each other for what felt like an eternity until Cook grinned and turned back into the brawl.

It was then that those eternally trusted instincts told Denton that he had to escape.

"Kill them all," Cook said to his two colleagues, still calm, still not breaking a sweat.

The reaction was instant. It was almost as if until then, they were doing just enough to fight off the other soldiers. Denton saw bones snapped. Eyeballs plucked from sockets, faces stamped on until they were no more than bloody pulps. The yard was fast becoming the site of a massacre. Cook was laughing, yellow veins standing out in sharp relief in his neck as he led the attack, his squad members destroying their fellow soldiers with vicious disregard for the fact that they were all part of the same side. Some had seen how things were going and had decided it was best to run. Denton was in complete agreement. He scrambled to his feet and ran towards the entrance to the base. Robbins was standing there, watching the carnage, unsure how to react, untouched bottle of Pepsi in hand. “What the hell's going on here?" He bellowed as Denton raced towards him.

"Go, run," Denton said, able to hear the fear in his own voice.

"What do you mean, run?"

"They've gone crazy! They're killing people in there."

A shadow of fear passed over Robbins's face, and he dropped his Pepsi to the ground and started to back away, trusting the same instincts as Denton which told him to put as much distance between him and the carnage in the yard as possible.

"It's the Apex guys, isn't it?" Robbins said as they hurried towards the entrance to the base.

Denton hesitated and tried to figure out what had shocked him more, the fact Robbins knew immediately what had happened, or that he didn't seem at all surprised. "Yes sir, it is."

"Inside," Robbins said.

"We need to restrain them, sir, we need weapons."

Robbins shook his head and gave Denton a look he had never seen from the commander before. It was a look of a man who was afraid. "Weapons can't help us. Come on, let's go."

"What about the others?"

"They'll have to fend for themselves," Robbins said, knowing how he must sound. Cold and callous.

"Sir, we have an obligation."

"Our obligation is to survive. Now get inside. That's an order."

Denton did as he was told, jogging up the steps and keeping pace with the commander as they headed back towards the base. "Did you see this happen?" Robbins asked.

"Yes, sir. I was right there in the thick of it. The one called Cook… he's….something's wrong with him."

Robbins nodded, brow furrowed. "You need to come with me."

"Where to, sir?"

"Away from here. Somewhere safe. Come on, my car is out front.

Robbins set off an alarm, and people were evacuating the building in unhurried groups. Only Denton and Robbins had any real urgency as they raced towards the front of the building.

"Why are we running sir? Surely we have enough numbers on site to restrain these people."

"If you understood what we're dealing with, you would know we can’t stop them. This was always a risk."

"I don’t understand sir, where are we going?"

The commander was pale, afraid. A shadow of the man Denton used to see striding confidently around the base. "Away from here. There are some people who need to hear what happened out there. You're our star witness."

As they pushed out of the air conditioned building and back into the baking Florida heat, the screaming and panic had already started from somewhere behind them. The evacuation which had started off as calm had now descended into chaos as admin and military personnel alike tried to escape the three monsters who were rampaging through the base. Smatterings of gunfire could also be heard now, but not enough to mask the screaming. There was more than enough screaming to go around. He remembered the way Cook had reacted when he was stabbed by the Asian man, the way he had barely reacted to wounds which should have killed him. He half wondered if the bullets would be equally ineffective, and if Cook would have that same look of enjoyment on his face as he rampaged through the base. Robbins climbed into a black jeep and started the ignition, the vehicle rumbling to life with a growl and heady smell of gasoline fumes.

"Come on, we need to get out of here," Robbins said as Denton climbed into the passenger seat.

Robbins floored it, the jeep snaking away through the gravel and out onto the access road leading away from the base.

"What's happening here, sir?" Denton said, glancing over his shoulder at the base as Robbins drove out of the grounds. "And where are we going?"

"Jacksonville, we need to get on a plane and get the hell out of here. As to what's happened, I'm not authorised to tell you anything yet, although I suspect if what I think is happening turns out to be true, you and everyone else will know all about it soon enough."

"What does that mean sir?"

"It means we could all be fucked," Robbins said, then turned his attention to the road, clearly not in the mood for any more questions which was fine with Denton. He didn't particularly feel like asking any. Instead, he leaned back in his seat and tried to make sense of what had happened, at the same time trying not to think about the fate of those left behind at the base.

# CHAPTER FOUR

## DEPARTMENT OF HOMELAND SECURITY
## WASHINGTON DC

### *14 days later*

THE NATIONAL TERRORIST ADVISORY System, or NTAS as it was known by those who were governed by it, is a simple colour coded scale designed to give an overview of the potential for any imminent threat to the country at any one time. Ranging from green which indicated low threat all the way up to red which meant 9/11 grade warning levels, the scale had, for the most part hovered between 'low' and 'guarded' as information was received, processed and acted upon by the Department of Homeland Security in order to keep the United States of America safe. It had come as a surprise to Director Marcus Atkinson when the scale was shifted over to the yellow coded 'Elevated' setting, which meant there was a significant risk of an attack for which people like him needed to be briefed. As the liaison between Homeland Security and the Secretary of Defence, it had to be a credible enough threat for them to call him in. His stomach knotted as he made his way through the glass and steel building, polished shoes echoing on marble floors as he headed to the meeting room. He had just turned forty-six, and with his daughters having fled the nest, he and his wife, Suvari, an Indian woman he had fallen for completely by accident, were finally hoping to find time to enjoy life a little for themselves.

His hair was still mostly black, his skin the unmistakable shade of brown of a man who spent a lot of time on tanning beds. Apart from the crow's feet at the corners of his blue eyes, he had a well-structured face and a square jaw with prominent cheekbones which had certainly helped him win over the attention of the opposite sex when he was a much younger, more promiscuous individual before he had chosen to settle down and start a family of his own. People often asked him how, with such a stressful job, he managed to retain his looks. He would respond with a shrug and tell them he was just lucky. The truth was, he had learned some years ago that the key had been to distance himself from the human aspect of his chosen line of employment. It was much easier to make a decision to send a team in to clear a building that was full of hostages if the actual hostages were thought of as statistics rather than people. Most of the time, he got it right. Sometimes it went wrong. He learned he could live with that just as long as his actions meant the country was safe again. However when it went wrong, the consequences were harder to deal with. Despite how he knew his colleagues perceived him – they called him the director of death behind his back - he didn't like to see people die, it was just an unfortunate side effect of the responsibilities he had as director. The cold harsh truth was that every operation involving extreme acts of terrorism carried with it a certain risk to the lives of both innocent civilians and the teams sent in to deal with whatever issue they were facing. He knew it when he took the job, and it hadn't changed since. He had learned to accept that saving lives sometimes came with the cost of innocent deaths. Usually, he got it right. Sometimes, a situation got so horribly out of control that even he, as detached as he had learned to be, had been affected.

Just thinking about it brought images of the past swimming out of the darkness of his mind's eye like phantoms chipping away at the wall he had built around his conscience just as fast as he could add to the defences. One image took precedence, one which hadn't been easy to forget. It all started with a man, a Polish immigrant called Greg who, after coming home early to find his long-term girlfriend in bed with another man, threatened to kill them both. When his girlfriend laughed at him and told him he didn't have the guts, Greg grabbed the illegally purchased shotgun from the trunk of his car and went straight to the elementary school where his son, Petr, was unaware that his father was about to make a life-changing decision. Greg entered the school, taking over sixty children hostage and barricading them and himself into the hall. Police were called, social media exploded, and before long, everybody was tuned into the ongoing siege at West Millburn Elementary School. Normally, such an incident would be a job for local authorities, however, Greg made one vital error. Frightened and realising he had gone too far, he grew desperate enough to do anything to stop the police from storming the school and shooting him dead. He sent one of the children out with a message to relay to the authorities, telling them that he had planted bombs all over the city which he would remotely detonate if anyone made a move against him. That statement, broadcast all over national, ensured that Marcus was notified. Anyone claiming to have planted explosives, no matter the motive, immediately became a threat to national security. Worse news for Greg was that his son, Petr, wasn't even in school on the day his father had decided to go to the extreme level he had due to a sickness bug. Greg's girlfriend, who had already made plans to take the day off work and spend the afternoon screwing the next door neighbour had shipped Petr off to spend the day with his grandmother. Without his son on hand and a room full of almost sixty frightened children, Greg demanded that his cheating girlfriend and his son were brought to him, or he would start to kill the children. The demands had of course been refused, and the siege went on with nobody able to make a decision on what to do to end the stalemate.

Marcus was certain the bomb threat was a bluff. He had interviews Greg's girlfriend and she had painted a picture of a man who was far from violent. According to her, he had acted in the heat of the moment. Nevertheless, he had sent men out into the streets, checking litter bins, scouring every alleyway, every parked car for any sign of hidden explosives. All the while, Greg sat in the hall growing more and more afraid and desperate. Marcus had also suspected that as a father himself, Greg wouldn't be able to bring himself to harm any of the children despite the threats he had made. Against the heated objections of local law enforcement and his advisors, Marcus made the decision to send in a team to bring the siege to an end one way or the other. Objections were made. It was suggested that provoking Greg would lead to a bloodbath. But Marcus was sure, confident he had made the right call.

He recalled watching the operation from the very meeting room he was about to go into on the bank of monitors across the back wall showing both TV coverage and the individual video feeds from the helmets of his team as they prepared to make their entry into the school. Marcus felt all eyes on him as he prepared to give the order to go in, knowing that each and every one of them would gladly throw him under the bus if things went wrong in any way. The orders were simple. Take the gunman alive if possible and kill him if they had to. Not Greg. Not a man anymore. Just a thing. An obstacle.

Just a gunman.

As soon as the team breached the school, breaking down the main doors and filing inside, Marcus realised although he trusted his judgement almost unconditionally, in this instance he had been horribly wrong. He could hear the sound of gunfire over the video feeds long before his team was anywhere near the hall. It was then as all eyes in the control room burned into him, Marcus realised he had made a gross misjudgement. The expected compassion he had been so sure Greg would feel towards children who were a similar age as his own son was lost behind fury and desperation at being forced into a situation he saw no way out of. Fear, it seemed had taken away any rational thought process. Backed into a corner, Greg did the only thing he felt able to do, which was to carry out his threat.

He started to fire.

It took the SWAT team six minutes to break into the hall, which was more than long enough. Forty-two of the sixty children were already dead, a further twelve were seriously injured. When he knew the end was near, Greg turned the gun on himself and blasted his brains all over the wall, making sure the six and seven-year-olds who were fortunate enough to survive would have a lifetime of horrific memories which they would never be able to rid themselves of. Vivid images of the carnage as they were fed in real time from the SWAT team's helmet cameras were burned into Marcus's brain, images nobody should ever have to see. They came to him now, as clear six years later as they were the day it happened, each of them driving home the fact that not only had he been wrong, but that he actually had feelings for what he had always seen as the expendable casualties of his operation.

Afterwards, there was a full investigation into what went wrong, but the government knew how valuable an asset Marcus was, and as someone with his natural instinct for making the right call nine times out of ten would go on to be forgiven even if that tenth time was a complete clusterfuck. Even so, Marcus never actually won. Not really. The images of those children took longer to banish into the dark recesses of his brain and needed a good few nights of heavy drinking to help them on their way, but eventually they went with the rest, and he returned to work, slowly feeling his way back onto that bicycle with the wheel that kept on turning no matter if Marcus Atkinson had a hold of the handlebars or not. People, the proverbial 'they' who everyone seemed to know, suspected it would be the end for him, that such a monumental mistake would forever affect his ability to do his job. In truth, it made him more determined to prove his methods worked. He still made the tough calls, and even if the guilt of that day was still there, it was his and his alone to manage. His own personal punishment which he would be forced to deal with in his own way, and although he had buried it deep, he had no doubt that from time to time, those ghosts would drift out of the dark to plague him one more time.

He snapped himself to the present, taking a deep breath and pushing aside the horrors of the past in order to concentrate on more pressing matters. He saw one of his senior staff members outside the closed door to the meeting room checking his phone as he paced the corridor. His agitation was clear, as was the look of relief when he saw Marcus approach.

"I'm glad you're here," the flustered man said.

"What's happening in there Mike?"

"I don't know, they won't say anything. They stonewalled me."

"I had the same thing on the phone. They wouldn't tell me anything apart from that I had to be here. Any familiar faces in there?" Marcus said.

"Oh yeah, Josh Harkins is in there, so is Susan Fring."

"From Langley?"

"Yeah. There are a couple of people I don't know too. They seem to be running the show."

Mike was nervous and seemed agitated.

"Any heads up on what we're dealing with would be nice."

Mike shrugged. "There's a commander from the Florida National Guard in there called Robbins. He seems to be in the know."

"How the hell did that happen? If we don't know, surely he shouldn't know either."

"Tell me about it. The other two guys running the show in there are strangers to me. They wouldn't even give me their names. Any idea who set this up?"

Marcus shook his head. "No, I mean it's obvious this has come from the top of the chain if that's what you mean."

"Presidential?" Mike whispered, leaning in, his cheap aftershave overpowering.

"Maybe," Marcus said, knowing something coming directly from the President had to be serious.

"Holy shit, they must have some credible intel to pull you in."

"Uh, thanks, I think," Marcus said, flashing his expensive veneers at Mike.

"What I mean is they wouldn't get someone as uh..."

"Emotionless?"

"I was going to say efficient," Mike muttered, "But if you like emotionless better, that works too. My point is they wouldn't get someone who was renowned for fixing problems if they didn't think they had a major problem to fix."

"Good point," Marcus said, his curiosity stirred. "You coming in?"

"Soon," Mike said with an exasperated sigh. "Got a god awful bladder infection. I can't seem to stop pissing. I'll take a leak and be right in."

"Make sure you wash your hands," Marcus said with a wink.

Mike just about managed a semi-amused smile then hurried off the way Marcus had come, change jingling in his pocket as he made for the entrance to the bathroom.

Pausing for a few seconds to enjoy the silence

of the corridor, Marcus took a deep breath and went inside the meeting room, curious as to what was so damn important.

II

He had selected the coffin himself, choosing to carry it on his back through the woods to the place where he was to be buried. The others watched in silence as he set it down and looked at them in turn. His brothers. His kin. One of them handed him a shovel. No words were exchanged. None were needed. This had been discussed enough.

The coffin bearer began to dig. The earth was hard, a heavy frost making the top layer hard to penetrate. He was strong, though, and with gritted teeth eased his way to the more compliant, softer ground below. Time passed yet he didn't pause, nor did they stop watching him. When it was done he climbed out of the hole and admired his work. Six feet deep by four feet wide. It would be more than adequate. He handed the shovel back to one of his silent observers, and then looked at each in turn.

"When I return, I shall be a new man," he said, breath fogging in the chilly night air.

They didn't respond, and only watched and waited for what was to come.

The man dragged his coffin to the hole, struggling to position it so it would land upright at the bottom. Again, no help came, just as he had instructed. With a last effort, he slid the coffin over the edge of the grave. It landed where he intended, its pale pink lining resembling the tongue of some kind of slumbering beast as it waited for him in the dark.

"Are you ready, Joshua?" the man with the shovel said. Joshua looked down into the hole without fear. He nodded. "When I come back to you, I will be a new man. I will have proved my worth."

"Are you sure you will rise again?" the man with the shovel said, his eyes shining like twin beacons in the gloom.

Joshua clapped him on the shoulder. "I do this

to show you my commitment to our cause. I enter the earth as your brother, and I will rise again as the father of the new world."

"When will you be back to us?"

Joshua considered the question, tongue flicking against the back of his teeth as he thought. "When the two of you become twelve in number, dig me out."

"How will they find us? The rest of our kind?"

"You have to believe they will, my brother," Joshua said. He looked at both men in turn and then clambered down into the hole.

"Remember, pack the earth tight," he said as he lay down in the coffin, taking a moment to get comfortable. “Pass down the lid."

The men responded at once, kneeling in the dirt and lowering the lid. Joshua took its weight and paused, staring up at the two men and the slab of sky above him.

"When I return, we give birth to the new world."

"Until then, we will wait for you here." The

man with the shovel said.

Joshua nodded and lowered the lid into place. The two men began to fill the hole, neither speaking to the other as they worked into the night. When it was done, they knelt, surrounded by the dense forest.

They waited.

III

The meeting room was dominated by a large oak table. On the back wall, a large TV screen surrounded by smaller monitors allowed presentations or live video feeds to be played as needed. Marcus looked at them, recalling what happened before then forced those ghosts back down into the place he kept them. He took his seat and waited for somebody to fill him in. There was a strange atmosphere in the room, a palpable nervousness which he supposed was directly linked to the increase in threat level. Even so, it was unusual for him to be out of the loop and he was feeling more than a little frustrated. He caught Susan Fring's eye across the table and was rewarded with a disgusted curl of the lip before she lowered her eyes and pretended to look at her phone.

Bitch.

As Mike had warned him, other than Josh Harding - a nice guy who worked in the White House with the secretary of defence- he didn't recognise anyone else. A man who looked to be aged anything between fifty and three hundred was standing at the end of the room reviewing a mountain of papers spread out over the desk. He was bald, and his pale skin had an ugly translucent quality giving the observer a sneak preview of the network of blood vessels and veins which lay underneath. His eyes were ringed in bluish purple, showing the distinct signs of a man who was suffering from a lack of sleep, a look enhanced by the white stubble which lined his gaunt cheeks. He reminded Marcus of some kind of zombie - the dead come to life and standing in a cheap suit at the head of the table. Marcus suppressed a small smile at the thought. Only the man's eyes showed any semblance of being alive and stared out from underneath bushy eyebrows like twin brown bottomless wells.

"Thank you all for coming," the man said as he looked at them. Marcus was surprised to hear he had an English accent. "It goes without saying what you are about to hear is extremely sensitive, and should be treated as being on a strictly need to know basis as far as your respective teams are concerned."

The man paused for a second, making sure his point sunk in. "My name is Robert Genaro, and I'm here to tell you about a situation which could have dire repercussions if we don't contain it and contain it quickly."

"Terrorists?" Marcus asked.

"Nothing so simple I'm afraid," Genaro replied, adding a thin smile which looked positively ghastly in the subdued lighting.

"Since when were terrorists simple?" Marcus fired back.

"If you let me go on, I'll tell you."

Marcus flushed, feeling both angry and a little put out that this stranger had come into his building, in his meeting room and belittled him. He considered saying something then thought better of it, instead choosing to remain silent until he, at least, found out what was going on. Genaro took his silence as the signal to proceed, and released Marcus from his gaze, glancing back at his vast array of papers on the desk. "In late nineteen ninety-nine, I was working as part of a special projects team commissioned by the government to explore the science of genetics and how they might be applied towards aiding modern warfare. That department still exists today, run in its entirety by me and my team of staff. Our objective was to look into ways of protecting our battlefield infantry from the wears and tears of life in the various war zones scattered across the globe. As you know, the United States is actively supporting and are directly involved on several fronts assisting peacekeeping operations around the world. Unfortunately, this also means we suffer losses. Every soldier who is killed in action represents, at its most basic level, a waste of resources, both time and money spent on training that individual who will never go on to repay that debt.

Marcus wanted to cut in and suggest that, perhaps by giving his life for his country, the soldier had already paid more than enough, but he didn't want to get kicked out of his own meeting room so he again chose to remain silent as Genaro went on.

"My team were tasked with exploring things which looked more like science fiction than anything we thought truly achievable. We were exploring genetic modification to enhance pain and temperature resistance, cell regeneration and things of a similar nature. Of course, technology at the time was grossly inadequate for such advanced experiments, and we struggled to make any headway. We had grand ideas, of course, just no means to execute them. That all changed in the spring of two thousand and one."

Genaro paused to take a sip of water, looking

around the table to make sure he still had their attention. Satisfied, he went on.

"As these things tend to be, it was quite by accident when I stumbled on something which would change the direction of my career and research, and what indirectly brings us all here today. That something was an article in New Scientist magazine written by a man called Richard Draven who was exploring similar technologies to my department but on a much smaller scale. His article claimed he had discovered a new species of monkey in the Congo with amazing regenerative properties. Of course, we know that species today as the tiger monkey so called for its distinctive yellow markings. At the time of its discovery by Draven, it was thought impossible for a population of creatures to remain undiscovered in a world which we humans wrongly assume holds no secrets to us. The article by Draven was borderline fiction, and he was universally blasted by his colleagues for indulging in such fantasy to the point where it damaged his career. I too scoffed, and yet, some of the things he mentioned rang true with our own research, which piqued my interest. As fantastical and indulgent as it seemed, I decided to seek out Mr. Draven in order to speak to him myself, if for no other reason than to satisfy my own curiosity. After numerous rejections of my requests to speak with him, he finally decided to meet with me, only because he was in London and had some time to kill between appointments."

Genaro paused for another drink of his water, and scanned his audience again, his eyes lingering for just a split second on Marcus.

"I wasn't sure what to expect from Draven before we met. I think I had half an idea he would be some kind of weirdo, or as you Americans might say a goofball. I was certainly surprised to find upon our meeting that he was a perfectly respectable, intelligent man. He was very humble, very wary of me, especially in light of the way his name had been dragged through the mud by everyone in the scientific community. He had done his research too and knew who I was even if he didn't know the nature of my work. Within half an hour of speaking to him, I was half convinced he was telling the truth in his article. By the time another hour had passed, I was absolutely sure and was offering him a place on my team. He, of course, declined. He said he was already worried about the damage the backlash would do to his already tarnished reputation, and didn't want to further aggravate the situation. He did, however, agree to take us to the location where this specific species of monkey could be found as long as we were willing to fund the trip, as he had spent pretty much all of his funds on his own research. Of course, with the ridicule of the scientific community came the stoppage of grants and funding. I assured him I would raise the funds needed and that he should stand by and be ready to fly out. Sure that my superiors would be thrilled with such a potentially monumental breakthrough, I requested a modest amount of funding to go and retrieve a sample of this particular species of monkey in order to see if we could use it to further our research."

He smiled, and Marcus thought it was a bitter expression rather than one of fondness, an intuition which proved to be correct as Genaro went on.

"Sadly, my superiors refused to authorise the trip, claiming it was a waste of valuable resources that would be better spent elsewhere, which, as we all know is ironic considering the trillions of dollars spent by the US alone on their military programs. Anyhow, that's not the issue here. The decline of the funding was final, yet fortunately, something was just around the corner which would change the lives of everyone and make those in power change their mind."

"Nine-eleven, right?" Marcus said.

Genaro nodded "Exactly. The most important day in recent history was, as we all know a terrible tragedy, and yet it opened the door to my research. With war looming and a world shell-shocked and frightened, the quarter of a million I had asked for to do my research which could directly help the war effort seemed like peanuts. In fact, I was given an open budget. For the first time, I was given free rein to do the work I had been trying to do on a shoestring budget for the last few years."

"Did you and Draven find the monkey?" Marcus asked.

"I did. Draven didn't come with me. He said he had changed his mind and was moving on to other projects. He had been invited to do some research in Antarctica and thought the isolation would be better to help repair his reputation. He did, however, give me extensive notes and directions which were enough for us to locate the animal, which we have since learned only inhabits that particular area of the Congo, or at least to the best of our knowledge."

"Was it true?" Harding asked. "About the regenerative properties?"

"If you mean was Draven lying, then the answer is no. In fact, he was quite conservative in his report."

"So he was right?" Harding said.

"He was more than right. He had discovered a creature which would change the face of genetics forever." Genaro knew they were all hanging on his every word and waiting for him to go on, yet he paused, clearly enjoying the attention. "We brought samples, both alive and dead, of the monkeys back to our facility in America and began our experiments. Almost immediately, we understood we were dealing with something far beyond anything we could ever have hoped to comprehend. This amazing creature had genetic markers which overnight made our prior research redundant. Cell regeneration. Self-repairing tissue. We showed our initial findings to my superiors, who in turn unrestricted our budget and told us to spend whatever we needed to further the research. As you can imagine, it was a dream come true. We were told to find a way to transfer the genetic properties of the monkeys over to humans as quickly as possible no matter the cost."

"Surely that's impossible," Marcus said, his mind boggling at the idea.

"Not only is it possible, we were successful. Humans and primate DNA is ninety-six percent the same. There are only minute differences between the two. There are actual examples of creatures in the animal kingdom who possess these same traits. Certain lizards, for example, can grow a new tail if one is lost during a fight. Starfish can also replicate themselves into a whole new animal just from an off cut of a leg. The problem had always been the vast difference in genetic structure. With the tiger monkey, that particular problem was eliminated. We were able to devise a product...call it a virus if you will based on the primate DNA. When delivered to a human subject, this virus would bond at a molecular level with its host, essentially fusing together to become a singular being and in doing so changing its properties."

"I'm not sure I understand," Susan said, glancing around the table to see if anyone shared her confusion. "You're suggesting you modified people's DNA?"

"It's really not that hard," Genaro said with a shrug of his narrow shoulders. "You would be surprised at the breakthroughs in science and medicine which have never been made public. For example, have you ever heard of a president or royal family member being diagnosed with cancer? Why do you think that is?"

Glances were exchanged around the table at such a crazy idea, and yet it made sense.

“Don’t look so shocked,” Genaro said with a grin. “We’ve had a cure for it since the mid-nineties. The only reason it hasn’t been released is because the pharmaceutical trade is worth billions of dollars a year and it’s more prudent to keep the cure under wraps.

A murmur went around the table at the revelation, all apart from Marcus, who remained unmoved. "What did the monkey virus change?" he asked, pulling the meeting back on track

"Everything," Genaro replied, this time with a grin that was of admiration for his work. "Normally, human trials take years to be possible. In this case, because of the genetic similarity between species, it was quite straightforward. The results were astounding. Our brief was to create a brand of super soldier. One who was designed for maximum efficiency with few needs as far as sustenance and care. We achieved that and more. We called it Project Apex. Essentially we took the current flawed human DNA and changed it. Improved it. Ironed out the flaws and made it better."

"You're talking about playing god here," Marcus said, unsure if he was more horrified or offended at Genaro.

"I don't believe in god," Genaro fired back. "Only science. Evolution. I deal in fact. Black and white. I deal in tangible absolutes. Surely, you of all people understand that? I'm led to believe your own work ethic is similar?"

For the second time, Genaro had shot Marcus down and put him in his place. Marcus was starting to develop a strong dislike for the Englishman.

"Back to your initial question about what our product changed. Let me put it into perspective." Genaro put a finger to his lips as he considered how to approach it. "Imagine a man who feels no pain. Imagine a man who is immune to extreme temperatures. A man who doesn't need to eat or drink. A man who doesn't need to sleep. Imagine a man given access to the full potential of his brain, giving him superior intelligence, decision-making skills and the ability to process and use information in real time at an almost computer processor like level. A man with unlimited stamina, a man who barely ages."

"You make it sound like they are invulnerable," Marcus said, feeling his stomach tighten.

"Essentially, they are. Stab him and the wound will heal itself. Cut off a limb and within three months it will grow back. They are physically and mentally superior to the rest of us in every single way. They are us, but with the flaws removed and the positives enhanced. If there is a god, this is surely the design he intended."

"How is any of this relevant?" Harding said. "Has someone discovered this technology and plans to steal it? If other countries were aware of the potential of this, it could be a disaster."

"It's entirely relevant," Genaro said. "You all need to understand, this isn't some kind of glimpse into what could be possible. This has been implemented already. We have Apex soldiers stationed in small units all over the globe."

"Wait, you're telling me there are people - genetically modified people out there right now?" Marcus said.

"Yes, which is why we called you all here today. It seems our testing was rushed, and there may be a significant problem with the programme."

"Not may be," Robbins snapped, speaking for the first time. "I've seen this first hand. Those bastards are out of control."

Genaro frowned and stammered, thrown off by the commander's interjection.

"This is Commander James Robbins from Camp Blanding down in Florida," Genaro said. "He was privy to an incident a fortnight ago which alerted us to a potential issue, one which I'm afraid to say has escalated enough for us to bring you all into this meeting today."

Marcus straightened in his chair. He had the feeling things were about to get interesting. The perpetually grumpy Genaro went on.

"Commander Robbins was on site when an argument at a basketball game at his base got out of hand between three Apex soldiers and several regular forces personnel. There was an.... incident which led to some unfortunate deaths."

"Let me jump right in there," Robbins grunted, shooting a glare at Genaro. "Let's not coat this in bullshit. It wasn't just an incident. Some of our guys got into an argument with your super soldiers and were butchered. Sixty-seven dead. Sixty-seven. Good men. Good soldiers trying to enjoy their downtime before your supermen came in and cut them to shreds."

"Butchered?" Susan said, flashing a worried glance at Harding.

"Yeah. It was a damn bloodbath." Robbins grunted.

"Did nobody restrain them?" Marcus said "All those people against three?"

"Who the hell are you?" Robbins snapped, glaring at Marcus, then continuing on before he could reply. "Of course, they tried. The base is a wreck. It looks like a fucking war zone. Thanks to these super soldiers this idiot created, we didn't stand a chance."

"The time for pushing the blame is long gone," Genaro said, trying to regain control of the meeting. "We need to find a solution to this problem."

"Can't you just call them back in?" Marcus said.

"You think we would have called this meeting if that was an option?" Genaro snapped. "We have over seventy Apex operatives stationed all over the globe. Days after the incident at Camp Blanding, as one they stopped following orders. It was some kind of coordinated mass decision which we don't yet understand. A few days after that, they went dark. They have gone off the grid."

"So they've gone rogue?" Marcus asked.

"Yes, that seems to be the case. We have no idea where any of the Apex teams are, what they might be doing or why they have become so aggressive."

"It seems to me you people didn't test this virus of yours before you starting screwing around with people's genetic codes," Marcus grunted.

"Look, this meeting isn't about passing the blame. It's about devising a solution" Genaro stuttered.

"No, he's right." Robbins cut in. "Seems to me like you and your people made a mess and now expect someone else to come in and clean it up."

Genaro took a deep breath and had a sip of water. Marcus noticed his hands were shaking as he screwed the cap on the bottle. "Look," he said, taking a deep breath. "I'm fully aware of my role in this. And not making excuses, I was also following orders. True, I was caught up in the possibilities and the excitement of the work we were doing, but please try and see it from my point of view We were breaking new ground. Pioneering new technologies. If anything, I'm guilty of losing focus. Did we speed through human trials? Yes, we did. Should we have devoted more time and money to thorough testing of the virus? Again, yes. In our defence, we were under pressure to deliver a product from the very highest rungs of the government ladder. Whoever is responsible, passing the blame won’t help us to deal with this situation."

"And what exactly is the situation?" Marcus asked. "Can you tell us what we're dealing with here?"

"Well, you are looking at a force of nature, unlike anything we have ever had to deal with before. They are regular men, so can hide in plain sight. Upon close inspection, yellow pigmentation can be seen under the top layer of the epidermis of the arms and neck as a result of the genetic modification, however, this would only be visible up close. These men were chosen for their intelligence primarily, which will have been boosted a hundred fold by the bonding of the virus. They don’t age, nor do they need to sleep. They are impervious to cold and pain and rarely need to eat. They also have an incredible ability to self-heal from almost any injury within a matter of hours. Sometimes minutes. They are essentially better versions of us with none of our weaknesses."

"We already know all that. The important question is, can they be killed?" Robbins asked.

"Oh, they are still human. The problem is the regenerative powers which make death by common methods so difficult. The only sure way is to destroy the brain. The other problem, which follows on from Commander Robbins's situation in Florida, is that the Apex team members had started to show increased levels of aggression, with the slightest incident sparking them to react with violence. We have received a growing number of reports of these 'Ragers' acting in groups and attacking civilians. Pack hunting, if you will. Some groups are stealing large quantities of cash and supplies. We suspect they are planning something, some kind or retaliatory event, although why we don't know."

"Could I ask you a question?" Marcus asked.

"Go ahead."

"All judgement and blame aside, how much do you actually know about this virus? What I mean is could whatever is happening, the pack behaviour, the group aggressions, be at all linked to the virus itself?"

"Possibly. In fact, it's likely." Genaro said, folding his hands in front of him.

"But you don’t know?"

"No. The real expert on this is Richard Draven. He has studied the monkeys themselves for years, certainly far longer than we had the time to. If anyone can help us to understand them and their behaviours, it's him.”

"Okay," Marcus said, finally seeing where he could help and take a little control. "Leave that to us. We'll find him and have him brought in to see if he can help. Do we have any intel at all on where these Apex teams could be hiding out?"

"No. I'm afraid to say we don’t know anything at all."

"We need to get teams on the ground. We need to look at anywhere large enough and secluded enough where groups of these soldiers might hide out. Josh, can your people cover the homeland locations? I assume we have reports on last known locations and the like?"

"Yeah no problem,"

"Okay, good. Susan, you have international contacts. Liaise with them and gather what intel you can. We need to find out where these people are and how they are communicating. I want emails and phone calls monitored. Treat this as high priority. We also need to make contact with local governments in affected areas and make sure they are on high alert. We can’t have this getting out into the media, so be sparing with the information. If you encounter any resistance, come straight to me."

Josh and Susan nodded agreement.

"What about the alert level?" Mike asked, wringing his hands.

"Leave it where it is for now. With luck, we can contain this without causing panic. Our top priority is finding Richard Draven and bringing him in." He turned to Genaro. "These lootings you mentioned. Do we have any recent intel as far as sightings of these Apex soldiers may be when they were last spotted?"

"We had a sighting two days ago in London, although it's unconfirmed."

"It's good enough. I'll need to speak to the British prime minister, see if we can mobilise a team over there to search the area."

"I can probably get that done for you," Genaro said. "The Prime Minister and I went to Cambridge together. We're old friends. I can have a word in his ear and get the SAS involved. They are the best of the best."

"Fine, let's make a move on this now. We need to deal with this before it gets out of hand."

# CHAPTER FIVE

RAF SPADERDAM
CUMBRIA,
UNITED KINGDOM.

THE RECREATIONAL ROOM was warm, a blessed relief from the near-zero temperatures outside. Stanhope burst through the door, his cheeks spotted pink from the cold.

"Fuckin ell' Stanny, shut the bloody door," barked Parker, his south London accent heavy with annoyance as he glanced up from the chessboard.

"Gimme a chance ya tosser," Stanhope responded as he kicked the door closed behind him. He crossed to the kitchen, switching on the kettle and dropping a tea bag into a cup with hands he could barely feel anymore.

"Cold?" Briggs said with a grin.

Stanhope gave Brigs the middle finger with his free hand. "Fuckin' freezin' out there mate," he said as he stirred his tea and sat beside Trig, who was busying himself with leering over the naked girl on page three of The Sun newspaper.

Without looking up from the silicon enhanced flesh on the page, Trig responded. "Tell me about it, dunno who we pissed off to get shipped all the way out here to the middle of nowhere. It was minus five earlier. Minus fucking five."

Stanhope pulled out a battered pack of cigarettes taking one himself, and offering the pack to Trig, who took one, popping it in his mouth. "Cheers mate."

Trig, known more formally as Jason Trigon, had just turned twenty and was the rookie of the group. His blue eyes stared out from beneath a permanently furrowed brow as he lit his cigarette, inhaling deeply. "Any action out there, Stanny?"

Stanhope shook his head, sipping his coffee. "Nah mate, not a thing. Patrol is a waste of fuckin' time if you ask me. What time are you due out there?"

Trig put his paper down on his lap, taking another deep draught of his cigarette. "I'm up next mate, three till five in the fucking mornin'. Ungodly to be outside in this sort of cold."

Stanhope nodded, lowering his voice. "I've half a mind to come back out with ya mate, these wankers in here are starting to drive me mad, especially Parker."

Both glanced towards Parker, obliviously playing chess in the corner, his scrub of facial hair making him look dirty.

"Look at him," Stanhope grunted. "Calls himself a soldier, the scruffy bastard."

Trig snorted a laugh as the two friends shared a grin. "Must be bad mate if you'd rather walk the perimeter with me in this cold than stay here."

Stanhope grinned and shouted across the room. "Oi, Parker, you ever heard of a razor ya scruffy cunt?"

"Get fucked Stanhope ya wanker." Parker fired back.

Stanhope flicked Parker the middle finger, then nudged Trig in the arm with his elbow, continuing in a voice loud enough for Parker to hear. "That's the thing Trig, these cockney cunts think they own the place, fuckin southern twats. We're up north now."

Stanhope could see Parker growing more and

more frustrated. The rest of the soldiers were watching, anticipating a confrontation that had been brewing for weeks.

Parker swivelled on his chair. "You got something to say to me, Stanhope?"

Stanhope stood, raising his own voice. "What if I do? What you gonna do about it?"

Parker swept the chess board off the table, striding across the room and going nose to nose with Stanhope as everyone jumped in to hold the two apart.

"You know your problem don't ya Stanhope?" Parker hissed with a smile as the rest of the group struggled to hold them apart. "You're still pissed off I knobbed that bird of yours."

They lunged for each other, individual insults lost in the noise as the two men tried to get to each other.

"What the hell's going on in here?"

The men as one stopped and snapped to attention where they stood, Stanhope and Parker breathing heavily as Staff Sergeant Mills entered the room. His salt and pepper hair was as always impeccably parted at the side, his grey eyes soaking in every detail of the room.

He strode towards Stanhope and Parker, glaring at Trig who stood in the middle, just about holding the two apart. He glared at each in turn, his face twisted into a scowl.

"New orders have come in," he barked. "Team of five needed. You three seem to be full of energy, so count yourselves in. Brigs and Johnson, you too."

"Yes Sir," Johnson and Briggs said in unison as Mills turned back to Stanhope and co.

"Since it seems you three have so much energy to spend, you can all go out and patrol until morning. First thing tomorrow I want you in my office for a briefing on the mission."

Stanhope opened his mouth, then closed it, remembering the stories of Mills which were well documented. By all accounts, he was a man not to be crossed.

Mills looked from one to the other, pausing at Parker.

"Parker, you are aware this is the British army, yes?"

"Yes, Sir" barked Parker, quick as a flash.

"And being a part of the British army implies you are representing your queen and country?"

"Yes Sir," said Parker, again robot like.

"Then why do you look like some kind of homeless vagrant?"

“I don’t know sir. Sorry, sir.”

“Get rid of it. Have a little respect for your position and pride in your appearance."

"Yes Sir," said Parker.

Mills glared at him for a moment more. "Go on then, do it now!"

Parker saluted, then left, heading out into the cold towards the barracks to shave.

"As for you two," Mills said, pivoting towards them. "Gear up and get out there."

In unison, they saluted. "Yes, Sir."

Mills stood for a moment, glaring at the two men. "Dismissed" he barked, pivoting on his heel and leaving the rec room.

"He's a fuckin wanker, that Mills" grumbled Stanhope, falling back into his seat. "Double fuckin duty. Parker's to blame, his fault for winding me up."

"Fuck it mate," said Trig, trying to diffuse the situation. "Let's just get out there and get it over with eh?"

"Suppose so," grumbled Stanhope. "What do you reckon these new orders are?"

"Dunno, can't be any worse than freezing our bollocks off in this shithole, though."

"True."

"Come on then," Trig said, grabbing his boots. "Sooner we start, sooner we can get finished."

II

It was sensory deprivation at its most extreme. A black void of absolute silence. With nothing to stimulate the senses, a person could go crazy. Joshua had been buried alive for almost two weeks now. Much like an animal in hibernation, he had slowed his vital functions down almost to a stop. He floated in an infinite inky limbo, straddling the line between sleep and consciousness, life and death, and for all he knew, heaven and hell. Time had stopped having any meaning the second he closed the lid of the coffin and the steady sound of dirt landing on the wood inches from his face became too quiet to hear as his grave was filled. Seconds felt like days, minutes like weeks, and hours like months. It was a virtual lifetime to contemplate not only the life he had lived to date but to think about the life he would lead when he was reborn.

The first half of his life had been uneventful. He was sure in time, people would compare him to Hitler or others who they deemed as vile beings who had committed awful deeds. If those people looked into his past expecting to find a troubled upbringing which would perhaps explain his actions, they would be sorely disappointed. There would be no eureka moments, no glaring entries in his history which psychologists could write papers on as to how violence was a product of upbringing. They would find he grew up as an only child of a father who was a preacher and a mother who worked as a clerk. They would dig for dirt, searching for evidence of abuse, and would find only examples of the love they showered onto him. His parents had brought him up well, taught him the value of manners, of respecting his elders. He was raised to believe in the good grace of God and the idea that by leading a good life he would one day be accepted into heaven. Somehow, Joshua thought his normal upbringing would probably be more disturbing to those who would look into his past than if they found what they had expected to. They would look in search of the next Jeffrey Dahmer or Ted Bundy and would find instead an all-American boy who excelled at school and was the apple of his parent's eye. They might skip on past his early years, hoping to find a trigger point later in life. They would see how he joined the army at eighteen, not because he had to, but because he wanted to serve his country and to protect it.

There would be no traumas to be found, no experiences which they could point to as the moment that sent him over the edge. In his mind's eye, he smiled. In the blackness of his coffin, his physical body barely twitched. It was at this point they would have to start accepting the truth that he wasn't insane or defective or even a monster.

He was just superior.

He was twenty-three when he was first selected for the Apex Project. He was working in administration at the time, the army preferring to put his brain to use in keeping their mountains of paperwork in order rather than have him flexing his muscles on the battlefield (and he did have them. At school he played college football to a standard good enough to turn pro if he wanted to). His job was to monitor the applications for men willing to test the cure and present the suitable candidates to Dr. Genaro. Three weeks passed without a single response. It seemed nobody was willing to try an experimental drug, even if it could potentially save countless lives.

Volunteering himself seemed like the most natural thing in the world, and it certainly didn't instil him with any fear. He knew well the advances in modern science and also had absolute and unconditional faith that god would protect him from any harm. Even so, confidence in principal was entirely different to confidence when actually faced with what he was about to do. His first meeting with Doctor Genaro was cordial, if tense. There were questions raised as to if Joshua was a little too intelligent to accurately represent their probable subjects, however with nobody else breaking down the doors to volunteer they went ahead. He was subjected to a number of physical and mental examinations measuring everything from height and weight to blood pressure and fitness. He recalled well that first meeting with Genaro as he was giving his blood sample. The scientist was incredibly thankful Joshua, at least, had enough faith in his work to volunteer his body. Genaro's words floated to him in the stifling dark of the coffin.

You will become a vessel Joshua, the carrier of something great which will represent the next stage in human evolution.

Joshua had said nothing, still firm in the belief that even evolution and the wonders of science were the work of God. How could they not be? Genaro had set the vial of Joshua's blood aside and told him he was done for the day.

"I thought you said I was to become a vessel?"

"You will, Joshua. All in good time."

It was after a further two weeks before Genaro called him back. Joshua entered the small office, detecting the faintest hint of antiseptic lingering behind the smell of lavender air freshener. Genaro was barely able to contain his excitement as he set a syringe on the table which was half filled with a clear liquid.

"Is that it?" Joshua asked, his throat suddenly dry.

"It is."

"Is it time?"

Genaro nodded.

"I'm afraid." Joshua had said, for the first time considering the magnitude of what was about to happen and the consequences if it went wrong.

Genaro had smiled at him and walked around the table, putting a reassuring hand on his shoulder. "You have nothing to fear, Joshua. I wouldn't be asking you to do this if I didn't have absolute faith in the project's success probability. This will make you into something nobody else can be, into someone who can make a real difference in this world. Of course, you are under no obligation to continue if you don't want to. There is still time to back out."

He shook his head. His parents were so incredibly proud of what he was doing, and he couldn't let them down. "No, I'm fine, it's just nerves. Go ahead and do it."

Genaro picked up the syringe and jabbed it into Joshua's shoulder, sending its contents into his bloodstream. He had waited for some kind of rush, some kind of euphoria. When nothing came, he stared at Genaro, who smiled at the confusion in Joshua's eyes.

"I don't feel any different." He mouthed the words again along with his memory as he lay in the darkness of his grave.

“You won’t, not yet at least. Soon you will. Believe it or not, as you sit here, you are a changed man."

"So what happens now?"

"You come back tomorrow and we give you another injection. We can’t do it all at once. It’s like building a magnificent structure, we have to do it one brick at a time."

For the next six week’s Joshua went to see Dr. Genaro. Usually on a Thursday morning, sometimes he would have to go again on a Monday. At first, he felt no different, and then, in the same way winter creeps up on summer and steals away the daylight, subtle changes were noticeable. His eyesight improved to the point where he could stop wearing his glasses. Asthma which had plagued him as a child was cured. He started to develop an incredible memory which was almost photogenic. New languages were learned in days. Like a sponge, he soaked up information. As his new bond with Genaro's medicine grew, the more he started to see the world with disdain. The more aware he became of the true possibilities which were inherent in the human body, the more it sickened him to see his fellow man throw away their precious existence. Worse, was the way they wantonly maimed the planet as if they owned it, rather than accepting their place in it like the parasites they were. Much like his time spent in his current underground solitude, those first months of bonding with the Apex virus seemed to change the way he perceived time. The more of it that passed, the more his hate for humanity grew.

It wasn't long before it became absolutely clear to him what he had to do. To what lengths he would have to go to in order to save the human race from itself, even if it meant doing something so radical, so extreme that it would change things forever.

That thought process had led him to where he was now, half comatose in the blackest of black, comforted by the chill, caressed by the crushing pressure of earth all around his private haven. The deprivation of his senses had let the bond between virus and host grow even more. The strain on his body forcing Genaro's medicine to work harder. Even though sight and sound were beyond him, he could sense the world, and within it his brothers, others like him, others who knew what had to be done. He could feel their presence, glowing entities out there in the world.

As he lay there, he imagined he could almost hear them marching towards him, coming to catch a glimpse of the father of the new world. Before he had entered his coffin, such a title was an idea, something he strived to be. But now after lying in the ground for... he hesitated.

How long had it been? Days? Weeks? Years? Perhaps even centuries? Maybe it had only been minutes and he still had a thousand lifetimes to wait.

No.

He didn't think so. He could feel the change. He had entered the hole as a man with something inside him to which he was a host. Now he felt no distinction between the two. He was it, and it was he, and together they were growing stronger and morphing into something incredible. He heard them again, the marching feet of a thousand men, his kin. His brothers.

Only....

It wasn’t marching. The sound wasn't in his mind, it existed in the real world.

It was the sound of digging, of shovels scraping on the wood of the coffin. That revelation had only taken seconds to sink in when the black veil lifted, and for the first time in almost two weeks, he saw the world.

They had come for him.

Strong arms lifted him from his exile and set him gently on the ground next to the grave.

He lay unmoving, feeling his body slowly come back to life. Blood forced its way through starving veins, muscles which had atrophied started to twitch as his body repaired itself from the inside. He blinked, his vision swimming into focus. There in the dark, he could see his brothers. His disciples, the two now twelve. It should have been impossible, and the look on the faces of his loyal followers suggested they agreed. Declining assistance, he stood, taking a moment to steady himself. His sunken eyes and gaunt face stared at them, each, in turn, making sure they understood.

"I am born again," he whispered, then staggered, almost toppling back into the hole. They steadied him, taking his weight as they led him to their sanctuary.

# CHAPTER SIX

## YUCATAN JUNGLE
## MEXICO

DRAVEN KNELT IN THE dirt, hunched over a small burrow in the ground. The sun was fierce against his back as he peered at the tiny ants scurrying around the jungle floor. Sweat gathered on the tip of his nose, which he wiped against the grubby sleeve of his t-shirt. As he knelt there with his knees and back screaming for mercy, Draven realised he wasn't a young man anymore. Or at least not quite as young. Years of exposure to the sun had turned his skin into a tough, leathery hide, and had bleached his hair into a not quite blonde, not quite brown mass which was wet with sweat and clinging to his face. Because of this, people thought he was older than he actually was and when he told them he was in his mid-thirties, eyebrows were raised in disbelief. He exhaled, trying to ignore the stifling humidity.

The Bullet ants went about their business, each inch long creature possessing a sting which delivered a potent neurotoxin which, in large enough dosage could cause paralysis and death. They were an aggressive species and the subject of Draven's current research. Until recently, they had only been known as native to Nicaragua and Paraguay, so to see them in the Yucatan was a surprise.

He had seen the aftermath of stings from these ants. The Satere-Mawe tribe, an indigenous group who live deep in the Amazon rainforest, have a unique use for the ants, one which Draven witnessed for himself. The rite of passage for a Satere-Mawe boy to become a man involves locating a bullet ant nest. Often they are found nesting at the base of trees (like the one Draven was currently observing), the ants swarming up into the tree in order to forage in the overhead leaves for small insects. Upon locating a nest, the Satere-

Mawe use smoke to render the ants unconscious and remove them. The ants are woven into a leaf glove with their stingers facing inward. In order for a Satere-Mawe boy to become a man, he must wear the glove for ten minutes, enduring the hundreds of stings of the angry ants inside. After the ten excruciating minutes are up, the glove is removed, often as the poor wearer convulses or slips into paralysis. Usually, within a week, the wearer will make a full recovery although in some cases death is the result of the bizarre and eye-watering initiation, which often has to be completed multiple times before the tribe accept the boy as a man. Draven himself had felt the sting of just one ant, more out of curiosity to see how it felt. The pain was excruciating to the point of incapacitating him for almost twenty-four hours. He lay in his bunk, arm throbbing, his insides on fire as the toxic venom ravaged his system. It was for that reason he kept a respectful distance from the nest which he knew could contain literally thousands of ants. His primary interest in the creatures was in how they attacked. An aggressive species by nature, the bullet ant had an ability to attack any intruder en masse. He had learned this was due to the first attacking ant releasing a pheromone to which all the other ants responded. Attacks on humans were often a case of a poor hiker accidentally kicking a nest open without realising it was there, only to find their legs covered with thousands of the tiny and aggressive creatures attacking in a frenzy. His train of thought was broken by the humanoid shadow which fell across the floor in front of him.

He looked over his shoulder, squinting against the sun. "Can I help you?"

"Are you Richard Draven?" the woman said as she stepped closer, blocking out the glare of the sun, her blue eyes trained on him.

"Yes. Who are you?" He said, getting to his feet with a wince as his knees popped in protest.

"You're a difficult man to track down."

"People don't often come looking for me. What can I do for you?"

"You need to come with me."

"Am I under arrest?" he said, finding time to appreciate her good looks. Her hair, in particular, seemed to glow as it was lit by the sun.

"No, you're not under arrest. Even if you were, I wouldn’t have the power to do it."

“You still haven’t told me who you are,” Draven said, keeping a close eye on the ant's nest to make sure they were keeping their distance.

“My name is Kate Goodall. I work for the government.”

“What does that have to do with me?”

“I’ll tell you on the way. Right now we have to leave.”

"I'm sorry, but I'm afraid I can't go anywhere. I'm busy here."

The woman scowled, pursing her thin lips and wiping a forearm against her forehead. There was a harshness about her which was both attractive and intimidating. He couldn't resist checking out the rest of her. Good figure, long legs poking out from khaki shorts.

"Homeland security sent me," she said, folding

her arms.

Draven hesitated, glancing down at the Bullet ant nest. "You sure you have the right guy?"

"We don't make mistakes. You're definitely who we're looking for."

"That's nice to know," Draven said. "I'm still not going anywhere until you tell me what you want."

She sighed, planting her hands on hips. "I work as a special liaison for the United States government. I need you to come and consult us on a developing situation back on US soil.”

"I'm afraid my consulting days are behind me. There are much better-qualified people out there I'm sure."

"Not about this," Kate said, holding his gaze.

"I'm not sure if the people at Homeland Security know this, but my reputation isn't exactly stellar in the science community these days. If it's a consultant you want, I suggest Sebastian Eller or Mary-Ann Palmer. I’m sure they would be more than happy to help you."

"I'm sure they're good, but I also know they don't know anything about the Tiger monkey you discovered in the Congo."

Draven stared at her, two people alone surrounded by thriving jungle and a couple of thousand Bullet ants. "I'm done with that part of my life. It nearly ruined me." He grunted.

"I know what happened and I know what was said. It turns out, you might yet have a chance to vindicate yourself and prove you were right."

"It's accepted now that I was right, or at least, it is, for the most part, even so, the damage is already done. Either way, it's a dead end. Science isn't in a position to do anything with my research anyway. Not only was I made a fool out of by my colleagues, it was all for nothing to boot. I'm sorry, I can't help you."

He knelt again, trying to concentrate on the ant nest but finding himself staring at Goodall's shadow, which was still thrown across the dirt in front of him and showed no signs of moving.

"What if I told you not only was your research

valid, it had also already been implemented into human subjects."

Draven turned to face her. "I'd tell you it's impossible."

"It's true," Kate said, staring at Draven.

"It's bull."

"You said so yourself, Mr. Draven. Why would they send me all the way out here for someone like you with your questionable reputation if your inclusion in this situation wasn’t absolutely vital?"

"That's a bit harsh, but okay. I'll admit, you have me curious. Tell me more." Draven said, again enduring the pain in his knees as he clambered back to his feet.

"I will, but not until we’re on a plane out of here and on our way back to Washington."

He stared at her and was definitely starting to change his perception of Goodall as just eye candy with security clearance. There seemed to be more layers to this particular onion than he first thought.

“What if I refuse?” he said, deciding to push her a little bit more.

"That's up to you. I'll report back to my superiors about your unwillingness to help and they will send out a team to arrest you. You can either do this of your own free will or via a prison cell Mr. Draven. It's your choice."

"When do we leave?" he muttered, taking a last look at the nest and thinking about all the research he was about to miss out on.

"Right now. There's a private plane waiting at the airport."

"Private plane huh?" Draven said with a sour grin "How can I refuse?" He was flirting, testing the waters, seeing if she would respond, which in a way, she did. However, stony silence wasn't the reaction he was hoping for. "Come, on lighten up. I said I'd come with you didn't I?" He added.

"If you knew what we could be up against here, you might not be quite so cheery."

"Well that just put me in a bad mood," Draven grumbled as he brushed dirt from his pants. He took a great gulp of water from the plastic bottle in his bag and then offered it to Goodall.

"No thanks," She said, slipping on a pair of stylish sunglasses. "Come on, we better go."

II

Five hours later, Draven had swapped the oppressive humidity of the Yucatan jungle for the air conditioned spaciousness of the private jet which had been sent for him. Feeling like a new man after a hot shower and a change of clothes, he looked out at the expanse of cloudless sky as they cruised at almost forty thousand feet. He and Goodall were the only passengers, and as she had disappeared up front some time ago, he was seriously considering trying to get some much-needed shut-eye. Taking advantage of the plush leather seats, he stretched out his legs and stifled a yawn. As if sensing his intentions, Goodall strode through the door from the cockpit area and dropped an overstuffed file on his lap.

"You better start reading. We don't have much time." She said as she grabbed the remote control for the flat screen TV mounted at the front of the cabin.

"What's all this?" Draven said, leafing through the reams of paper.

"That's why we brought you here. That folder is what became of your discovery."

She scowled and sat opposite, watching him intently.

"Have I done something to offend you?" He asked, unable to ignore the hostility aimed at him.

"No, why?" She asked in the way women always did when no meant yes.

"Well, you've been short with me ever since you found me. Remember, I didn't come looking for you."

"It's nothing personal."

"So what is it?"

"I don't like having to come all the way out here to babysit you. It's a waste of time."

"Well, I'm sorry to hear that, but it's not my fault. Take it up with your boss if you have a problem."

She straightened in her seat, perhaps not expecting such a response.

"Sorry," she said with a sigh, relaxing a little. "It's been a rough few days. You have no idea how much is riding on you being able to provide us with some answers. It irks me when you joke around and make light of things."

"Don't take it personally. It's a defensive thing. Some kind of coping mechanism or so my therapist told me. I make jokes out of serious situations. It's how I get by. It doesn't mean I'm not interested or paying attention. In fact, I'm more than a little curious. To be fair, you haven't been very forthcoming in handing over information. I still don't even know why I'm being dragged to the other side of the world."

She tucked her fringe behind her ear and folded her hands on her lap. "I'm supposed to wait until my boss briefs you."

"Based on the size of this file you just gave me, any head start will be appreciated."

"Give me a minute," She said, standing and

taking her phone back through the door towards the cockpit.

Draven leafed through the first few pages of the file, which didn't appear to be in any kind of order. He made a mental note to complain to Goodall about it, if only to see if he could push her buttons a little more for his own amusement, when she came back, shoving her phone into her pocket.

"Okay, you want answers, you'll get them direct from my superiors," She said as she switched the channel on the TV. "It's a live webcam link, so you might want to sit up straight," She said as she activated the camera. Draven ignored her, slumping further down in his seat just to be annoying. On the screen was a dreary looking office desk, behind which was an equally dreary looking man dressed in an ill-fitting grey suit. He had the look of a school teacher in everything apart from his eyes, which were a sharp and brilliant blue.

"Mr. Draven," the man on the screen said. "Pleased to meet you at last. My name is Marcus Atkinson, Homeland Security director. It's me who gave the order to bring you in."

Draven was barely paying attention. Something in the files had caught his eye, and he was furiously leafing through the pages, a deep frown on his brow.

"Mr. Draven?" Marcus said again.

"Am I reading this right? You mixed the primate DNA with a human?" Draven said, staring at the television screen.

"It's not quite as simple as that, I'll explain in full when we meet but-"

"This won't wait. Did you or did you not merge the primate DNA with people?"

"Yes, we did," Marcus said. "That's why we need to speak to you. It seems we are having certain issues with our test subjects."

"Let me guess," Draven said, sneering at the screen. "These people you modified are showing extreme increases in aggression. I'd bet my house I wouldn't be a million miles away if I suggested they had also stopped following orders? Maybe gone into business for themselves?"

"How did you know that, Mr. Draven?" Marcus asked, shifting his gaze towards Goodall.

"I'm asking the questions," Draven snapped. "Am I right or am I wrong?"

Marcus squirmed in his seat. "Yes. That's exactly right. Are you suggesting you know why this has happened?"

"I know exactly why. Who was in charge of this? The genetics project, I mean."

"A scientist called Genaro, he's supposed to be the best," Marcus said.

"Robert Genaro?"

"Yes. Do you know him?" Marcus said, glancing towards Kate.

"I only met him once, but I know his work. He's supposed to be brilliant, which is why I'm surprised he missed such a huge and obvious flaw."

"What are we dealing with here Mr. Draven?" Marcus said, straightening a little in his seat.

"Is Genaro there?" Draven said, ignoring the question as he started to separate some pages from the rest of the file.

"No, he isn't.

"Get him there. I need to talk to him."

"He's unavailable until at least tomorrow. Anything you need to say you can do so now. This conversation is being recorded so I can relay it back to him straight away."

“That’s not good enough. I need to speak to him. I have questions.”

“He seems to think you are the most knowledgeable on this subject, Mr. Draven,” Marcus said with more than a hint of irritability. “That’s why we came all this way to get you.”

“As far as research about the Tiger monkeys goes, yes I am. Most of this relates to Genaro’s work after my involvement ended. No disrespect, but I don’t have time to dumb it down for you. I need to speak to him directly.”

Marcus cleared his throat and straightened his tie. Draven could see he had pushed a little too far and hoped it served to relay how urgent his request was. “Mr. Draven, please. I appreciate what you’re saying. However, we can’t reach Dr. Genaro right now. Could you please give it to me in simple terms so I can at least give the rest of the people working on this some kind of idea about what we're dealing with?"

Draven sighed, tapping his fingers on the file. "Okay fine, I'll give you the simple version. It seems to me that Genaro based his entire program on the single paper I published in nineteen-ninety-nine on the specific healing properties of the tiger monkey. What he wouldn't know is that there was much more to my findings than made the article. Long story short, this species of monkey had all of these amazing regenerative properties and a killer immune system, but it all came at a price."

"Go on," Marcus said, his brow furrowed.

"I conducted experiments on these creatures and found that along with the increased resilience and seeming unlimited regeneration, the monkeys also had flaws. Something put into the creature's genetic makeup by nature to counterbalance its amazing abilities. My experiment's showed the male monkeys possessed incredibly inflated levels of testosterone, so much so that they would go into a frenzy and fight to the death with other members of the group for little to no reason, often with no provocation. Have you ever heard of the term roid rage?"

"Yes," Marcus said, folding his hands on his desk. "That's what they call increased aggression in long-term steroid users."

"Exactly. Now imagine that a thousand fold and you will see why I'm so concerned. In the wild, the Tiger monkey aggression was controlled in a sense because they had a definite hierarchy within the community with one male acting as the Alpha to which the rest of the species deferred. Also, due to the harshness of their environment in the Congo, they were forced to exist together in a form of uneasy alliance. What you, or should I say, Genaro has done, is take those traits and merge them with the volatile and complex human machine."

"What does that mean for us?" Marcus asked.

"Humans as a species are an incredibly selfish, violent and bloodthirsty race. We are ruled by greed, jealousy, anger, selfishness and every other flawed emotion you can imagine. Think about it from the point of view of those who have been changed for a second. What would you do if you had almost unlimited power, and a volatile no tolerance temper to boot? To put it a better way, what would you do if the restrictive rules of society, of right and wrong no longer applied to you? What if you were superior to your fellow man and knew nobody could do anything about it? Would you still take orders from those you deemed beneath you? Or would you decide for yourself what you wanted to do?"

"This is worse than we thought," Marcus muttered.

"Not to heap more misery on you, but I can see it getting worse before it gets better," Draven said.

“In what way?”

“You said they've gone rogue, is that right?"

"Yes, we’ve lost all communication with them. Intelligence has picked up a possible sighting going into the Tremont tunnels in Boston. We have a team en route and about to engage. Other than that, we have no leads. Any idea why?"

"I think so, but I need to read these files first to check my info. In the meantime, please contact Genaro as a matter of urgency. This is important."

“Absolutely,” Marcus said. “Is there anything we can do in the meantime to help from this end?”

“All any of us can do now is pray it’s not too late,” Draven said.

“Alright,” Marcus replied. “Call me back on this line if you need anything else. I’ll have a car waiting for you when you land.”

The connection was broken as Kate stood and switched off the TV. She looked at Draven, perhaps hoping for him to elaborate. He however simply turned away and stared out of the window and for the first time in as long as he could remember, prayed he was wrong.

# CHAPTER SEVEN

TREMONT UNDERGROUND TUNNELS
BOSTON, MASSACHUSETS
USA.

TRAFFIC CRAWLED THROUGH THE thriving streets of Boston as locals and tourists alike went about their daily routine. Little did they know they walked above a secret which had been beneath the city since the early nineteenth century. The Tremont subway system was initially built to ease street car traffic. Opened in 1897, they are officially the oldest tunnels in North America. As the city grew, and traffic from the city's four railway stations was rerouted and diverted, new tunnels were built, leaving the Tremont line as a relic of a time gone by. Abandoned and forgotten, it had drifted out of the consciousness of the local residents as modern technology paved the way for a faster, more efficient service.

The SAS team led by Johnson had been indulging in their unique and vulgar brand of banter right up until their unmarked van stopped at the tunnel entrance. As Parker, Briggs, Stanhope and Trig had pulled their black balaclavas into place, hiding all but their eyes, it was as if a switch had been pressed and full on business mode had been activated. Personal differences were pushed aside, individual grievances forgotten. Now, they were at work, and would live or die together and for each other. Johnson had crouched with them in the back of the van as they double and triple checked weapons.

"This is the wanker we want," Johnson said, showing them a grainy photograph of Joshua.

"CCTV got him at a petrol station a few days ago. This is hush hush which is why our yank friends have called us in to deal with this."

"Who is he?" Stanhope said, adjusting his grip on his weapon.

"Names Joshua Cook, the yanks want him for offing some soldiers at one of their bases. They want him alive, and because yanks tend to get sensitive about this kind of thing and might get trigger happy, they want us to come in and clean up their mess."

"Any idea how many are down in the tunnels with him?" Briggs asked.

"No, not exactly. Let's go in expecting shit and hoping for sugar." Johnson grunted. "Trig, I want you ready with the explosives on the off chance they've barricaded themselves in down there. Low impact stuff, though, yeah? Not like Syria."

"Got it, boss," Trig said. "I know what I'm doing."

"I hope so. The last thing we need is for you to bring the city falling down on our fuckin' heads whilst we're underneath it."

"Got it boss. Low impact." Trig repeated.

"Alright," Johnson said with a sigh. Most of you have been in situations like this before. You know what to expect. You know what to do. Watch each other's backs. Make use of the flash bangs. Clear your corners. One room at a time boys, alright?"

The men nodded.

"Stanhope!" Johnson said.

"Sir?"

"You keep your eyes and ears open. You have the least experience here, so it's in your interest to watch and listen and try not to die."

"Got it, boss," Stanhope said, his eyes flicking to the others. "I'm ready for it."

"Just don't go in there like fuckin' Rambo and thinking you're invincible. You're a cog in the machine. A new one at that. Don't forget it."

Stanhope nodded, glancing at the others and feeling all eyes on him.

"Okay then," Johnson said. "Let's do it.

Remember, it's likely going to be close combat down there. We only want this Joshua character alive. The rest are expendable. Intelligence says these guys are likely wearing body armour, so remember to double tap these pricks. Any questions?"

He waited, looking into the eyes of the men. "Okay then, let's go."

They bundled out of the van, Johnson in the lead, the others in twos behind, keeping low as they ran towards the tunnel entrance.

II

The network of tunnels had proved perfect for Joshua and the rest of his growing following as a base of operations. In just a few short weeks they had gathered supplies and weapons in great numbers, stealing without detection when they could, taking by force if they had to. Joshua was sure he would be able to put his plan into action without distraction, so was surprised to find their sanctuary breached by assailants who were, for the time being unknown. He walked through the curved main tunnel, veering off into one of the many sub-chambers towards his most trusted disciples. Already the steady crackle of controlled gunfire was echoing through the vast chambers.

"We've been compromised," Peter said, watching Joshua and waiting to be told what to do.

Joshua smiled and ran a hand through his hair. "Who are they?"

"We don’t know. There are five of them. Very organised. We outnumber them, but they are better trained than us." Simon said, lowering his gaze.

He was one of those who had been present when Joshua had gone into the ground and had held vigil until he rose again. In the old world, he was called Eric, however after his resurrection, Joshua had personally rechristened him, dousing his head with water and renaming him as Simon. He and the rest of the twelve men had been ordered to shave their heads to a buzz cut, told their new life began with abandoning the vanity of the old. Only Joshua was different, with long black hair which touched his shoulders. His narrow face was now thick with the beard which he had been growing since he first volunteered his body to the earth as a short haired, clean shaved man.

"What should we do, Joshua?" Simon asked, glancing towards the tunnels as another sporadic crackle of gunfire erupted.

"Are you prepared to fight?" Joshua asked, showing little concern at the sound of gunfire which was growing ever louder as his woefully overmatched men were pushed further back.

"You know all of us will die for you," Simon said, looking him in the eye. “Whatever it takes."

"Good," he replied with a small smile. "Now pull your men back."

"But Joshua..."

"Do as I say, Simon. I wouldn’t ask you to do for me something I’m not prepared to do for you. Take them and flee. If it’s me they want, then it’s me they shall have."

"You’re staying?"

Joshua nodded.

"But why?" Simon said, visibly flustered. “We need you. You’re our leader. Our father.”

"Remember our mission,” Joshua said with a smile. “Remember how it is bigger than any one of us. I don’t want you to see me as a figurehead who only gives orders. I need to show you how I’m prepared to do for you anything I ask you to do for me."

"Who will lead us?"

"You all know what to do. You know what the mission entails. Take the men into the world, find the others. The twelve of you are my generals. Lay the foundations for the new world. Go to the sanctuary, the one we discussed."

"I don’t know what to say..." Simon replied his voice wavering.

"Then don't say anything. Pull the men back."

"Please, let me go in your place, I’ll give myself up so you can escape."

Joshua smiled and put a hand on Simon's shoulder. "I appreciate the sentiment, but I have given my orders. It has to be me who goes with them. If they are to have a prisoner, then I must be it."

"Why? I don't understand?"

The chatter of gunfire was close now, and amid the smoke and the screams, the voices of their assailants as they grew closer increased in volume.

"I don't ask you to understand," Joshua said, "only to follow. Go now. Do as I ask."

Simon hesitated, then stepped back. "You can count on me."

"I know. Now go, hurry. Escape through the tunnels you and the twelve. Make me proud."

Glancing one last time towards the sound of the gunfire, Simon jogged into the tunnels, leaving Joshua alone.

He stood for a few moments, eyes closed and listening to the sound of the destruction as it came closer. There was a beauty to those sounds. The screams, the zing of gunfire, the shouts of the men who had invaded the tunnels as they methodically cleared each sub-chamber. Joshua clasped his hands behind his back, and whistling a happy tune which was inaudible over the roar of gunfire, walked towards the chaos.

III

It soon became clear as they moved through the tunnels that the resistance, although determined, was both unprepared and untrained to deal with the close combat expertise of Johnson's team. Room by room, chamber by chamber, they pushed deeper, killing those who resisted with the routine double tap method as instructed. (One shot to the heart, another to the head to make sure)

It was Parker who first saw Joshua as he walked out of the smoke, strolling towards the centre of the tunnel right in front of them, a serene calm amid the chaos. The two locked eyes and Joshua smiled, holding out his arms to the sides.

"Down, fucking get down!" Parker screamed, aiming his M16 assault rifle at Joshua. The rest of the team had joined him now, and all were screaming the same instructions. Joshua smiled.

"On the ground, on the ground right now!" Johnson said, eyes bulging as he looked beyond Joshua to ensure the way was clear.

Joshua dropped to his knees, folding his hands behind his head and closing his eyes.

Briggs and Trig moved in, pushing Joshua to the ground and cuffing his hands behind his back as Stanhope and Parker took up defensive positions.

"We've been looking for you," Johnson said as Joshua was pulled to his feet.

"And now you found me."

Johnson faltered at the completely relaxed and unafraid nature of Joshua's reaction. "Come on then, there are a few people keen to have a few words with you."

"I'm sure there are."

Johnson hesitated again, unsure how to take Joshua. There was a magnetism about him, and he had to remind himself he was dealing with what was by all accounts a very dangerous individual.

Johnson tore himself away from Joshua's

piercing gaze and tried to get his mind back on the job. "Let's get out of this fuckin' shithole. I don't like it down here."

"What about the rest of the tunnels sir?" Stanhope said.

"Fuck it. We got what we came for."

"Yes sir," Stanhope said.

The men led Joshua away. Johnson waited for a few seconds, trying to control the tight gnawing in his guts. Something wasn't right. The operation had gone smoothly. Too smoothly. It was almost as if Joshua had wanted to be captured. Either way, he decided the sooner they handed him over to the Americans, the better he would feel. Taking a deep breath, he jogged to catch up with the rest of his team. Joshua allowed them to lead him. Still smiling, still whistling that jolly tune from his childhood.

# CHAPTER EIGHT

CITY OF BAGHDAD,

IRAQ

THE PEOPLE OF IRAQ have long been used to unrest. In an almost perpetual state of conflict, the people on street level who simply want to live their daily lives are often forgotten amid the globally televised presence of the British and American forces (who were either seen as saviours or invaders depending on who you spoke to) and the Taliban insurgents, who had as many supporters as they did detractors. With neither side willing to back down, it was the public who suffered, living in constant fear. Akhtar had never known peace, and so the rattle of distant gunfire and constant military presence were perfectly normal to him. However, something had changed in recent days, something which he couldn't quite understand and liked even less.

He led his brother by the hand through the maze-like streets, skirting around fellow citizens who were in just as much of a hurry as he was. He looked into the faces of these strangers as he passed, and saw they too wore the same tense expression which had been brought about by the recent change in the atmosphere. Akhtar glanced at his brother, who was devoid of any concern or panic. His face was a picture of simple wonder, his mental deficiencies blocking out the wider problems of the world. Akhtar didn't know exactly what was wrong with him, only that he had been born a lot earlier than he should have been, and spent a lot of his early months in the hospital. Now aged seven, he relied on the care of others. Sometimes, Akhtar would look at him and be sure he could see intelligence in his eyes, and with it frustration at not being able to articulate it. Youness mouthed words, which to most would be a series of unintelligible grunts. Akhtar and his family had learned to understand his brother's unique language perfectly, though, and looked at the source of his sibling's distress, which in this case was an untied shoe.

"Come on, in here," Akhtar said, leading Youness to an open arched passageway off the main street. He knelt and started to tie his brother's shoe, still unable to shake the uneasy feeling in his stomach. Someone sprinted past the doorway, making Akhtar draw a sharp breath. He leaned out of the passage, watching the man go on without stopping, looking over his shoulder every few seconds before disappearing into the crowd. Akhtar looked back the way the man had come and saw people craning their necks as they looked down the street. Others, like the man who ran past them, were moving on, hurrying away from whatever they could see.

"Wait here, Youness. Don't move." Akhtar said, getting to his feet and giving the crowd his full attention. Something was definitely going on. He could tell by the activity at the head of the narrow street where he stood. The main thoroughfare was now jammed with people who were, for the most part looking back over their shoulder. With the agility possessed by most children of Akhtar's age, he clambered onto the window ledge of the building where they had stopped and cupped his hand around his eyes so he could see against the glare of the sun. There appeared to be some kind of commotion in the middle of the street. There were five men, all armed and dressed in black. He recognised the uniforms as the same ones worn by the soldier at the checkpoint who had taken out the terrorist attack single handed. The five men were arguing with a team of US soldiers, who outnumbered them by at least ten. Snatches of words came to Akhtar through the still air, but the general chatter of those around him made it impossible to pick out what was being said.

An older man down on street level saw Akhtar's vantage point and joined him on the window ledge, gripping the inside of the open frame to steady himself so that he too could see what was happening. The two shared a second of eye contact, before turning back to the face off in the street. The U.S soldiers were now gesticulating with their weapons, faces set into determined grimaces. The men dressed in black pointing in response to the insignias on their shoulders. Even from so far away, Akhtar could sense the danger as memories of what happened at the checkpoint a few weeks earlier came flooding back. It was normal to see the military here in the city, however, it was not usual to see them undermined or otherwise disobeyed.

One of the soldiers levelled his weapon at one of the men in black, shifting smoothly into a firing stance. Feet spread apart, rifle glimmering in the sunshine. The man in black who was the subject of the soldier's attention seemed unconcerned, and Akhtar even saw him smile.

It happened quickly, almost too quickly. The men in black moved as one as if they were a single entity rather than separate people. They darted forwards and attacked the soldiers, the coordinated pattern of their movements reminding Akhtar of the way flocks of birds would change direction in unison. The soldier who had been aiming his rifle was dead before he had a chance to react. The man in black had stepped forward, pushing his shoulder against the barrel of the gun. The soldier reflexively fired, Akhtar clearly able to see the explosion of blood and bone as the bullet tore through the man in blacks shoulder and out of the other side. In the same instant, the black-clad man unsheathed his hunting knife and drove it up under the soldier's chin, burying it up to the handle, the tip of the blade pushing the soldier's helmet up as it exited the top of his skull. The man removed it, as bright red blood began to soak into the sandy desert floor. As the soldier fell back, the man in black grabbed his weapon with his free hand, sheathed his knife and turned the assault rifle on the crowd. The rest of his team made equally short work of the other soldiers and commandeered their weapons. Without reason or provocation, the men in black started to fire into the crowd.

The man on the window ledge with Akhtar had seen enough, and leapt down, racing away from the carnage. Akhtar, however, was frozen, too afraid to move. The crowd of onlookers were now fleeing from the men in black and were charging towards where he perched like an undulating wave. The sounds of footfalls reverberating off the walls was deafening and only broken by the incessant gunfire as the men in black gunned down people at random. There was no way Akhtar could get down. People were running past at too high a speed, too afraid to pay attention to where they were going and who they might hit. Akhtar took a last look down the street, trying to ignore the rivers of blood pouring from the corpses which lay twisted at the feet of the men who were leisurely continuing their rampage. The leader of the men, the one with the shoulder wound grinned as he shot a young woman in the face from just a few feet away, disintegrating her head in a shower of blood, hair and bone. It was the nasal whine of his sobbing brother which spurred Akhtar to action.

Youness was crouched in the doorway, chin slick with drool, cheeks wet with tears. Unable to understand what was happening, he held out a hand to Akhtar, pleading for his help. Without thinking, Akhtar jumped down into the crowd, barely noticing the explosion of sandstone as the window frame exploded in the space which had just been inhabited by his head as a stray bullet hit home. He was being pushed now by the surge of people trying to flee, past the alley where his brother cried and waited expectantly. Akhtar reached out, grabbed his brother's wrist and pulled him into the crowd.

"Come on Youness, we must run," he yelled over his shoulder. The gunfire was closer now and was intercut with more screaming.

Akhtar did his best to drag his brother along but knew it was impossible. Youness didn't have the dexterity to keep up on his own. Somehow without stopping or losing his footing, Akhtar scooped his brother up, holding him tight and doing his best to run along with the flow of people. Youness was heavy, and with the added weight, it was impossible to keep the pace with the terrified throng of people. The ground had become softer underfoot, uneven. Akhtar knew it was because he was standing on people, and he forced himself not to look, knowing to do so would resign both he and his brother to the same fate. Youness was still whining, screeching in Akhtar's ear, drooling against his cheek. Someone shoved them, desperate to get past the slow moving pair. With the additional weight of Youness in his arms, he was unable to maintain his balance and felt himself pitching forward amidst the tangle of fleeing legs. He managed to retain his balance, stumbling a little and almost reaching the point of overbalance, then somehow managed to right himself. A fresh patter of gunfire zipped overhead, driving the already terrified crowd to increase their speed - something which he himself could not. Another shove from the rear, this time harder and with more intent, ensuring any chance of retaining his balance was little more than a hope replaced by blind panic as he struck the ground, his knees taking the brunt of the impact. He fell atop his brother, cupping his head and trying his best to protect him from the army of feet which were around them. Someone stood on his leg, someone else on his back as the people desperate tried to flee the attack, either not caring or too horrified to notice what they were doing as they systematically crushed him further into the dirt. He glanced to the side and saw someone who had suffered the same fate. The man was lying on the floor, head turned to one side, dead eyes wide and staring. Blood seeped from his nose and ears, and his teeth were shattered. Even so, Akhtar recognised him as the man who was perched alongside him on the window ledge just minutes earlier. In a surreal display, Akhtar watched as every few seconds, a foot would stand on the man's face, bugging his eyes out of his skull which looked to already have been severely softened by the constant trampling. Someone kicked him in the ribs, stumbled, glared back at the two boys then carried on running. Akhtar knew they had to move, to fight to their feet if they wanted to survive. Without grace or worrying about hurting his brother, he lurched to his feet, grabbing his sibling roughly by the arm and yanking him upright, ignoring the sting of pain where he had been kicked and stood on, all in the name of survival. A quick glance over his shoulder renewed his urgency, as the men dressed in black were closer, now just twenty feet away from where they stood towards the rear of the thinning crowd. Akhtar dragged his brother towards a narrow alleyway between two buildings, hoping it would, at least, offer them a chance to regroup. The gap was smaller than it looked, Akhtar having to turn side on to squeeze between the buildings at either side. The alley appeared to lead towards a sewer drain of sorts, a circular drain pipe which was wedged at the rear of the alley, the blackness beyond their sanctuary from the horror in the streets. Akhtar shoved his brother in first, hating himself for bringing more panic and upset to the screaming seven-year-old. He was aware that they had backed themselves into a dead end, and if the men in black happened to glance into the alleyway as they walked past, they would be unable to escape death.

"Go further into the tunnel," Akhtar hissed at Youness, shoving his head down and pushing him into the filthy, dark opening.

Youness whined and cried, scratching at his brother.

“Do it now, Youness. Please.” Akhtar hated to do it. He knew his brother was terrified of the dark, and that this was probably terrifying him. A crackle of gunfire reminded Akhtar that he could deal with a brother who was afraid and upset as long as he was alive. He shoved his brother into the dark ahead of him, gasping for breath and falling to his knees, not caring what might be floating in the water as long as they were safe

Youness was sobbing, his face streaked with a combination of tears, drool and sweat. Akhtar grimaced at the amplified sounds of his brother's cries, as they bounced off the walls and spread deeper into the sewer system. It was too loud, and would surely draw the attention of the men in black. Hating himself for doing it, Akhtar covered his brother's mouth, restraining him as he struggled in confusion.

"Shh, you must be quiet, please Youness, be still," Akhtar whispered in his ear.

The younger boy simply didn't understand what was happening and continued to kick and thrash and try to wriggle from his brother's grip. Akhtar was about to try a different method of silencing Youness when he saw the men in black walk past the gap between the buildings. He drew breath and increased the pressure on his brother’s mouth, backing further into the darkness of the tunnel. The men walked past the alleyway, none of them casting a single glance in their direction. As they followed the direction the bulk of the crowd had gone. Akhtar waited, counting to sixty in his head and listening to the screaming and gunfire move away from him. Realising he was holding his breath, he relaxed and released his grip on Youness, who responded with a fresh torrent of tears, glaring at Akhtar with eyes which were confused and afraid. Akhtar let him cry. After all, he deserved to feel guilty for putting his brother through such an ordeal. When Youness eventually calmed and his sobs morphed into occasional moans, Akhtar turned his thoughts to what their next move should be. The city was no longer safe, of that there was no doubt, and even if he did try to go back the way they came he doubted he could get Youness to go with him. He looked over his shoulder into the inky darkness of the sewer tunnels. It seemed it was their only option.

"Come on Youness, let's go," Akhtar said, holding a trembling hand out towards his brother.

Youness looked at it, still confused as to what was happening. Reluctantly, he grabbed Akhtar's hand, and the two boys stood, Akhtar having to hunch over in the small tunnel.

"Let's see if we can find a way out," he said as they walked, immediately noticing that rather than stay level, the tunnel seemed to decline, sending them deeper below ground level. As they inched further into the foul smelling underground, Akhtar couldn't shake the feeling that what they had experienced was just the beginning, and things were about to get much, much worse.

# CHAPTER NINE

GENTEC LABORATORY
WASHINGTON D. C

FROM THE OUTSIDE, GENARO'S lab

looked like nothing more than a modern glass and steel building on the outskirts of Washington DC. As one of the many unlisted government buildings located all over the United States, its purpose was neither advertised nor queried and ran mostly off the books. Genaro's research which started off in the office of the home he used to share with his late wife and funded by the little cash he could beg or borrow from those showing interest in his work, had grown into a laboratory covering five hundred square feet of real estate and contained the very latest (and most expensive) equipment which was provided to Genaro without question upon request. A lot of the equipment he didn’t actually need and were the result of the early weeks when the budget cap on his project was lifted. He ordered the most expensive equipment he could, not because he would need it, but because for the first time he was able to be so indulgent and wanted to see just how much leash he would be given. His staff of forty was made up of some of the brightest brains in genetic research, and all answered directly to him.

What his staff weren't aware of, was the secondary laboratory which was accessed via Genaro's office and located in the sub-basement. It was here where his own private research took place, away from the prying eyes of his staff who he knew were only a stolen idea away from being rivals. It was here, in the fifty-foot square lab space where Joshua was being held. The holding chamber was made of bulletproof Lexan, which was the same material which was used in the Popes bubble car and the presidential limousine. Joshua lay on his bunk, slender hands folded behind his head. He glanced towards the door as it opened and Genaro walked in accompanied by two men who he recognised. Curious, he stood and watched them approach.

"Is this him?" Genaro said to Robbins.

"Yeah, that's the guy," Robbins grunted, walking to within inches of the reinforced Perspex and looking Joshua in the eye.

"You were at Camp Blanding," Joshua said, a flicker of a smile on his lips.

"Yeah, I was. I saw what you did to those men. Our men."

"They started it. I did try to warn them, but they wouldn't listen."

"Don't try to justify it you prick, you killed them in cold blood."

"To call it cold blood would imply I cared. I can assure you, that wasn't the case. It was an unfortunate accident."

"Don't give me that crap. Trust me, you'll get the chair for this. Executed like you deserve." Robbins grunted.

"I don't think so," Joshua said, letting the smile grow to its full width. "I don't think so at all."

"Commander Robbins," Genaro said, cutting in before Robbins could respond. "I think it might be a good idea to go upstairs and get some fresh air."

"Yeah, I think so too," Robbins said, glaring at Joshua. "Just remember what I said, asshole. You'll fry for this."

Genaro waited until the commander made his leave, then grabbed his tattered desk chair, rolled it in front of Joshua's holding cell and sat down.

"How are you, Joshua?" He asked, taking off his glasses and slipping them into his breast pocket.

"I've been here for almost seven hours now. This is the first time you've been to visit me. Have I offended you so much?"

"I've been busy. There is nothing personal in it."

"I'm sure you have," Joshua replied, sitting on the edge of his bunk, watching the scientist carefully.

"Your hair got long," Genaro said, an almost wistful smile forming on his ancient face.

"I'm growing it."

"It goes well with the beard."

"I know."

"You look very....biblical."

Joshua smiled and folded his hands together. For a moment, Genaro thought he was praying, then saw that he was, in fact, waiting for the scientist to go on.

"Look, Joshua, you've caused a lot of trouble

and there are people who are demanding answers. Now you and I have a history, and I hoped you would open up to me and explain your actions. Believe it or not, I don't want to see you hurt. I want to help you."

"I appreciate that Doctor Genaro. You were always good to me. My father always said you were a good man." Joshua's smile was warm and genuine as he spoke, his voice amplified through the speaker on the front of the cell.

"Then let me help you. Of anyone, you know I won't hurt you. You know how much I appreciate what you did for me by volunteering for the Apex programme." Genaro said.

"Yes, I know you have good intentions. I also know I mean more to you alive than dead. But you need to understand, that I'm not the naive boy you remember who started this journey. Things have changed."

"I mean no disrespect. I think of you as a son. You know that."

"And in a way, I am. You took the boy I was

and turned me into the man I am. Mary Shelley would be proud."

"You're no monster, Joshua. No matter what they tell you."

"Nor was the creature in the Shelley novel. He was a bright, misunderstood individual who was feared because he dared to be what his creator had made. Only when the book was translated to film did he become grotesque and frightening. I wonder if this tale will have a similar conclusion."

"I'm sorry, I meant no disrespect, I'm just doing as I was asked. As I said, I want to help you."

"And to do that, you need information, I presume?"

Genaro nodded. Joshua smiled. "You want to know how it's working, don't you?"

"I'd be lying if I said no. They shipped you off to Afghanistan before I could see the results. You have no idea how I fought to have them leave you behind so I could continue to work with you."

"Yes, I never understood why they sent me off to a war zone so quickly. I suppose the governments of the world wanted a return for their investment, to try out their new toy. Still, this isn't quite how I imagined us meeting again. I’m unsure if I’m disappointed or not."

Genaro readjusted his position in the creaky seat, captivated by his charismatic prisoner.

"Your father was so proud of you for helping us to make this a reality, or, at least, he was until he found out how they intended to utilise you."

"Yes, he told me the military should value my brain rather than my trigger finger." Joshua's eyes glazed over as he said it, and he averted his gaze. "Of course, he had no idea exactly what you had done to me. I suppose it was my fault for expecting anything else."

Genaro squirmed. He opened his mouth, closed it again, and then stared at the desk full of papers as he searched for the right words.

"I know why I'm here, Doctor Genaro. I also knew they would bring me back here, to you, to this place. I have to admit, I preferred it when it was less cluttered with people and equipment."

"It's the downside of progression I'm afraid. After seeing your initial test results, Project Apex suddenly became interesting to those who had been so desperate to close us down before."

Joshua nodded and watched the scientist, waiting for him to find a way to ask the question he really wanted to. Realising it wasn't going to come without prompting, Joshua decided to help, if only because time was so short, even if those outside of the cell didn't know it yet.

"Do you remember my IQ when I first started the Apex treatment?"

"Of course," Genaro said. "I read your file so many times it became second nature. You scored 109 as I remember. High end of average, just a hair below superior."

"Yes, I remember. Would you like to know what it is now?"

"I would," Genaro said, the scientist in him unable to help himself.

"Just after I was shipped out to Afghanistan I tested at a hundred and twenty-two. I did another test recently and scored a hundred and fifty-nine."

"Such an improvement is impossible, that puts you in the Einstein range."

"Not quite, he was around a hundred and eighty I believe. Although, if you were to test me now, I wouldn't be surprised if it had grown again. I suppose I have you to thank for that. ‘Behold the great Creator makes himself a house of clay, a robe of virgin flesh he takes which he will wear for ay."

“What was that?” Genaro said, unable to help but smile.

“Thomas Pestel, circa fifteen eighty-six to sixteen-sixty, I believe.”

“You believe me to be this creator?”

Joshua nodded. “Yes. You moulded your house of clay on my innocence. I suppose I thought it might be a fitting reference to this situation.”

Genaro flushed and lowered his eyes, staring at his scuffed leather shoes. "The serum shouldn't have been so potent," Genaro said, shaking his head. “It was supposed to be a steady and controlled increase. Nobody expected it to bond so completely and quickly with its host."

"Ahh, but you made one critical error, or, more accurately, oversight," Joshua said, standing and pacing the room, hands clasped behind his back.

"We know something went wrong, my team and I just don't know what exactly."

"Wrong?" Joshua said, pausing and staring at Genaro with raised eyebrows.

"Yes. No disrespect intended, of course, but based on the initial intention of the project, I think it's a fair assessment."

"I disagree. In fact, I think you have developed something which will go on to change the future of mankind for the better, even if it seems that wasn't your intention."

"That was my hope, but the government have pulled our funding. Backed out. Project Apex is done."

"I sense a little bitterness in your voice, Doctor. I take it you blame me for this?"

"Not just you, no," Genaro said with a shake of his head.

"You mean the incident at Blanding? They were given every opportunity to avoid a confrontation, and instead, they pushed and pushed and pushed." Joshua hissed, lashing out and punching the steel frame of the holding cell.

"Calm down, please," Genaro said, fear for the first time coming ahead of his thirst for knowledge. "This isn't like you, Joshua, you were always so calm."

Joshua was glaring, eyes wild, breathing in ragged gasps. Blood wept from his knuckles where he had punched the wall. Genaro had no doubt despite their previously close relationship; Joshua would have killed him if not for the physical barrier between them. Taking a deep breath, Joshua sat on the bunk, elbows on knees, head hanging low.

"I'm sorry about that," He whispered, his voice barely picked up by the two-way intercom. "Another side effect of your treatment I'm afraid.

"The aggression?"

"It seems along with enhancing my physical attributes, it also increased my testosterone output to dangerous levels. Anger. Aggression. Violence. These things which were once so alien to me are now part of my nature. Your product is brilliant, Doctor Genaro, but it is also flawed. All part of the balance of nature, I suppose."

"Then let me help you, let me go back and fix it."

"You can't fix it, we both know that. It's a part of me now and that can't be changed."

"The alternative is death. You must understand that?" Genaro said, desperation creeping into his voice. "Please, Joshua, my superiors' want an example made of you. If I can prove to them your actions were the fault of the product, we can delay any decision indefinitely. I can save your life and stop them from sentencing you to death."

Joshua smiled, and Genaro wondered why he looked so unconcerned. "I appreciate the sentiment, Dr. Genaro, but I'm afraid I won't be staying long enough for those government pigs to get their hands on me."

"I don't see how you have a choice."

"There's always a choice, doctor. Always." He replied the sinister edge to his voice impossible to ignore. "After all, isn't that how this all began? With a choice? You see life is all about perspective. Finding a hundred dollar bill on the street to a poor man might change his life, and yet a rich man would give the same amount as a tip in a fancy restaurant without a second thought. Do you remember when I first came here? How afraid I was to have the injection and you put a hand on my shoulder and told me I could change the world?"

Genaro nodded, trying to decide if he was more fascinated or afraid.

"I didn't know what you meant, at first, but as my strength increased and my weaknesses faded away, I started to see the world in a new perspective. I saw it for the first time with open eyes. I saw how fragile man is, and how much better it could be. I see a different future for this planet, Doctor Genaro. One free of the current mindless creatures which pollute it on a daily basis."

"That sounds like something Hitler would have said," Genaro whispered. "Come on Joshua, no one man can change the world, as much as we would like to. Sure enough, we may not like the way mankind behaves, but that's part of life. We just have to deal with it. No man has the power to change that."

"An ordinary man, no. But we both know I'm no ordinary man."

A tightness in Genaro's gut brought a fresh surge of fear at the calm and casual manner in which Joshua was speaking.

"What do you mean?" Genaro asked.

"I'm talking about wiping the slate clean, Doctor Genaro. Starting again. The world is a mess. Wars. Disease. Famine. Global warming. People killing each other to fight over scraps whilst the rich buy real estate and overpriced art just because they have more money than they could ever spend. The world is unbalanced. It's broken."

"You can't fix it, Joshua. It's impossible."

"Nothing is impossible. You told me that once."

“Let’s say you could if you had the infrastructure and the ability to make people listen. How would you do it?”

Joshua smiled, the expression without any emotion whatsoever which made Genaro cold. “Like I said, I’d wipe the slate clean.”

“How. Exactly how?”

Joshua leaned closer to the Lexan, smiling at Genaro. “I wish I could tell you, but it seems we are out of time.”

"I don’t understand. Out of time for what?"

Joshua smiled and lay down on his bunk. "As I said, I won't be staying and letting those pigs get their hands on me. My brothers will be here for me soon. I know they will."

"Nobody knows you are here. Face it, Joshua, they won't find you. You will either let me help you, or you will be sent to trial and executed. It's your choice." Genaro barked, the fear in him manifesting as anger.

"I wish you could see things as I do. Do you think I'd be here now if I didn't allow myself to be taken?" Joshua almost looked sad that Genaro didn’t see the bigger picture.

"The extraction team would have taken you anyway. There was no way out of those tunnels."

"No, they wouldn't. My brothers were willing to die for me. We could have fought them off with ease if we had so chosen."

"So you let them capture you?"

“Of course,” Joshua said with a thin smile

“Why would you do that?”

"Because I had to come back."

"Why?"

"For you."

Genaro froze, staring open-mouthed at Joshua, who stood and approached the Perspex, stopping inches from it.

"Why me?" Genaro whispered.

"Because it's your project. I want you to see what the world could be. I want you to join my cause. I want you to be everything you can be," he held his fist up to the glass as he said it, wiping away the blood to show the wounds on his knuckles had already almost completely healed.

"Listen to yourself Joshua, I know you believe what you're saying, but its madness. The virus has done something to you, given you some kind of unknown side effects, maybe some kind of narcissism complex. We can fix it, you and me together just like at the beginning."

"I understand how difficult it must be to believe me. Which is why I'm willing to ask you again when you know for sure I speak the truth."

"I don't understand."

"You will."

"How?"

A dull thud followed by the sound of screams and broken glass drifted to them from upstairs.

"Because they're here," Joshua whispered as Genaro stood and backed towards the wall.

II

Draven had read and re-read the file and was utterly convinced he was right. He glanced at his watch, then to Goodall who sat on the opposite side of the aisle from him.

"How long until we land?"

"Still twenty minutes yet. Relax." She said, half wishing for the return of the less uptight version of Draven.

"You don't understand, we need to get there now. If these notes are accurate, I need to speak to Genaro right away."

"Do you want me to try the video link again?"

"Please. Anything you can do to get in touch with them."

She stood and tried without success to establish a link, then with a frown headed towards the front of the plane. "Wait here, I'll see if I can radio in," she said, before disappearing through the curtain.

Trying to ignore the giddy somersaults in his gut and the prickle of fear which had given him goosebumps, he turned back to the folder, checking his theory for the tenth time and getting the exact same cast iron results. There was no doubt in his mind.

Goodall came back through the curtain, wearing a frown which echoed his own.

"There's no contact from the lab, which is odd. I got in touch with Homeland to see if they can get a team out there. What's so urgent?"

"I need to check my findings with Genaro first, but if I'm right, this is a lot worse than I thought," He said, glancing out of the window as the plane banked slightly towards its final destination.

"Can't you give me the short version?" she said, not hiding her irritation as she sat opposite him.

"According to these notes, Genaro wanted to control the virus."

"Virus? You mean Project Apex?"

"It's still a virus whatever you call it. It was designed to enter the bloodstream and alter the host's DNA and with it the traits which go with the virus itself. He knew human antibodies were never going to be strong enough, and so did all he could to engineer a virus which was non-contagious as a safety measure."

"That's a good thing, right?"

"It is and it isn't. You see what he didn't take into account was the tendency of nature to change in order to adapt to its circumstances. We see examples of it the world over. The virus is so strong, so bonded with its host that it has the capacity to change, to mutate from its initial state."

"I'm sure Genaro would have seen and adapted for it. He's too good for that."

"I don't doubt his brilliance, and under ordinary circumstances, I would agree with you. However, look at the time constraints he was under. If anything, it would have been an afterthought. There is certainly nothing in his notes to say he has made contingency for mutation."

"Okay, so let's assume, for the sake of argument, he hasn't, what does that mean?" Kate asked.

"This virus is essentially a living organism in itself. The specific breed of monkey which is the basis of the virus carried a low-grade version of rabies. It wasn't as potent as the version we know of today, but it was present across the entire species.

Those same markers are present within the Apex serum."

"You're losing me here, what does that mean?"

"It means this Apex virus is not only incredibly dangerous, it's also contagious."

Kate blinked, taking a few seconds to digest what Draven was telling her. "How? I mean, it can't be possible."

"That's why I'm hoping there is more information that Genaro hasn't provided in his notes. Some kind of missing information which means I'm wrong."

"What if you're right, how can this thing be spread?"

"I can't say for sure, but if I base it solely on the Tiger monkey, my best guess is that it can be transferred through bodily fluids. Blood and saliva being the most obvious."

"Could it go airborne?" Goodall asked, her features taut with worry.

"No," Draven said with a shake of his head. "It would need immediate delivery into the body to allow the virus to begin the bonding with its host. We, at least, have that in our favour. Either way, I need to speak to Genaro. I don't need to tell you how quickly this could get out of hand. Based on the aggressive nature of those affected in the reports and the speed in which the virus is able to bond and change its host, we could be looking at a global epidemic here."

"Jesus," Goodall muttered, staring at Draven. "According to Homeland, there are Apex operatives stationed all over the globe that have gone dark. We don't know where they are."

"As long as they don't know they're contagious, we have a chance. Besides, right now the virus likely won't feel the need to replicate itself. It's still in its infancy."

"What does that mean?"

"It means we still have time. But it's absolutely vital I speak to Genaro."

Goodall nodded and stood.

"Where are you going?" Draven asked.

"To radio in. We need an emergency pickup to

get us as soon as we land and to take us straight to Genaro's lab. Do you think you can stop this?"

"Me? No, not alone at least. I've been out of the game for far too long. With Genaro's help, though, it might be possible."

"In that case, let's get you there as soon as we can."

III

The sound of chaos and gunfire from upstairs filtered through to Genaro, where he cowered in his underground lab. Joshua made no effort to call out, or to alert them of his whereabouts. Genaro experienced another wave of nausea and sat on his chair before his legs gave.

"If you're thinking they might not find us down here, I can assure you they will," Joshua said, his conversational tone almost mocking.

"How did they find you? It's impossible." Genaro muttered, sure his life only had a few minutes left before it was snuffed out.

"Nothing is impossible. Miracles happen all the time. Just look at me. When people know who I am, what I represent, they will say I too am impossible. That I'm some kind of living, breathing miracle."

Genaro shook his head. "Your father would hate to see you like this Joshua. Although, I must take some of the blame for it, which is why I don't try to escape. Perhaps, knowing what I've done, I deserve death." He heard footsteps descending towards the lab and knew his time was up.

"I'm going to let you out now Joshua," Genaro said. "I know it's pointless to resist this. I only ask one thing of you, one favour for old time's sake."

Genaro activated the controls, unlocking the heavy steel door. Joshua casually opened it and stepped out.

"What is it you ask?" Joshua whispered as his men started to break down the door.

"Kill me quickly. Don't let me suffer." The doctor whispered, his lip trembling.

The door gave up its fight, allowing Joshua's men to enter.

"Kill you? Whatever in the world makes you think I want to do that?"

"Then... what do you want?" Genaro stammered.

"Like I said, I came back for you."

"Why?"

"Because you're going to help me build my army."

Joshua lunged, biting Genaro on the arm, shearing away a great chunk of flesh. Blood spewed out of the wound, as Genaro fell to his knees and wailed.

"What have you done to me, what have you done!" Genaro screamed.

"I just made you immortal," Joshua said as he released his grip and wiped the blood from his chin, looking at his brothers with a smeared, crimson grin.

"Today, the birth of the new world begins."

## IV

Genaro's arm was on fire. He lay on his side, listening to the sound of his blood spew out onto the floor. He was incredibly aware of his body, how every cell was working in unison. He imagined he could feel the blood as it was blasted around at incredible pressure via the heart, terminating at the gaping wound in his forearm. His main concern wasn't with what was coming out of him, but more what had gone in the other direction.

He had long suspected the Apex virus had the potential to become contagious far too late to do anything about it. Like the rest of the project, he had become a victim of the time pressure he was under, and things which should have been meticulously checked had been skimmed at best, ignored at worse.

My god, I'm dying.

The thought came to him not in the blind panic he imagined, but with a calm sense of finality which he knew he was powerless to alter or otherwise affect. At least in death, he would be spared dealing with the consequences of his actions. For all of his good intentions, he had been reckless, and now the world was about to pay the price. He imagined the virus surging through him, visualising the microscopic and quite brilliant building blocks with the ability to rebuild a human with none of its flaws merging with the man he was, enhancing what was already there. Changing him from the inside.

What if it goes wrong? What if my body rejects the virus?

It was certainly something to consider. He listened to his body, blocking out the sound of Joshua's men as they removed equipment and took whatever they could carry.

Could he feel it? If he turned his senses inwards, could he know where the virus was in his bloodstream? The rational side of him, of course, knew it was impossible. Yet it didn't stop him listening anyway.

He couldn't feel anything.

Not even pain.

He drew a sharp breath, and opened his eyes, focusing on his arm. It was, of course still a bloody mess. However, it was a mess which didn't hurt. It was a mess which was no longer bleeding.

With a shaking hand, he reached out to touch the wound, bracing himself for the raging fire of agony as his fingers met with ravaged flesh.

There was no pain. It was as if his eyes were lying to him and showing him an injury which didn't belong to him. He felt strong arms pick him up from the ground, then Joshua's comforting voice whisper in his ear.

"Have no fear brother, I have you now."

Genaro murmured in response. Perhaps a protest, maybe an agreement, he wasn't sure enough how he felt to make a decision. Even so, he didn't fight or struggle. It seemed there was little point.

# CHAPTER TEN

## DEPARTMENT OF HOMELAND SECURITY
## WASHINGTON DC

MARCUS HAD STEPPED OUT of his office and dialled home for the third time, hoping not to get the machine again. He knew Suvari would be there just as much as he knew she usually let the machine pick up if she were busy. He was desperate to get to her to the point where he was considering driving home to catch her in person before she left. The machine picked up, and he waited, tapping his foot as he waited for the beep.

"Suv, it's me. Pick up if you're there. I need to talk to you right now."

He waited, and was about to hang up when the line connected. "Sorry, I was in the other room. What's wrong?"

Relief washed over him, and it took a few seconds for him to regain his composure. "I know you're all set to go out to Mumbai tonight, but –"

"I was just about to leave. I'm running a little behind schedule."

"Suv, listen, I want you to cancel the trip for a while."

Silence, something that from Suvari usually wasn't a good sign.

"What for?"

Marcus hesitated, knowing he had to choose his words carefully so as not to either cause alarm or divulge classified information. "We have a situation that's developing over here. I don't want you so far away until it's under control."

"Marcus, you know how long this trip has been

planned. I can't let these people down. They are hungry and need food."

"I know, and I wouldn't ask you not to go unless I had a good reason."

"They're relying on me. You know why it means so much to me to go back there."

"I do, believe me. I just… I can't go into detail, but I want you to be safe that's all."

"Isn't that why I married you, to keep me safe?"

He could hear the smile in her voice and realised with dismay that she had no concept of how dangerous the situation could be. "It is, and I'm doing all I can from here it's just… it's so far away Suv."

"Don't worry about me. You know I'm as stubborn as you are and will just go anyway. I trust you and your team completely. You're a brilliant man Marcus Atkinson, and I trust you to handle whatever it is you're facing down there."

He closed his eyes, knowing as all married men do when there was no point in arguing anymore. "There's nothing I'm going to be able to do to talk you out of this is there?"

"No, although you already knew that when you called."

That smile in her voice again. He wished he could tell her how there had never been a less appropriate time for that particular gesture. "What time is your flight?" he asked, hating himself for not forcing the issue.

"Seven. I was just about to throw my case in the car when you called."

"Do me a favour, call me from the airport then again when you get there."

"It will be late over there when I arrive are you sure-"

"-I don't care what time it is. Just call to let me know you're safe, okay?"

"Marcus, is everything alright?"

The lead in question. The one that might give him an opportunity to sway her, and yet maybe, under the circumstances, being over in India might prove to be safer than staying on U.S soil. Still, the desire to tell her, classified or not what was happening was great, almost impossible to fight off.

"Marcus, are you there?"

"Sorry," he said, coming back to the present. "I was miles away. I'm here and I'm fine. You have a safe trip, and please be careful."

"I will. I'll call you when I get back. I love you."

"Make sure you do. I'll talk to you soon." He replied, feeling that, under the circumstances telling the wife he had just sent halfway around the world that he loved her too when they were on the brink of what could be a global catastrophe, seemed inappropriate. Instead, he hung up the phone and found a whole new level of self-hate. There was no time to dwell on it, however, as personal life aside, there was still a crisis to contend with. Taking a second to compose himself, Marcus slipped his phone back into his pocket and went back into the situation room.

II

Smoke billowed from the broken windows of the lab as the black Mitsubishi Shogun skidded to a halt at the police barrier. A crowd of onlookers were being held back by angry-looking soldiers, whose weapons were enough to deter anyone who might be tempted to pry too much. Goodall and Draven climbed out of the car and approached the barricade.

"No access," grunted a giant hulk of a soldier in a t-shirt so tight it looked to have been sprayed on.

Draven winced as Kate tried to shove past him anyway.

"Hey," he repeated, grabbing her arm with his shovel-sized hand. "I said, no access."

"I’m with Homeland security. They're expecting us inside," she said as she flashed her I.D, shoving the black folding wallet in the soldier's face.

"I still can’t let you in. It’s not safe yet."

"We need to get inside, now."

"Hey, maybe we should hang back a little and let these people do their job," Draven muttered as he stared over at the smouldering building.

"You should listen to your friend. Once the building is secure I'm sure you -"

"Commander Robbins," she yelled over the barricade, waving to get his attention and pointing at Draven. Robbins was holding a bloody towel to his head and speaking to three men in black suits who Kate was sure were CIA. He waved her towards him as he half listened to one of the black-suited men he was with.

The hulk of a soldier stood aside and let them through. Draven followed Kate into the crowd of soldiers and high-level military officials milling around outside and realised just how out of his depth he was. His life wasn't meant to be like this. He was used to working alone, and although the natural dangers of the world were things which he dealt with and accepted as part of his job, standing on the frontline of what looked to be a war zone definitely was not.

To Draven's surprise, the commander walked straight to him. "Mr. Draven?"

"Richard," he said, shaking the commander's hand. Despite the nasty wound on his forehead, he was still incredibly composed.

"What happened, commander?" Kate said, glancing at the burning lab.

"Some kind of attack. We think it's more of these super soldiers. The assumption is they came to break out the one we captured."

"How could they do that? Nobody knew he was here."

"Damned if I know, but that's what happened. I was inside when they hit. They were like damn machines. I shot one of them from twenty feet away and the son of a bitch just kept coming."

"Where's Doctor Genaro?" Kate asked.

"They have him."

"They're still in there?"

"We don't know. That's what we're discussing. We need to sweep the building, but frankly, I'm not willing to send men in there unless I have a hell of a lot more of them and all these people are clear."

"Do they have hostages? Apart from Doctor

Genaro, I mean." Kate asked.

"No, everyone else is either injured or dead," Robbins said, wincing as he dabbed at his wound.

"I just don't understand this. Why would they attack this place? More to the point, how did they find it?" she said to nobody in particular.

"No idea. All I know is I've never seen anything like this before." Robbins muttered.

"What do you mean?" Kate asked.

"I mean the way they moved, the way they attacked, it was... well they were fucking slick. Makes our very best look like rank amateurs. I don't know how to explain it."

"Did they attack like a single consciousness?" Draven asked, averting his gaze as Robbins looked at him.

"I'm not sure what you mean."

"I mean as if they were separate parts of the same thing. An extension of the same organism."

Robbins looked Draven up and down, then nodded. "Yeah, that's exactly it. How the hell did you know?"

"It fits with the research. It also explains how they found this place."

"Okay, now you have me curious," Robbins said, giving Draven his full attention. "Go ahead and explain.

"When I studied the species of monkey from which the Apex virus was created, I saw behaviours which closely replicate what's happening here and the reports I read on the plane."

"Go on," Robbins said.

"The one you captured, he was the first one to be administered the Apex virus, correct, the one from Genaro's report?"

"Yes."

"According to Genaro's research, Joshua's blood was used to enable the initial bonding of the Apex virus to a human host."

"Plain English please Mr. Draven," Robbins grunted. "I'm a soldier, not a scientist."

"Essentially, Joshua is the alpha of a new human subspecies."

"Subspecies? That's a little extreme isn't it?"

Kate said.

"No, actually, that's exactly what we're dealing with. The genetic mutation brought on by the virus has essentially created a new evolution of mankind."

"The attack Mr. Draven. You were talking about the attack."

"Yes, sorry, I got sidetracked. As I was saying, because Joshua's blood formed part of the building blocks of the virus, part of him is in all the other Apex subjects. He's their natural leader by design."

"That still doesn't explain how they located him," Robbins grunted as more soldiers arrived at the scene.

"Actually, it does."

"I'm all ears," Robbins grunted.

"When they attacked, was there a smell in the lab?" Draven asked.

For the first time since they had arrived, Robbins seemed flustered." Actually, there was. It was nasty, like stale sweat or something. How did you know that?"

"Some species of animals secrete a pheromone when they attack, instantly allowing others of its kind to locate the prey and assist the attacker. It's most prevalent in certain species of ants but also present in the Tiger monkeys that formed the basis of the virus. Combined with the theory Joshua is their Alpha, much in the same way as a queen ant is in sole control of their nest, so Joshua is in control of them. They can communicate without speaking, and if my pheromone idea is true, they have an advantage no team, no matter how well they are trained, can overcome."

"I think you might be underestimating the abilities of our forces."

"With all due respect Commander, I'm not," Draven said, avoiding the commander's stare. "You have to understand these men are superior in every way to us. They think as one, almost as if they have a shared consciousness. To put it into real world terms, it would be the equivalent of regular people like us going to war with a species of chimpanzee."

"Jesus, it sounds like you're their biggest fan,"

Robbins grunted.

"It's not that, I just respect them, that's all. For what they are if not for their behaviour."

"And I take it you have some grand revelation about that too?" Robbins spat.

"Hey, I'm just doing as I was asked. I'm trying to help you here."

"Just remember these bastards have killed a lot of good men. Soldiers with families. I don't agree with hyping them up as if they're fucking supermen."

"Look, Commander," Draven said, unsure why he was becoming so angry. "You might not like it, but the fact is these are supermen, compared to the likes of us anyway. They have all of our strengths and none of our weaknesses."

"Okay, I can buy that. My next question is what the hell do we do about stopping them?"

"I need to speak to Doctor Genaro. He designed the virus, he alone will know its weaknesses."

"We haven't heard or seen any activity from inside for a while now. No contact." Robbins said as he stared at the smouldering building.

"Are you sure they're still inside?" Kate asked.

"We have the building surrounded and nobody has come out or made any contact with us regarding Dr. Genaro, we are assuming that to be the case."

A wiry soldier in full military fatigues approached the trio. He gave Draven a cautious glance, one which Draven presumed was because he probably did look so out of place amid the swarms of police, fire crews and soldiers in his baggy T-shirt, knee-length shorts and pumps.

"Commander, we've completed initial recon of the building. It looks to be empty."

"It can't be empty. We know there are targets inside. Check again." Robbins said.

"We did sir. Three times. Whoever was in there looks to have gone."

"Commander, I need to get inside that lab," Draven said, enduring another glare from the soldier.

Robbins took a moment to consider. "Okay, here's what we're going to do," he said, turning to the soldier. "Get a team in there and do a complete sweep of the building. Do it quickly."

"Yes, Sir."

"As for you," Robbins said to Draven. "You can't go in there dressed like that."

"Sorry, I didn't expect...this."

"None of us did. I take it you brought a bag with you? Spare clothes?"

"Uh, yeah. It's in the car."

"Good. Go change. We'll get you some armour and a helmet. As soon as they finish sweeping the building, you're going inside."

"Commander, is that wise considering the potential risk?" Goodall said, glancing towards Draven.

"Under ordinary circumstances, I'd agree with you. A lot has happened since you went to find Mr. Draven here, and things are escalating quickly. The sooner we get him into this lab, the sooner we can start to formulate some answers."

III

Twenty-five minutes later, Draven stood outside the entrance to the lab alongside Goodall and Robbins, wondering quite how he had managed to be talked into such craziness. Even though the lab was swarming with soldiers, there were still bodies on the floor along with bullets and slick pools of blood belonging to the unfortunate victims of the massacre. Broken glass and lab equipment littered the ground, and the pungent, stale sweat smell Robbins had mentioned was still there. Draven whistled through his teeth as he followed Robbins and Goodall over the threshold.

"Jesus, they did a number on this place," He muttered.

"Any survivors?" Goodall asked as she skirted around a body covered in a bloody white sheet.

"None. It's a goddamn massacre. I'd have been dead too if I hadn't left the building." Robbins said.

"You were in here?" Draven asked.

"Yeah, I was with Genaro in his lab waiting for you. He was talking to the one they'd captured. I stepped outside for a smoke. Next thing I know there are bullets flying and people screaming."

"What about Genaro?"

"No sign of him. We haven't found a body yet though either, so take that as you will."

"I don't understand," Kate said, glancing at the carnage. "If they were only interested in breaking out the one we captured, why did they have to kill everyone?"

"It's not just that," Draven replied, pointing at the banks of computers and expensive equipment. "It looks like they deliberately destroyed all this equipment. It seems like they took the time to make sure it wasn't useable."

"Why, though?"

"I don't know," Draven said with a shrug. "Whatever the reason, I don't like it."

"Agreed," Robbins said, leading them past the bulk of the massacre towards the back of the building. "Genaro's private lab is down here. This is where he did all his research."

Draven and Goodall followed Robbins down

the steps, away from the smell of smoke and blood. Draven was curious to see the lab, and more importantly, gain some kind of idea where Genaro was with his research.

"Something's wrong," Robbins said as she stood at the threshold of the room. Draven didn't need ask what. The entire lab had been ransacked. Equipment had been removed, files and folders scattered across the floor. The larger equipment which couldn't be taken was damaged beyond repair.

"What the hell happened down here?" Robbins muttered.

"They took the research," Draven replied, leafing through a few papers on the desk.

"There's some blood on the floor here," Goodall said, crouching at the spot where Genaro's wound had dripped onto the floor. It looks like they got out this way," she added, pointing to a steel door behind a cabinet which had been slid aside to allow access.

"Shit, this exit wasn't on the plans for the building," Robbins grunted. "I need to go call this in and get some teams out on the road, see if we can pick these assholes up."

Robbins sprinted upstairs, leaving Draven and Kate behind.

"What do you think?" she asked as he made his way around the lab, looking for anything which might help.

"Looks like they picked the place clean."

"Why would they do that?"

"Seems to me they don't want anyone to find out what Genaro was doing," Draven said.

"Or they want him to continue his work elsewhere."

Draven looked at Kate across the desk. "It's possible I suppose."

"Think about it," she went on. "Genaro isn't here. We know that much. It looks to me like they took him with them along with the equipment they thought he would need and his research. To me, that seems too much to be just coincidence."

"You think they might force him to continue to work? Why would they do that?"

"I don't know," she said with a shrug. "Maybe

so we can't use his research to formulate a cure."

"Surely there are backup servers, though? Outside of here?"

She shook her head. "No. It was a condition of his. He didn't want anyone interfering or accessing his work. The entire reason this place was so well hidden and off the books is because it's the only place the research exists."

"You're telling me we're now flying blind?" Draven said, not quite able to believe what he was hearing.

"Yeah, it looks that way."

"Why wouldn't the government insist on an off-site backup? What if there was a fire or something?"

"This lab is protected. Even if the building upstairs went up in flames, this place would survive."

"Even so, couldn't the government access the data anyway? I know they have the means to do it."

"You've watched too many movies. Besides, how could we ever know things would get like this? Genaro's work was never seen as something which could potentially become such a security risk. At the time, there was no need to monitor him."

"This is crazy," Draven said, flopping down into Genaro's swivel chair. "So you're saying without Genaro, we have nothing."

"I don't know," She snapped. "We brought you in as the expert. Is that the case?"

"Pretty much," He replied, adding a sigh to emphasise his annoyance.

"So what do we do now?"

"We need to get Genaro back, or at the very least his research. I can't do anything without it."

"What if-"

There was a noise from the cabinet by the escape door. They both heard it at the same time, Kate standing and drawing her weapon with well-practiced smoothness, Draven almost falling as he stood, the chair rolling back and clattering against the wall. Kate put a finger to her lips and inched towards the cabinet, gun arm straight and trained on the steel sliding door.

"Whoever is inside the cupboard, please step

outside now," Kate said, her voice sharp and clear. She waited, adjusting her grip on the weapon and glancing at Draven.

"There are weapons trained on you, and if you don't respond we will be forced to open fire," She said. Of course, there was only one weapon trained on the cupboard, but whoever was inside wouldn't know that, and weapons sounded more intimidating than the singular form.

What if it's Genaro?

Draven was about to voice the idea when a muffled voice broke the silence.

"Alright, alright, don't shoot. I'm coming out."

The door slid open, and a dishevelled man stumbled out, squinting at the light.

"Down on the ground right now!" Goodall said her training kicking in.

Draven could see well enough the man was no threat. He was bloody and frightened. Even so, procedure had to be followed, so he didn't speak up. Kate patted him down with one hand, keeping the one holding the weapon trained on the man at all times.

"Who are you, what are you doing here?" she said as she stepped back and returned both hands to the weapon, satisfied the man was unarmed.

"Please, you don't have to point that thing at me," the man grunted from the floor.

"Until I get some answers, you better get used to it. Who are you?"

"I work here."

Draven looked at the man. He was dressed in shabby overalls and had scruffy hair to the nape of his neck. His beard was patchy and without style, and his blue eyes bugged out of his head, reminding Draven of a chameleon.

"You're a scientist?" Kate asked.

"No, I'm the janitor. I came down here to hide."

Kate seemed satisfied with the answer, and stood down, training her gun on the floor instead.

"What are you doing down here?" she asked, catching Draven's eye and nodding towards the chair. Draven grabbed it and rolled it over towards the man, who gratefully clambered to his feet and sat down.

"Thanks," he said, running a hand through his dirty hair. He had a bloody lip, but other than that seemed otherwise okay. "Name's Herman. I was upstairs when those guys came in and started shooting up the place. I hid in the toilet until one of them found me. They dragged me down here to ask the leader what to do with me. "

"The leader?" Kate said.

"Yeah, the one who they had locked in that thing," Herman replied, nodding towards the holding tank.

"And why did they let you live when everyone else was killed?"

"I don't know, lady."

"I do."

They both looked at Draven. "It's because he isn't a scientist."

"I don't think I understand," Kate replied.

"You told me on the way here everyone who works for Genaro were high-level talents, the best in their field. It seems to me our...friends didn't want any of those minds existing in the world that might be able to stop them. I'd bet everything that the leader got himself captured on purpose because he knew they would bring him here. It was the perfect plan. Without being captured, there was no way they would have found the lab and had access to both the staff and equipment at the same time. Our friend here survived because he wasn't a threat to them."

"You don't have to talk in code. I know these guys are Ragers." Herman said.

"Say again?" Draven replied.

"Ragers. That's what Doc Genaro called the angry ones. Those were the ones he wanted to fix."

"How do you know about this?"

Herman lowered his head, and then scratched his beard. "Okay, I'll tell you, but you gotta believe me when I tell you I'm not involved, okay?"

"Understood," Kate said, catching Draven's eye.

"You should know, it's crazy, though," He said, flicking his chameleon eyes from one of them to the other. He reminded Draven of the crazy person who always got on a bus or train at night and would come and sit next to you to tell you about how he was abducted by aliens.

"Please, in your own time," Kate said.

The bug-eyed janitor leaned forward on his chair, licking his lips and speaking in a near whisper.

"Don't patronise me, lady," Herman said, glancing at Draven. "My guess is you're here to find out about Project Apex."

Draven and Kate's stunned silence spoke volumes to Herman. Clearly enjoying being the centre of attention, he relaxed and went on. "Lucky for you two, I know all about it. Believe me, this shit will blow your goddamn minds."

"In that case, I think you better start from the beginning," Kate said, giving Herman her full attention.

"Okay, sure thing. But not here."

"Why not?"

"Bugs," Herman whispered, then pointed to the

roof and lowered his voice to a whisper. "They're listening through the walls."

He wore an elastic grin whilst he waited for some kind of acknowledgement. Kate and Draven shared a worried glance.

"Uh, I'm not sure there are bugs in here pal," Draven said, somehow hiding his smile.

"Oh, they are. They're always listening. Big Brother. Using alien technology lifted from Roswell. Trust me, I know about this stuff."

Draven and Kate exchanged another quick look, and this time, Herman saw it.

"Hey, now I'm not one of those crazy conspiracy loons you know."

"Nobody said you were," Kate said.

"No, but I saw that look in your eye. I'm different to those guys. I have direct sources if you know what I mean," He said, rolling his eyes towards the heavens. "No speculation from Herman, just honest to god facts."

As much as Draven thought getting into a long conversation with Herman about his supposed sources of info could be all kinds of fun, he knew time was critical, and they had to push on.

"Look," Kate said. "If we could just stick to the current situation it would help. What do you know about Project Apex?"

"Are you kidding me? What don't I know? I've been janitor here for years. I see things. I hear things. People think I'm dumb because I push a mop instead of a pen. But I was chosen for a reason. I'm supposed to make a difference. It's my destiny."

"Okay, relax," Kate said. "Just tell us what you know."

"No, sorry. I don't trust the government." Herman said, his eyes darting nervously around the room.

"So where do you suggest we talk?" Kate said, trying to hide her irritation.

"My place. At least, I know it's safe there."

"I don't think we can do that. We don't have time." Kate said.

"Then make time. Believe me; you are going to

want to see what I have to show you."

Draven shifted in his seat, picturing Herman as the nice guy who lures you into his house before chopping you up and feeding you to his pet cat. It was always a pet cat.

"It looks like we have no choice," Kate said, moving towards the door. "I'll clear it with Robbins. You better not be wasting our time."

Draven and Herman watched her leave.

"Don’t worry about her. She's cranky." Draven said, deciding for as odd as Herman was, he quite liked him.

"I like it. Strong women do it for me," Herman replied with a grin.

"A word to the wise. That one has a temper. You might want to give her a wide berth."

"Noted."

"Well, we better go upstairs and get moving."

"Sounds good. Hey, any chance we can go to the drive through on the way? I’m starving."

"I don’t think they’ll go for that," Draven replied with a grin.

"Should have known. Damn government." Herman muttered as they left the lab and headed back upstairs. Seeing the hellish scene made them forget their jovial tone, and reminded Draven at least why he was there.

“What a mess," Herman muttered.

"This is bad, but it’s only the start," Draven replied.

"What do you mean?"

"If I’m right, this is just a drop in the ocean compared to what's to come."

IV

Harmony Place Trailer Park was exactly the kind of location Draven had expected Herman to live at. As they drove across the Pontiac Bridge towards Virginia, none of them spoke. Kate concentrated on the road, her face taut and focused. Draven sat beside her, watching the impressive architecture of Washington give way to the urban landscape of Virginia. He was wondering just how bad things must be if they were forced to invest so much time and energy on the word of a man like Herman – who on face value seemed to be as mad as a box of frogs.

Draven glanced at him in the rearview mirror. To his surprise, Herman was looking back at him. He sat in the centre seat, arms resting palms up on his thighs.

"Did you know the government is filling the air with chemicals?" he said.

"Say again?" Draven replied, only half listening.

"Chemicals. Contrails. You know when you see those trails coming from aeroplanes? It's not friction or air resistance or any of that crap. It's a chemical they pump into the atmosphere to keep us docile. To stop us asking questions."

Draven half turned in his seat, curious and amused at the same time. "Come on, that seems very farfetched."

"No, it's true. Man, people need to wake up to what's happening. Society now is too happy to sit and stare at their TV's whilst the governments rule the world. You ever hear of the Illuminati?"

"Yeah, I have as it goes. I don't believe in it, though."

"Figures. You government types never do." Herman grunted.

"Actually, I'm civilian. I'm only here as a consultant."

Herman's eyes lit up, and Draven half wished he had kept his mouth shut.

"Well, in that case, you and I have stuff to discuss my friend. When we get inside, I can show you things- tangible evidence of government cover-ups that will blow your mind."

"Where am I going here?" Kate grunted as she rolled down the dusty track lined with grubby trailers.

"Right down at the end. There's a red pickup parked outside. You can't miss it." Herman replied, and then turned back to Draven.

"I tell you, man, there's stuff out there in the public domain that gets deflected or pushed aside by the press."

"In my experience, the press are a bloodthirsty bunch who would kill for a hot story," Draven said.

"That's what they want you to think. In reality, they're just puppets. Pawns to the Illuminati and the other higher powers. I'm talking about inter-dimensional communication with beings on a different plane than us. The world is due a wake-up call, and based on what I know about Project Apex, this could be it."

"You believe this crap, don't you?" Kate snapped.

"Absolutely I do. You should too. "

"You people are always so quick to throw the conspiracy crap around, but you forget about how people like us protect you."

"In what way?" Herman said, refusing to back down.

"Terrorists for one. If you only knew the number of times the government have stopped attacks before they happen in order to keep people safe, you might change your opinion."

"A fair point," Herman said, leaning forward in his seat. "To which I ask why is this country under a terror threat in the first place?"

"What do you mean?"

"Well, the way I see it, if Uncle Sam had kept his nose out of the business of other countries, all this hostility would probably be aimed elsewhere."

"Are you seriously suggesting we brought it on ourselves?" Kate said, unable to hide her anger.

"That's exactly what I'm saying. This country would be a hell of a lot better off if they just stopped poking around in the affairs that don't concern us."

"That's the biggest load of shit I've ever heard," she snapped.

"Hey, how about we all take it easy and concentrate on the job in hand, okay?" Draven said as the car rolled to a stop at Herman's trailer.

The tired motor home suited their zany passenger to a tee. Everything from the grubby whitewashed outer walls to the tattered American flag hanging from a broom handle screwed to the roof screamed weirdo.

"Here we are," Herman said with a grin. “Prepare to have your minds blown."

He tried to open the door, glaring at the back of Kate's head when the handle moved freely in his hand. "Are you kidding me? You put the child locks on?" he grunted.

"For your own safety," Kate said, just about hiding a smile.

Draven hid his own smile just long enough to hop out of the car and release Herman. He walked towards the trailer, shoulders sloped and bobbing his head, reminiscent of a chicken. Pausing to fish a key out of his pocket, he unlocked the door and went inside, switching on the lights.

"Come on in," he yelled over his shoulder before turning towards the kitchen area. Draven followed Kate up the two creaky steps and into the compact trailer. There was a vague smell of beer and old farts. Draven wrinkled his nose. He watched for Kate's reaction but saw only a blank canvas. He joined her in looking around the camper. To their left was a seating area of sorts with a fold away breakfast table. A dirty pillow and grubby blanket were on the end seat. It appeared from the wear in the imitation leather seats, that this was where Herman spent the vast bulk of his time. Pinned to the wall were two posters. One depicting a grainy photograph of the Patterson Bigfoot, the other was a shabby X-Files poster, complete with a brooding Mulder & Scully, and the tagline 'The Truth is out there'. Draven was starting to think their host was pretty out there too. Beyond the sitting room were two doors which Draven guessed contained the bedroom and bathroom. To their right, Herman was in the small kitchenette, washing out some cups.

"Coffee? I'm all out of milk but if you don't mind taking it black you can knock yourself out."

"No, thanks," Kate said.

"I'm good," Draven added.

"Suit yourselves."

They waited until Herman had made himself a coffee in a cup with rings on the inside which wouldn't look out of place on Saturn. He walked into the seating area, and waited, watching them with a grin on his face.

"So, you were going to tell us what you know about Project Apex?" Kate said.

"I can go one better. I'll show you. Come on," He said, walking his chicken walk towards one of the closed rooms at the end of the trailer. Draven went to follow and felt light fingers on his arm. Kate shook her head ever so slightly and made sure to go in front, hand hovering near her weapon which was holstered inside her jacket.

Message received, he let her go next as he followed behind, taking a moment to acknowledge the impressive array of conspiracy documentaries and DVDs which were scattered around the TV.

Herman paused at the door, turning to face them with that familiar self-amused grin.

"Project Apex has been a pet project of mine, something of an obsession. It's one of those things I was so close to, it was too tempting not to research if you know what I mean."

He waited for a reply, and when none came, his

smile faltered for a second. "Well, anyway, here is the sum of my work. Welcome, to the Apex room."

He opened the door and bobbed inside. What used to be a bedroom had been stripped bare of furniture, the window boarded over. A small coffee cup ringed desk and chair were positioned in the centre of the room amid the mountains of papers and cuttings. Every surface of the walls was covered with articles, photographs, theories. Draven couldn't help but be impressed. A lot of the documents had notes directly written onto them in Herman's spiky hand. Others were highlighted and underlined in yellow or pink from fluorescent pens.

"Wow, this is...extensive," Draven mumbled as he tried to take in the sheer volume of information.

"As I said, it's become an obsession."

Kate was over by the wall, leaning close to some of the papers pinned there. "Are these official homeland security documents?" She said, turning towards him.

"It depends on how much trouble I'm in if they are," he replied, shuffling his feet.

"Don't worry, I won't haul you in. I just wanted to assess the validity."

"In that case, let's just say they're real enough."

"How the hell did you get all this?" Draven asked.

"It wasn't hard. As I said, I work in there and nobody would ever suspect the lowly janitor of having the mental prowess or the desire to pay attention to what was going on. See, I'm smarter than people give me credit for."

"So why are you a janitor?" Kate said. There was no malice in her question, but Draven saw Herman flinch as she asked it.

"Circumstances worked against me. Let's call it a youth spent wasting time doing things I shouldn't be doing and never really giving a second thought to getting a formal education. By the time I realised what I was doing, it was too late and I had to educate myself. That's when I started to see the world for what it really was, and the lies it's built on."

"And you think Project Apex is part of it?"

"Damn right I do, lady. All the evidence points to it."

“It’s obvious you have a great interest in this project and have shadowed Dr. Genaro's work closely. With him missing, we need you to fill in the gaps."

"He's not dead, you know."

"Genaro?" Draven said.

"Yeah."

"How do you know that?"

"I heard them. After I was presented to the leader, I was pretty sure I was gonna die. Genaro was on the floor, bleeding from the arm. The leader, Joshua, asked me if I was a scientist. I told him I wasn’t and I’m pretty sure that's what saved my life."

"Smart move," Draven said.

"No, you don’t get it, man. Even if I was and tried to tell him otherwise, there was no hiding it from him. He has this intensity, this look in his eyes that lets you know he will see through any lie. Physically he wasn’t much to look at. At the same time, he's probably the scariest guy I have ever seen."

"What happened when you told him you weren't a civilian?" Kate asked.

"Well, he believed me of course. Dressed in my overalls, I suppose it was easy. He told me he was sparing me because sometimes it took more strength and power to let live than to kill. He touched my shoulder and leaned close enough that I could feel his breath in my ear. He told me to prepare for the new world. He told me the end of everything we know was coming."

"Then what happened?"

"He looked at one of the others and they put me in the cupboard where you found me."

"Did he say anything?" Draven asked.

"No, they barely said a word to each other. It was almost like they could communicate without words."

"I have a theory about that relating to -"

"Sorry, we can't discuss that. National security." Kate said, cutting Draven off.

"Oh yeah, sorry," Draven mumbled.

"Typical government. All take and no give." Herman grumbled.

"Standard protocol. Now please, you were telling us about Doctor Genaro?" Kate snapped, steering Herman back on track.

"Yeah, I was. So, they locked me in the cupboard and started ransacking the place, taking stuff with them. I could see a little through the gap in the door, and saw one of them pick the doc up and carry him out of here."

"Did you see any other hostages?"

"No, Just the doc."

"Any idea why they would take him?" Kate asked.

"I do," Draven said.

"Go on," Kate replied.

"At first, I thought they destroyed the lab and killed all those people to make sure nobody could look for a cure for Project Apex. Now, knowing they took all the equipment and the doc, I think there's a good chance you were right and they've taken him for the sole reason of having them continue his work."

"My biggest issue with that is why would they?" Kate asked. "It's already proven to work. I don't get what else they could hope to gain from it."

"To make it better," Herman said, taking the words right out of Draven's mouth.

"Go on," Kate said.

"One thing I gained from all my snooping around and uh, my research is that the doc was under pressure from the people further up the ladder. They were happy with the basic virus, and yet the doc was hell bent on making it better. Improving the formula."

"Unlikely," Kate said. "He told us in a meeting recently he had ceased all Apex research."

"I promise you he hadn't. Up until yesterday, he was still working on the possibilities of mutations. New strains of the virus designed to give specific abilities or traits."

"That's surely not possible, it would take years of research," Draven said.

"Agreed. And in fairness, as far as I could tell, the doc was struggling to make any headway. It was just too complex."

"Well, that's one thing at least. God knows we have enough to deal with." Kate replied.

"Don't be so sure. I have a theory of my own if you want to hear it." Herman said.

"Go on."

"Okay, let's just say the only reason Genaro wasn't having any success was because the skill to do so was beyond him. By that I mean as brilliant as he is, his natural ability has stonewalled him."

"Okay, that seems plausible."

"What if the reason they've taken him and his equipment is to change him into one of them so he can continue his work?"

Draven felt ice rush through his veins. "Jesus, I think you might be right," he said as he turned to Kate. "We know what the Apex virus can do to an ordinary man. It boosts their natural traits. Even on a common soldier, the research papers you presented to me showed a marked increase in intelligence. What if the Apex virus was given to someone with an IQ at the level of Genaro's? What kind of avenues could that open up?"

"There's more," Herman said as he walked back towards the sitting area. "Come take a look at this."

Kate and Draven followed as Herman grabbed the TV remote. "Have you guys been watching the news lately?"

"I've been out of the country. I haven't seen any TV for weeks." Draven said.

"What about you?" Herman asked Kate as he switched the television on.

"I'm too busy for TV. A lot has happened lately."

"Yeah, well, maybe you should take a few minutes and look at the bigger picture."

Herman switched to the news channels and started to cycle through them. On every station were reports of disturbances in cities the world over. At the bottom of the screen, the yellow news ticker scrolled across with headline reports of skirmishes and rioting at street level in locations the world over. Paris. London. Russia. Iraq. As they watched, more news broke, the ticker announcing unconfirmed reports of mass shootings in Iraq by a group of unidentified men. Eerily similar reports were coming in all the time as the watched.

"Jesus," Draven said, perching on the cracked faux leather seat.

"This is happening now people," Herman said, eyes wide as they watched the news. "We might be watching it on TV, but you can bet your asses it will be happening outside our windows soon enough."

"You think this is all related?" Kate asked Herman, for the first time without condescension.

"Absolutely."

"That's impossible," Kate said, joining Draven on the sofa. "There are only a small number of Apex operatives out there right now. It isn't enough to coordinate something like this."

"No, it actually makes sense. You know how when you found me in Mexico I was studying ants?"

"Yeah."

"Well, the reason was to consider a theory that the monkeys were using a similar system. In essence, they exist solely to serve a queen, or in this case, an alpha male."

"Joshua," She said.

"Exactly. His DNA is a part of them now. What if some primal instinct has bonded them to him?"

"I get it," Herman said. "Kinda like when birds or whales migrate. They don't know how they know where to go, they just get there."

"Exactly," Draven replied.

"But for what purpose. Even if they are doing this, there are so few of them that any kind of resistance would be futile. It's only a matter of time before they are stamped out."

"It would be if they weren't contagious. I mean, that's why you people are involved, right?"

"The research notes said it wasn't airborne. I had considered the possibility it could be transferred by a bite or scratch. But again, it was speculation. I was hoping to speak directly to Genaro to confirm it." Draven said

"Forget the notes, they were wrong."

"You're absolutely certain it can be transferred?"

"Hang on, it's easier if I show you," Herman said, hurrying to the converted bedroom and snatching some documents off the wall. He returned and handed them to Draven.

"This virus not only bonds with its host, it also replicates. It's almost like a parasitic organism. It's the replication which makes the Apex virus work in the way it was intended."

Draven skimmed through the pages handed to him by Herman.

"Where did you get these?"

"Genaro's wastebasket. You wouldn't believe the sort of stuff people throw away. I'm supposed to take them straight to the incinerator, but I always look first, just in case there's anything good in there."

"What's happening?" Kate said, peering over the shoulder of Draven at graphs and equations which made no sense to her.

"According to this, we have a hell of a bigger problem than we first thought. In the monkeys I discovered, the healing and resistant properties were genetic. They were a part of the creature itself. Genaro tried to isolate this aspect and administer it as an injection in much the same way as a person might get a flu shot. A little of the virus was injected, just enough to allow it to become part of the host's system. Genaro assumed the virus would give the desired effects, the strength, the resistance and then dilute away. The initial program called for repeat injections of the virus to top up the effects, almost like a booster jab of sorts. What he didn't know was that once administered, the virus was aggressive enough to self-replicate exponentially."

"So what does that mean in real world terms?"

"Well, for one it explains the aggression. The increase in testosterone from repeated injections was because the virus had never diluted or faded. Every new injection simply boosted its effectiveness. The downside for us is the virus will by now have infiltrated the body of the host in every way. Every cell will be adjusted. In essence, those who received the injection are the virus. "

"Holy shit, this is bad," Kate said. "So let's say you're right and like we suspect, they're contagious and making more of their own kind is their agenda. They would need needles and the virus itself, right? Samples of it at least."

"No, they don't," Herman said, pointing at the paper in Draven's hands. "You have to understand. The virus is part of them. A scratch, a bite, anything where cells or fluids can transfer from infected to non-infected will do it."

"This could become an epidemic?"

"Worse. This could be the end of the world as we know it." Herman said.

An hour earlier, such a statement would have been shrugged off as another one of his outlandish, conspiracy theory led ideas. Now nobody was laughing.

"I think we need to keep this in perspective. End of the world seems a little extreme." Kate said more to convince herself than the others.

"Just look at the TV," Herman said. "This is only the start. It's like a giant game of chess. Joshua is working on getting his pieces into position before he delivers the killer blow. Think about it from their point of view. If you were genetically superior in every way to your fellow human. Stronger. Faster. More intelligent. If pain and fear of death were a distant memory. If you were a god on earth, and you looked upon the rest of us, people like you and me, what would you see?"

"I don’t know what you're saying," Kate said.

"I do," Draven cut in. "Think about it. To them, we are inferior in every way. Parasites. If you look at it objectively, we - the regular bog standard human being - are now obsolete, and in my experience, nature always finds a way to get rid of the obsolete species. The bottom line is we're in big, big trouble."

"I need to call this in," Kate said as she walked towards the door to the trailer.

"Robbins?"

"No. We need to go higher. This is a game

changer."

# CHAPTER ELEVEN

## BAGHDAD SEWER SYSTEM
## IRAQ

THE BAGHDAD SEWER SYSTEM had fallen into disrepair. Despite promises from the US government that the military presence would lead to a better quality of life for the residents of the city, if anything things had gotten worse. Several sections of the sewer section were severely blocked and spewed their contents onto the streets. Others were cracked and broken, waiting for the inevitable collapse which was to come. Akhtar and Youness walked deeper into the darkness, both able to hear the screams and gunfire from above. Youness had calmed and held his brother's hand as they delved deeper. "Not long now," he whispered to his brother. "Soon we will be home and safe."

Youness didn't reply, he simply allowed himself to be led deeper, completely trusting of his brother. Akhtar should have been happy; however the fact his brother was so trusting scared him, especially with what was happening up on the surface. He had no concept of right or wrong, of who to trust and who not to. He would trust anyone who was an adult. Akhtar's thoughts turned to his parents, and not for the first time, he wondered how they were and what they were doing amid the chaos in the streets. He prayed they were safe. A dull explosion at street level rocked the sewer pipe, and the two brothers drew closer to each other as they inched further into the darkness. Youness emitted a whine, one of the involuntary sounds which Akhtar always took for granted on the surface. Down in the sewer, however, it was an incredibly loud sound, and it rolled away from them, echoing from the walls.

"You have to be quiet Youness," Akhtar whispered.

Youness responded with a blank stare, still not understanding what was going on. Akhtar was starting to think that was a good thing.

They went on, trudging through ankle deep water and trying to ignore the things which touched their legs as they waded. At every access ladder to the surface, Akhtar would pause and listen, trying to gauge what was going on up on the streets. It seemed that as lost as they were, they were definitely heading away from the violence. The explosions which had seemed frighteningly close were gradually growing more distant. The tunnel inclined ahead before levelling out, and Akhtar thought it was as good a place as any for them to rest. At least the higher ground would get them out of the filthy water for a while. Leading his brother up the slope, Akhtar slid down the wall, stretching his legs out in front of him. Youness also sat, exhausted and unused to walking for such long distances. Usually, he was kept in his wheelchair because it was easier to travel that way. Such luxuries were behind them, though, and Akhtar mentally chastised himself for leaving it behind. The brothers sat in silence for a while, listening to the steady drip of water and the distant rumble of explosions and chatter of gunfire.

Perhaps because stopping had given him the first opportunity to think about it, he started to consider why the city was under attack. The people of Iraq had always been a background element of the war, an inconvenience or a statistic to throw around when news agencies or terrorists were talking about how many were killed, either as a means to gain viewers or to brag about the impact of their most recent attack respectively. Never had such direct action been taken at street level. He wondered how many had lost their lives in the last few hours. Surely many must have been slain before they could escape.

Youness grunted and mouthed half-formed words which to anyone but his brother would be nothing but gibberish.

"I know," Akhtar replied. "I'm hungry too."

Youness replied with more half-formed words which cut Akhtar to the bone.

"I know, I'm scared too. I'll look after you, don't worry." Akhtar said, giving his brother a gentle squeeze of the hand. "Do you want to rest here for a while or go on?"

Youness replied in his own unique way, and Akhtar nodded. "I agree. We'll stay here for a while and rest."

The brothers got comfortable, Akhtar sitting upright with his back against the wall so he could see in both directions down the tunnel, Youness lying on the ground, head on his brother's lap. Akhtar stroked his brother's hair, knowing it helped him to relax. He was surprised when after a few minutes, Youness was sleeping, for the time being free from the fear and worry. Akhtar's own eyes started to grow heavy, the steady trickle of water soothing him as he let his body relax.

Part of him knew that he too should get some sleep and that his body needed the rest, especially with the uncertainty of what the future held. Another voice in his head reminded him how he was solely responsible for his brother, and falling asleep would put them both at risk from anyone else who had happened to escape the chaos of the streets for the sewers.

It was as he was trying to decide which argument was more compelling that his body took over, and without realising it was happening, Akhtar too drifted off to sleep.

He didn't dream as such, but drifted between scenes from his life, his subconscious mixing them into a bizarre melting pot of experiences and emotions. He saw his home, a humble apartment in a block of hundreds which looked the same. His father and mother were inside, smiling, laughing. Akhtar saw himself and his brother, only in his dream Youness had none of his mental ailments. He was aware and happy, and the two brothers were chatting, having a real conversation. The joy of seeing Youness happy and normal was overcome by the sound. They all heard it, and as a family walked out onto the balcony overlooking the busy rooftop jungle beyond. On the horizon, a cloud of dust was approaching. They could barely see it from their tenth-floor apartment, but as it always was in dreams, Akhtar knew exactly what it was. The sound of a thousand marching feet intercut with sporadic gunfire. Akhtar watched as his mother and father shared a worried glance as the cloud relentlessly drew closer.

"Don't worry, Brother," Youness said, grinning at Akhtar. "I'll look after you."

The dust cloud was closer now, and the screams and gunfire were frighteningly real.

"Why does nobody run from them?" Akhtar's mother whispered.

"Because there are none left alive to run, are there Akhtar?" Youness said, grinning at his brother.

"No, they're all dead," His dream self-said.

A blast of air hit them, warmer than the baking forty degree heat. No sooner had they drawn breath than they saw them. The plague. A swarming mass of those men in the black uniforms. They were winged, half men half locusts, complete with deformed, sharp-toothed jaws. They decimated everything in their path. The building began to shake and rumble as they swarmed into it, kicking more dust into the air. He saw himself watching from another building in the distance as his own apartment block was devoured and collapsed into its own footprint, leaving nothing but a smouldering cloud of rubble. The dream Akhtar squeezed his eyes closed from the horror, knowing that when he opened them, the entire dream started again, and he was once more with his family on the balcony, impossibly watching his own demise again and again.

"It will go on like this," Youness whispered as the relentless cloud again came towards their building. "They cannot be stopped."

For the second time they came, the half man - half locust cloud, and again the building began to shake as they swarmed inside.

"Please, make it stop," Akhtar gasped, turning to his brother.

But Youness was gone. In his place was one of those black-clad humanoid locusts, saliva dripping from its maw as it hovered next to him, its wings pushing the dry air towards his face.

"It will never stop," gurgled the thing that used to be his brother. Akhtar screamed, and once again was on the balcony, looking across at himself as the building was devoured and the perpetual loop of a nightmare went on, each time slightly different to the last. This time, the locusts were all Youness, twitching and buzzing as they swarmed towards the building. Akhtar screamed and wondered how long he would have to endure this hellish dream when he was yanked into consciousness by heavy hands pulling him to his feet.

He blinked away his dream and began to thrash

and kick at the people who had picked him and his brother off the floor and were carrying him deeper into the tunnels. Akhtar caught a glimpse of his brother, who was back to his usual self, frightened and sobbing. It was the last thing Akhtar saw before a hood was pulled over his head and he and his brother were carried deeper into the network of tunnels.

# CHAPTER TWELVE

THE WHITE HOUSE

WASHINGTON D.C

PRESIDENT RON FITZGERALD WAS in the middle of his second term in office and was just two days shy of celebrating his fifty-ninth birthday when news of the Apex uprising first broke. The white haired, blue eyed republican walked down the corridor towards his meeting with the vice president; sure it was a case of over cautious national security blowing things out of proportion.

Before he came to office, he had a reputation as a no-nonsense man who spoke his mind, and unlike many of his political colleagues, did everything he could to avoid the tangled spider web of lies and bullshit that came with a career in politics. He had promised his wife, Helen, when he first entered the race for the presidency that he would try to retain his dignity and be a good man no matter who tried to influence his decision making. It was something, that two years after her death from ovarian cancer, he tried to do every day, not only in tribute to her memory but because the country needed stability and a leader who was prepared to do what must be done for the good of the country. Like those who had come before him, the nature of the role meant it was impossible to please everyone and it was something which had taken him a little getting used to. He recalled how during a game of golf with his predecessor, Harold Ramell, he had been told something which had stuck with him. As they teed off on the seventeenth, Ramell had turned to him with a wry smile and told him the words which had stuck in his head ever since.

"Ron, you can be sure of two things if you get the big job. First, that your hair will go grey and go quick. Stress of the job, it's just one of those things. Second is you better get used to pissing people off. Remember, damned if you do, damned if you don't."

The words had, for the most part, proved to be true. His hair was already starting to lose its brown hue when he was first sworn into office and now was almost completely white. He had also managed to piss off just about as many people as he had gained the support of. Some of his decisions, like increasing funding for health care and education had been met with praise and support. Others such as maintaining a military presence in Iraq and Syria, and refusing to back down from increasing the pressure on the Koreans and Russians were less popular with some sections of both the public and his own government. According to the latest opinion polls, he was somewhere in the middle of the road as far as popularity went.

Everyone stood as he entered the meeting room, something which he was still embarrassed by even if it was protocol.

"Take a seat, gentlemen," the president said as he took his place at the head of the table. To his left was Eamon Morrison, who was the president's chief of staff. He looked at the president from eyes which seemed too widely spread across his face. Seemingly impatient, he was rotating his pen through his fingers as he waited for proceedings to begin. To the right was Vice President Paul Carter. Twenty years Fitzgerald's junior, he was ambitious and didn't make any secret of it. He was free of the presidential white hair curse and sported a thick mane of jet black hair which was slicked back with enough oil to power a small country. He peered over his glasses with a look of perpetual apathy, and unlike Morrison, was a picture of calm.

"This better be good gentlemen. I was enjoying

a much-needed vacation when you called."

"Sir, we have a situation which is escalating by the hour," Morrison said.

"Go on."

Carter slid a document over the desk to the president. "Do you recall the Apex Project, Mr. President?"

"Yes, of course. Genetic enhancement. Cost us a small fortune."

"Yes, well, as you know it was deemed a success and modified agents were sent into the field to start active duty."

"Yes, I recall," The president said as he leafed through the papers. "We sent some to Syria recently, and another group to India on a training exercise as I recall."

"Yes, that's correct sir," Morrison said. "In fact, we had a total of forty-seven agents on active duty across the globe as of two weeks ago."

"Had?" The president said eyebrows raised.

"Yes, sir. It seems something has happened and the teams stopped responding to commands. In fact, they stopped responding at all."

"What happened to them?"

"Well sir, at first, we weren't too sure. We put together a small team at Homeland security to investigate and report back with their findings."

"Come on Eamon, spit it out for Christ's sake."

"They've gone rogue sir," Carter cut in, glaring at the less confident chief of staff across the desk.

"What the hell does that mean?"

"It means they've gone into business for themselves. We hoped we could keep a lid on it and fix it before things went too far, but the press are asking questions and we can't hold them off for much longer."

"What the hell's happened for the press to get involved?"

"Sir, we don't know. Reports are sketchy right now, but there are some alarming consistencies with our intel the world over."

"So why am I only hearing about this now?"

"We failed to see a pattern at first. It started as a few isolated incidents which seemed unrelated. It seems we were wrong.”

"Go on," Fitzgerald said, imagining he could feel a few more hairs lose their hue as he sat there and listened to his chief of staff.

"They're attacking people, sir."

“The Apex teams?”

“Yes, sir.”

"Civilians?"

"And military. It seems completely random right now. We have reports of seventy dead in Baghdad and growing. Similar reports from Paris, London and Germany."

"Wait, let me just take a second here. You're telling me our assets are firing on civilians?"

"Mr. President," Carter snapped, sliding another document across the desk. "I don’t think you understand the magnitude of this. We have new information that suggests these rogue assets are actually incredibly dangerous and should be considered as a serious biological terror threat."

"Terror threat? Are you out of your damn minds?"

"No sir, in fact, we're quite certain."

"Find Genaro, I want him here within the hour to explain."

"Sir, Genaro is gone. His lab was raided by a small group of infected assets and he was taken."

"Taken where?"

"We don't know sir."

"Well someone better god-damn find out." Fitzgerald raged, scouring the reports off his desk.

"Homeland has an expert sir – a man called Draven who first discovered the species of monkey the Apex virus was taken from. He believes not only are the Apex teams unstable, they are also incredibly contagious. This could be an epidemic if we don't deal with this now."

"Why the hell am I only just finding out about this?" The president said, glaring at his chief of staff.

Morrison squirmed in his seat and glanced across the table at Carter, who was looking right back at him. "Sir, Vice President Carter thought it wasn't something worth troubling you with."

"Is this true?" Fitzgerald said, turning his attention to his arrogant second in command.

"Mr. President, let me explain-"

"Jesus, Paul, cut the Mr. President crap and speak freely for Christ's sake."

Carter looked flustered and shoved his glasses back up his face. "Okay, I'll give it to you straight, if that's what you want."

"Go on. I want to hear this." Fitzgerald shot back, not sure why he was allowing Carter to get under his skin so easily.

"Well, the truth is, I didn't want to trouble you with it for two reasons. Firstly because I underestimated the situation and thought it would be quickly fixed. I take full responsibility for that. The second reason is because..."

He hesitated, licking his lips as he tried to find the words.

"Go on, don't stop now," Fitzgerald said, watching Carter intently.

"Well, the truth is, you've looked tired of late. You looked like you could use the break. After the decision on military funding last month, some people were worried you might be struggling to cope."

Fitzgerald smiled, the rage inside making him tremble. "You mean the fact my decision to scale back on our occupation of foreign countries didn't suit your idea of what should have been done?"

"Not just mine sir," Carter fired back, some of the arrogance replacing his discomfort, "But for the record, yes. I think you made the wrong call. I didn't want to call you back from your holiday unless it was absolutely necessary."

"So I see," Fitzgerald sneered. "Look, Paul, I get it. I know how ambitious you are, and I know you think you can do a better job than me."

"No sir, absolutely not, I-"

Fitzgerald raised a hand and went on. "No need to deny it. I always suspected it, and it was confirmed when you and I got into the near argument about the foreign occupation policy. Be that as it may let me make one thing crystal clear to you." Fitzgerald leaned forward in his seat, pointing at Carter as he spoke. "Until the day you sit in my seat, until the day something happens to me and you get to hold the reigns, this is my horse. The responsibility to make the right call is mine to make. You don’t get to decide what's good or bad for me, what I should and shouldn’t deal with. You might think I’m an old fool who doesn’t know any better but don’t make the mistake of confusing my kindness with weakness. I'm more than prepared to make the tough calls as and when they need to be made. Understood?"

"Look-"

"I said is that understood?"

"Yes, of course. I'm sorry." Carter said, lowering his eyes to the table top.

"Now because of you trying to decide what's best for me, we're already on the back foot. I need options. I hope you have some."

"We could engage them at street level. Small arms fire, keep it controlled. We need to take into account the public perception of this." Morrison said.

"All due respect," Carter cut in, giving the chief of staff another sour glare, "I think we need more decisive action here."

"What did you have in mind?" Fitzgerald asked.

"I can't stress enough the need to contain this quickly. If the reports of these individuals being contagious are true, we need to destroy them immediately."

"That seems a little excessive," Morrison cut in.

"It has to be. Just imagine how quickly this could escalate. If our experts are right and these things can infect someone with just a bite, we could be looking at an army of these things in a matter of weeks."

"Mr. President, it's important we don't overreact to this situation. Although Vice President Carter has a point, right now it's too early to tell what will happen, if anything. As we said, intel is still hazy on this. I genuinely think small scale ground forces in the affected areas to restore order is the best move right now."

"Come on Eamon," Carter said, taking off his

glasses and setting them on the polished oak table top. "This isn't something we can afford to get wrong. If we wait too long and these things start to spread, it will be almost impossible to stop them. Remember, this isn't just an isolated incident in one location, we're talking about mass uprising across multiple countries. We need to act now to avoid paying the price later."

"What do you suggest Paul?" Fitzgerald asked.

"Well, for me, the preferred action is targeted air strikes. Civilian casualties will be minimal and we are assured of a swift and, more importantly, permanent solution. As you know, the traits of these Apex soldiers mean ground based combat is less effective than with regular enemies."

"Mr. President," Morrison said, finding his voice at last, "With all due respect, surely you can't see this as a viable option. The loss of life would be astronomical, not to mention the structural damage to the target locations."

"This is bigger than structural damage," Carter spat. "This could be a global level disaster. A few dead civilians and damaged buildings seem like an acceptable level of risk to me."

"I've heard enough," Fitzgerald snapped.

They waited whilst he came to a decision.

"Alright, here's what I want to do. I want to go with Morrison's idea. Small arms teams, keep it subtle."

"Ron, come on, you're making a big mistake here," Carter whined.

"Maybe so, but it's my mistake to make. The last thing I want is to frighten people by sending in goddamn air strikes and potentially causing more tension with the other nations of the world. Those acceptable casualties you mentioned so off the cuff are people with families. I won't put the people I'm sworn to protect under threat unless it's as a last resort."

"This is just like last time, you're making the wrong call, Ron," Carter said.

"And I say again, it's duly noted. Do we have an understanding?"

Carter shuffled in his seat. He wanted to say

more but knew he had already overstepped the mark. "Understood, Mr. President," He muttered.

"Good. Now I want action on this right now. We are already behind, so I want teams pulled together who are the best fit for low key small arms fighting."

"What about the media sir?" Morrison asked. "Speculation is rife. News outlets are already covering the situation."

"Well, we can't do anything about that now. From here on in I want a full media blackout. We need to limit the damage as much as we can."

"Yes sir," Morrison said.

"These experts you mentioned, with Genaro missing they are our main source of knowledge on this. We need them involved every step of the way."

"Do you want them brought here sir?" Morrison asked.

"No, not here. They're in Virginia right now, correct?"

"Yes sir, they are."

"Okay, tell them to wait there for further

instructions. Have Homeland coordinate with them and feed the information through to us. I need to speak to the rest of the world leaders to discuss our options within the global community."

"Understood sir."

"Alright then, let's go. Update me hourly."

"Yes sir," Morrison said, gathering his things and leaving.

Fitzgerald also stood, and turned to Carter.

"Paul, consider this a word to the wise. Don't bite the hand that feeds, and never assume you know everything."

"Yes, Mr. President. Apologies for my outburst." Carter said the words sour tasting.

"I'm not a man to hold grudges, Paul. I'm sure you know I'm disappointed with your actions. Now all I care about is you doing everything you can to put it right. You're a good man, even if you can be a hot-headed asshole sometimes. Just remember, we're on the same side here."

Fitzgerald waited for a moment for a response, and when none came, left the vice president alone in the meeting room. Carter watched the older man leave, and promised himself even if it was the last thing he did, he would prove the old bastard wrong at least once. Gathering his papers, Carter followed the president out of the room and went directly to his office.

# CHAPTER THIRTEEN

ADIRONDACK STATE PARK
SANTIAC RIVER VALLEY
NEW YORK STATE

KNOWN AS THE SILOHOME, the innocuous looking building nestled in the barren Saranac valley held a secret. The isolated home offered breath-taking views of the valley from all directions and was the ultimate in privacy. The real secret, however, was what lay underneath the building. Accessed through a discreet interior door, a staircase leads directly to a nine storey two thousand three hundred square foot decommissioned underground Atlas-F missile launch facility. Purchased by an ambitious property developer in the mid-nineties, the underground facility had been renovated into multi-level living quarters accessible only by passing through several steel blast doors. Deeper still was the missile launch area. A relic of the cold war, the immense launch bay offered another 12,000 square feet of space. Completely secure and undetectable, it was a perfect base of operations, the house above ground giving little clue to the sheer scale of what lay beneath. It was here where Joshua and his men had set up home. The building security had been laughable at best and were quickly dispatched. It was on the second underground level where Genaro's new lab had been set up. Joshua's men went about their business with frightening efficiency, some working at renovating the missile launch bay, others stocking weapons and supplies as per Joshua's instructions.

Genaro ignored the noise as best he could and concentrated on his work. His injured arm had healed in just fourteen hours, and now there was little evidence of Joshua's bite, although he could feel its effects surging through him as his body adjusted to its new parasite. As a man who had never done drugs, he had no idea how it felt to be high, yet was sure the pure euphoria he experienced during those first few hours was close. Subtle things made all the difference. The nagging pain in his knee as a result of early onset arthritis was gone completely. As was the dull ache in his wrist following a break when he was seventeen and came off his motorbike and slammed into a tree. In fact, he had never felt stronger or more aware of the world around him. It was as if a veil had been lifted from the life he used to know, and he had been ushered into a new place where the possibilities were endless.

"Addictive, isn’t it?"

Genaro turned to see Joshua as he walked into the makeshift underground lab. He looked quite regal with his hair tied back, arms clasped behind his back.

"It's incredible. I could never imagine it would feel this way."

"Now do you see? Now do you understand?" Joshua said, smiling at the scientist as he stood at his side.

"Yes, I don’t think it's something you could ever express in words. This feeling is one which has to be experienced first-hand to truly understand."

"And many will," Joshua replied, his eyes sharp and aware as they scanned the myriad of equipment on Genaro's workstation. The scientist saw where he was looking and stepped aside.

"The work you asked me to do, the work I said was impossible..." Genaro trailed off and lowered his head.

"You are able to do it now, correct?" Joshua said.

"Yes, I don't understand how, though. The equations and methods which seemed alien to me just a few days ago now make perfect sense. The work is almost racing ahead on its own. In truth, I feel like I'm hanging on to the handlebars of a runaway motorbike with my legs trailing out behind me."

Joshua clapped a hand on Genaro's shoulder and widened his grin, immediately making the scientist feel better. "Don't worry about that, it's just the adjustment to the change. You are still growing into the man you will become. I have every faith you will do as I ask. I wouldn't have brought you here otherwise."

"And I promise you I won't stop until it's done. I won't let you down, Joshua."

"I know you won't. I have every faith in your

ability."

Warmth rushed through Genaro's body. A euphoric adrenaline rush of pure devotion to Joshua. Love was a word he didn't like to use, however, it was as good a description as any for the emotion he felt. He knew then and there that he would, without question do anything Joshua asked of him, even to the point of giving his own life.

"Are you alright?" Joshua asked.

"Yes, I'm sorry I was just overwhelmed for a second. My brain is alive with thoughts, ideas. It's quite remarkable."

"And it will only get better. These new emotions will grow as your body adjusts to the gift."

"I wish everyone could feel this way."

"I'm afraid that's not possible."

Genaro hesitated, and then looked Joshua in the eye. "Can you live with the guilt Joshua, of what you have to do to the world?"

"I feel no guilt. I do what I have to in order for humanity to survive. And you are a key part of that process. A brilliant mind further enhanced by our special gift. You can make our task easier."

"How will you do it? Surely we don't have enough men. We're outnumbered by far."

"Indeed, we are. But remember, one man alone can create an army."

"An army?" Genaro said, a flicker of uncertainty crossing his face.

"Yes. An army. A force to usher in the new world and rid it of the cruel, barbaric creatures which inhabit it." The bitterness in Joshua's voice was hard to ignore, and Genaro felt a stab of fear.

"Is that necessary? I mean, is there no other way?"

"Do you remember, Doctor Genaro, way back at the start of all this when you asked me to trust you?"

"Of course I do. I was impressed by your courage." Genaro said, meeting Joshua's eye. "If not for you, my work would never have started."

"Then I ask you to remember that and give the same courtesy to me. Trust me when I tell you there is no other option. We have to purge the weaker species. It's nature's way. The strong survive, the weak become extinct."

"But Joshua, there are over seven billion people on the planet. Surely it's impossible."

"Some will be shown the light. Some will join us. Some will be spared from death to work for our cause."

"You will never convince them," Genaro said. "I've worked for the government for long enough to know that anyone different will be perceived as a threat, and threats are often crushed before they can gain a foothold."

"And who will crush us?" Joshua said with a smile. "Do you think a soldier will stay loyal to his country when he sees his bullets penetrate us and we still don't stop? Will his love for his country be enough to keep him fighting when he knows he can't win?"

"What are you saying?"

"I'm saying the physical fight, the warfare, the dirty work, isn't where the battle is won." Joshua tapped his temple with a bony index finger. "Winning the psychological battle is the key to victory. First we break their spirits, and then we purge their physical form."

"And how will we break their spirits?"

Joshua smiled and clasped his hands behind his back. "Don't worry about that. I have something in mind that will show our intentions to the world. Something that will turn the current confusion at street level into terror."

"It sounds like something Hitler would have said," Genaro replied with a nervous snort.

"Yes, it does, doesn't it? He had the right idea. You see, he knew fear was the key to success. He only failed because he made a couple of small but critical errors. We will not repeat them."

"When? When do we put this into action?"

"My friend, it's already started. The world doesn't yet know it, but it is enjoying the final days of life as they know it."

Genaro nodded, feeling a mixture of pride and fear racing through his veins. Breaking away from the hypnotic gaze of Joshua, the scientist returned to his work.

# CHAPTER FOURTEEN

## DHAVARI SLUMS
## MUMBAI
## INDIA

YOU COULD NEVER FORGET the smell. Food waste rotting in the gutters, stagnant sewer water running freely down the same roads people walked, baked into a disgusting throat burning stench by the intense pollution heavy air. And the desperation. The helplessness. That was a smell all of its own. With a population of up to a million, the almost unbearable living conditions were a way of life many of the areas would have to endure until their death – an event which could happen at any time through starvation, conflict, or from one of the countless epidemics which scourged the closely knit ramshackle dwellings. Flies and rats thrived in abundance amid the haunted faced people for whom just making it through the day was seen as a huge achievement.

Thirty-nine-year-old Suvari Tam grew up on these streets. An exception to the rule, she had been one of the few lucky ones to find a way out and make a life for herself, to flee to America and find a good man who she loved dearly. Even though it was to help, she found it incredibly strange to be back. She wasn't sure what to make of the whirlwind of emotion she could feel stirring inside her. Part of it was a deep sadness that nothing had changed. Some of it was fear that she had come back to the place where so many memories were bad. Another aspect was the conversation she had with Marcus just before she left. He had sounded distant and withdrawn, and although they had both tried to forget it, she couldn't help but compare his mood to the immediate aftermath of the incident at the school which had changed him forever. She also thought of her sister for the first time in years, the guilt of that revelation cutting deep. Like Suvari, she had wanted out and shared the same determination to make a difference. However, like many of the residents of the slums, she was sold into a prostitution ring at just eight years old and spent the next three years being forced to endure horrific sexual acts from men who would gladly pay the minuscule fee her owners would charge, knowing nothing was off limits as far as what they would be allowed to do to the fragile young girl. Suvari last saw her sister on the day of her eleventh birthday. She was emaciated and her once bright eyes were dead and devoid of hope. She had asked Suvari for a few rupees to get some food and disappeared off into the maze of buildings. Two days later her body was found by the river with her throat cut. It was a ghastly end to a pitiful existence, and the worst part of it for Suvari was that nobody cared. One dead underage prostitute in a community full of them wasn't news. It was part of daily life.

What it did, was give Suvari the extra motivation she needed to ensure her own life wasn't wasted in the same way. Knowing it was a case of either die in the slums or take a chance by moving on, she chose the latter, and with nothing but the clothes on her back, set off as a thirteen-year-old child into the world with no clue how far she would get or what the future held.

Now here she stood, back where she started, an educated woman who against all odds had found a loving family in Bangladesh who took her in and gave her all the tools she needed to make the most of life. She was never the brightest and sometimes struggled to keep up with her classmates who had been afforded the luxury of education from a much younger age. However the desire to be a success burned inside her, and drove her to make as much of a success of herself as possible. She had moved to America, hoping to find the path to whatever life intended for her and in doing so met her future husband, Marcus. They had met by chance at a local bar and immediately hit it off. She was taken in by his good looks and sharp personality but never anticipated that he would feel the same way, even less that they would go on to marry and have two wonderful children. Now working as an aid worker, she was determined to help as many children as possible to a better life and ensure as best she could that they avoided the same fate as her sister. She walked through the crowded streets, surprised at how little she had forgotten about how awful it was. Her internal navigation took over, guiding her down alleyways and through the winding, filth-laden roads. Outwardly she showed little emotion. Inside she wanted to weep for the horror of an existence these poor people had to endure.

The claustrophobic walls of the slums gave way to the rubbish-strewn banks of the river. The stench of the filthy water was almost overpowering, a smell that instantly triggered memories from her childhood. She couldn't forget that stench. It had ingrained into her skin and even after leaving Mumbai for pastures new, it seemed to linger, somehow in her skin no matter how often she washed or tried to scrub it away. She watched from the bank as children who knew no better played in the rancid water which was in truth little more than an open sewer filled with human waste. It was little wonder disease was so rife. She approached the edge of the water walking through ankle high rubbish at its edge and disturbing mosquitoes and rats alike.

She pushed her jet black hair out of her eyes and slung her backpack off her shoulder. Inside were bottles of clean water and bread.

"Children, come here," She said, holding the bread and water up for them to see. She knew most of the children were orphans, either through abandonment or due to the death of their parents. As she had arrived back in the city she had seen them sleeping on the ground and in gutters, devoid of anything which might resemble pride. They flocked to her, eyes wide, grins plastered onto their emaciated faces. There wasn't enough for them all, it was impossible. She had only six bottles of water and there were twelve children.

"Share it around, share it around," she said as she handed the water to the children.

The ones who didn't grab the bottles were grabbing at those who did, desperate to get a taste.

"Hey, share it," Suvari said in the native tongue. "If you don't, you won't get any bread."

That seemed to do the trick, and she waited

until all of them had taken a sip.

"Oaky, now the bread," She said as she began to tear chunks from the loaves and hand them to the hungry children.

She waited as they ate, feeling both elated and sad as she looked across the river. In the distance, through the perpetual shroud of low hanging pollution, she could see the tower blocks of the city. Although the Dhavari slums were right in the middle of India's financial capital, it was a place forgotten and ignored a place –

Her thoughts were broken by the flash of light across the water. The rumble of the explosion followed seconds later and she watched as a black edged fireball rose into the sky from between the tall buildings of the city chased by a thick plume of black smoke. She was starting to wonder if it was some kind of traffic accident or some other explainable occurrence when two other similar explosions happened within seconds of each other in different parts of the skyscape, and a fourth from behind, somewhere out of sight beyond the slums.

Rolling across the still air, she could hear the steady chatter of gunfire, which was enough for her to know something was desperately wrong.

"Go, home to your families," she said to the children. A few did as they were told, running into the maze of hovel like homes, the rest stayed, watching Suvari, waiting for her to do something. She could tell by their dishevelled appearance these were the kind of children who had no homes or families – the type who were forced to live on the streets and faced an uphill fight every day to survive. There were six of them in total and although she wasn't sure where it came from, she felt an overwhelming desire to look after them.

"Come with me," she said to the children. “I’ll get you to a safe place."

Another explosion, this one much closer rattled the earth and Suvari felt a tiny, dirty hand grasp hers in fear.

"Come on, this way," she said, fighting the urge to run as she walked back the way she had come, leading the children away from the river. She met people coming in the opposite direction, curious faces interested to see what the commotion was. Two more unseen explosions rattled the city, and the people gasped. She looked over her shoulder just as one of the tower blocks on the horizon collapsed, throwing a huge cloud of concrete dust into the air. With increased urgency, she turned her attention back to the narrow streets and tried to push against the flow of people who were all now trying to get to the river for a closer look at what was happening. Suvari led the children through winding side streets, hoping they were still following and at the same time having no clue where she was even leading them. She had come to the slums via bus and had no transport of her own.

Another explosion erupted, this time uncomfortably close. Now those who were curious at the riverbank were unsure, and some were starting to double back, causing a bottleneck in the narrow streets. Suvari led the children towards one of the main thoroughfares through the slum. Dubbed ' 90 feet road' so named because of its alleged width (although most residents knew the neighbouring '60 feet road' was actually wider). Here the noise was deafening, the street gridlocked with battered taxis trying to bully their way through traffic to reach their destination. Horns honked, and the air was filled with acrid black smoke spewed from sick sounding exhausts. She had hoped to find transport out of the slum from here, an idea which was quickly abandoned. She heard another dull explosion, although amid the constant drone of shouting, revving engines and honking horns it was barely audible. She saw their opportunity, a rusty flatbed truck idling by the side of the road, its driver leaning against the cab and smoking as he watched the traffic crawl by. She ushered the children to the back of the pale blue vehicle and started to help them inside.

"Hey, what are you doing?" The driver said. He was old and leathery, with a thick moustache, hard eyes and crooked yellow teeth.

"Please, you have to take us out of the city," She said, not stopping as she helped the children into the truck.

"No, I'm not a taxi. I can't help you." He replied, then leaned inside the truck. "Come on, out of there," He barked, reaching for the child nearest him.

Before she could help herself she grabbed his wrist.

"No," she said, wondering if she had finally overstepped the mark. "Please, help us," She added, pressing a handful of money into his hand.

The man looked at the money, then at the children and back to Suvari.

"Where do you want to go?"

"Just get us out of the city." As she said it, there was another explosion, this time, close enough to shake the buildings of the slums. The people were now starting to spill onto the street, and Suavari saw a flicker of understanding in the man's eyes.

"Okay, come on," he said, helping the last of the children into the back of the truck.

Suvari went to the passenger side and was about to climb in when the man hurried around to where she stood.

"Wait a moment," he said, opening the door. The foot well and seat was covered in food wrappers and other assorted garbage which looked to have been accumulated over the years. The man scooped it out onto the street and then turned to her with an apologetic shrug.

"Sorry, I'm used to travelling alone."

She climbed into the truck, desperate now to be anywhere but there. She could see arguments breaking out as desperate people tried to find someone to give them a ride to somewhere safe. She could sense how things were just a hair away from spilling into chaos, and she didn't want to be there when it happened.

The owner of the truck climbed into the driver's side, cigarette jammed into the corner of his mouth. She thought it would be an absolute miracle if the truck even started, let alone was able to get them out of the city. Heated arguments were taking place all around them as those who had seen what was happening across the river grew increasingly desperate to flee. Some had already given up on securing a vehicle and were running, which in turn caused more confusion as people started to wonder what was happening.

"We need to hurry," Suvari said to the driver.

"Yes yes, just a second," he replied, taking a last drag of his cigarette and tossing it out of the window. He turned the key, and to Suvari's elation and surprise, the truck sputtered to life at the first attempt. It sounded sick, but it was running. The gearbox groaned as the man found drive and inched them forward into the slow flow of traffic.

"What's your name?" he asked as he squeezed past a shirtless man on a scooter.

"Suvari."

"I'm Rakesh," the man replied as they picked up a little speed.

The panic was palpable now, and more explosions came from the city. More disturbing still was the rattle of gunfire which seemed to be closer than ever.

"We need to go faster," She said, glancing at the

older man in profile as he concentrated on the road.

"This is as fast as I can go in this traffic. What's happening in the city?"

"I'm not sure. I saw explosions and one of the tower blocks collapsed."

"Let me see if I can get something on the radio," He said as he narrowly avoided hitting a group of teens as they ran out in front of the truck. Cursing under his breath, he let them pass and turned up the volume on the radio, filling the cab with static.

"Broken?" Suvari asked.

"No," the man replied, frowning at the display. "That should be the radio station."

"What do you mean?"

"It's gone. Whatever has happened, the radio isn't broadcasting."

They sat quietly for few moments as they inched through the traffic.

"I think we need to get as far away from the city as we can," Suvari said as she looked at the increasing panic which was all around them.

"Yes, I agree," Rakesh replied. They broke free of the bulk of traffic and were, at last, able to pick up a little speed. As the landscape of slums rolled away, they were able to see the city and for the first time the full scale of the problem. The skyline of Mumbai was alive with multiple fires and thick plumes of smoke rising into the sky. Rakesh sucked air through his teeth as he watched another tower block crumble and implode.

"Terrorists?" He said as they navigated the traffic.

"I don’t know."

"We need to get out of here," he replied, picking up speed.

"We can’t go too fast. Remember the children."

"What's that up ahead?" Rakesh said, squinting through the filthy windshield to try and get a better look.

At the end of the street, a rough roadblock of sorts had been erected, and armed men with crew cuts and black tactical uniforms were pulling people out of their cars to question. The driver at the head of the crew was arguing his case to the man, who looked completely unimpressed.

"I don't like this," Suvari whispered.

"Nor do I," Rakesh muttered, joining the line and putting the car into park. They watched as the man at the head of the line was ordered to pull off to the side and let the others through. Reluctantly, he did as he was told, letting the next car approach the checkpoint.

"Is it some kind of military coup?" Rakesh said, keeping a close eye on the conversation at the roadside between the driver and the black clad soldier. The soldier wore a plastic grin and nodded as the driver spoke and gesticulated.

Suvari couldn't shake the swirling butterfly feeling in her stomach. Every instinct screamed at her to get away from these people, and she realised she feared them more than the explosions in the city. As she watched, more men clad in black started to line up behind the roadblock, all armed, all watching the snake of cars shimmering in the sunlight with apathy. There were just five vehicles ahead of theirs before they would reach the head of the line. She had no identification with her. No paperwork to say who she was or why she was there. How would she explain the truck full of children to them?

The answer came to her immediately, and it was one she had tried to deny for the last few minutes.

They don't intend to let anyone go.

It all clicked into place then. The roadblock wasn't to process people or to check their identification. It was to stop them from leaving until the rest of the black-clad men were in a position to open fire.

"Drive," she whispered, the words so quiet they barely left her lips.

Rakesh didn't hear her. He was staring at the argument by the side of the road, which was growing more and more heated from the driver's side. The man in black was still wearing the same Cheshire cat grin as he listened without reacting.

"Drive," she said again. This time forcing the

words out.

"What was that?" Rakesh asked, turning his head towards her but keeping his eyes on the argument.

"I said drive!" she croaked.

"Drive where? Where can I go?"

"Anywhere. It isn't safe here, it-"

Glass exploded from the passenger side window showering Suvari with broken pieces. The truck rocked on its tired old suspension as another car - presumably one from further back in the line - had also realised they were all queuing up to wait for their deaths. The rusty red Fiesta scraped down the side of Rakesh's truck, clipping the wing mirror and knocking it off as he snaked towards the front of the roadblock.

"Hey! What the hell?" Rakesh said as the red Fiesta picked up speed.

Suvari watched as if she were somehow outside her own body, hands trembling on her glass covered lap as she looked on in half fear, half curiosity to see what the men in black would do. Her answer came just seconds later.

As if they were some kind of synchronised swim team, the men behind the roadblock lifted their automatic weapons as one and started to fire at the car.

Screams.

Chaos.

Confusion.

All words which barely scratched the surface of how Suvari felt. Something in her forced her to react. Maybe it was the survival instinct which helped her to escape the slums in the first place, or perhaps some other unexplainable thing. She threw herself into the foot well of the truck, covering her head as bullets tore through the air. Glass exploded all around her. Something warm and wet hit her on the back. She glanced up to see Rakesh, limp in his seat, the top portion of his head missing where the bullet had hit him full in the face.

The children.

The children.

The children.

It was all she could think about. She couldn't hear them in the back of the truck and hoped the reason was simply because of the sheer volume of everything else that was going on around her. Something happened then. Something in her mind clicked and the fear was gone. She crawled over the foot well, ignoring the hair, bone and brain matter all around her as she leaned across Rakesh's body. The gunfire was incessant, yet she didn't dare look for fear of what she might see. She reached across Rajesh's corpse, grasping for the door handle. She missed at the first two attempts, not quite able to reach. She lurched one last time, digging her feet in and shoving herself across his lap. The door clicked open. Suvari shoved Rajesh's body as hard as she could, blinking through tears as it flopped out onto the road with a wet thud, ejecting more brain matter from the exposed cavity. His legs were still inside the car, blocking her way. She grabbed the ankles of his trousers and shoved them out, then shuffled into the driver's seat, ignoring the fact she was sitting on brains and hair. Keeping her head low, she turned the ignition, praying the vehicle would start and half expecting the old horror movie cliché of the car refusing to turn over. The beaten old van sputtered to life, and she shifted into gear, still hunched down in her seat and hoping the general din of the gunfire and explosions from the city would mask the sound of the engine.

She risked a peek over the dashboard to get her bearing, and couldn't believe the devastation. Bodies littered the ground, smoke billowed from damaged cars. Broken glass glittered under the sun in the street. There was no resistance, and yet still the men in black fired indiscriminately, mowing down people who were too confused to know where they were going. Miraculously, the way ahead was clear apart from the three men with automatic weapons who stood in the middle of the road, taking shots at people as they tried to hide. She watched as one man somehow avoided being hit, and skirted past the black clad men. Rather than try to shoot him, the man in black charged after him and tackled him into the dirt, then in a single fluid motion, bit the man's throat, sending a jet of incredibly bright blood arcing through the air.

The man screamed and writhed, then stopped moving altogether. Suvari was sure he was dead, another victim of the massacre. She flicked her eyes back towards the road, knowing there was no way she would make it, and even if she did somehow get past, they would turn and shoot, exposing the children to almost certain death.

It was the proverbial rock and a hard place situation. Damned if you do, damned if you don't. If she stayed, she would surely be picked off and murdered along with everyone else. If she went for it, she could still suffer the same fate but the children were at much more risk. As she battled over what to do, the day erupted with the sound of an explosion overhead. She watched as a military jet was hit by some projectile from the city – the smoke trail clearly visible in the still air. The jet lurched towards the ground, huge chunks of burning metal raining down on the slums. Now on fire, the jet slammed into the ground, slicing through the tired old buildings with ease and sending an enormous fireball into the air. Suvari's truck was rocked by the concussion wave, and a rush of hot air blasted through the shattered windows. The men in black were gawping at the spectacle, their guns by their side as they watched. She knew it was likely the only chance she would get. She floored the accelerator, the truck slewing across the road as she pulled out of the line towards the roadblock and freedom beyond. One of the men turned towards her as she accelerated, smiling at the vehicle and swinging his weapon towards her.

She picked up speed and hit the man hard, crushing him under the van which lurched as it drove over him. Blinking through tears, she scraped the van between the two cars parked in the middle of the street and then was free, speeding away from the chaos and the explosions. She waited for the rattle of gunfire to cut the van to ribbons, yet it didn't come. As she turned into the maze of city streets, she looked back towards the scene roadblock. The men watched her go, smiling and making no effort to chase her down. More disturbing than that, however - perhaps, even more, disturbing even than the explosions or the sheer violence and death which had surrounded her – was the sight of the man. The one who was chased down and bitten in the throat. She had been certain he was dead, and yet there he was. Standing with the men in black. Showing no fear, and them no aggression towards him. He too watched her go, a local from the slums who just moments ago was as desperate as she was to flee the city, and now stood side by side with his attackers.

# CHAPTER FIFTEEN

## THE WHITE HOUSE
## WASHINGTON D.C

THE BANKS OF MONITORS in the White House situation room were alive with a mixture of news reports and live non publicised feeds from various locations around the world. The president's conference call with his fellow world leaders had for once been without the usual posturing and pushing of political agendas for the simple reason that they all knew they were dealing with something new which was a threat to all of them.

The president sat alongside Vice President Carter and listened to the Secretary of Defence - a sharp, proud man with white hair and a steely eye called Ronald Rose - as he gave them the latest update.

"We have several new reports of attacks Mr. President, most recently in Mumbai, London and

Tokyo."

"I thought these Special Forces were only stationed in a few locations? This is going global."

"Sir, we believe this uprising has been in the works for some time. We think this group had sleeper agents waiting to begin turning people just as soon as they received the go ahead."

"Turning people?"

The secretary of defence squirmed and pushed a brown folder towards the president. "We have confirmation of deliberate and targeted infection. They are biting civilians and turning the ones they think they can use. The rest are being murdered."

"Jesus," The president said, shaking his head. "How long?"

"For the turn?"

"Yes."

"It varies sir. Some reports are saying anything between a few minutes and a few hours. All the same, whoever this group are, they're getting bigger. At this level of growth, it won't be too long before our forces are outnumbered."

"What about resistance? Are we engaging these people?"

"Well, we have men on street level as instructed fighting back, but truth be told we're stretched thin. We lost contact with Iraq two hours ago."

"For now, I want to hear about our own soil. What's happening here?"

"Not as much as we expected. A few isolated incidents, but nothing on the scale of the other attacks. The problem here is the public. Despite our best efforts, we couldn't keep a lid on this. It's all over the news and people are starting to panic."

"This is the last thing we need," Fitzgerald said, rubbing his temples to try and stave off the headache for just a little while longer. "How serious?"

"A few sporadic riots at first, but the more news breaks, the more panic on the streets. People are already looting. Local law enforcement agencies are struggling to cope. They haven't experienced anything on this scale before. None of us have."

"What kinds of numbers are talking about for

our troops over here? Surely we have enough to fight back against these bastards."

"Some. A lot of our men are deployed as per your instructions to help overseas."

"What about reserves?"

"Already called in sir."

"Good," the President said, glancing at the TV screens which were showing news footage from all over the world. "Get them out assisting local law enforcement. I want this contained."

"Sir, we don't have enough reserves to stretch to every area with rioting."

"Then prioritise damn it!" Fitzgerald said, glaring at the Secretary of Defence. "It's your job to make sure the country is safe, so send them to the heaviest hit areas until we can get some assistance. The French and British are sending whatever troops they can spare, but as you know they're having their own issues. The Russians refuse to release anyone and insist on dealing with their situation alone, so it doesn't leave us many options."

"It's not too late to go with the air strikes sir,"

Carter said, staring over his glasses at the president.

"Come on Paul, let’s not have this shit again. I already told you, as long as we can control this from the ground, I’m not prepared to send the jets in and cause even more panic."

"Forgive me sir, but I think the situation dictates a more direct response. You've already lost the public. Things are only going to get worse."

Fitzgerald didn’t answer at first. He took a moment to control his temper and remind himself he was in a position where he had to retain control. Despite the fury which raged inside, he spoke calmly when he addressed the vice president. "Look, Paul, we discussed this earlier. Frankly, I’m getting tired of you trying to push your idea of what we should do on to me."

"I'm sorry, I didn’t mean anything by it, I’m just trying to stop you from making a mistake."

"It's my mistake to make! I told you this earlier. If you can’t do your job then you better get the hell out of here. In case you haven’t noticed, we have a situation on our hands here that we don’t need to add to by sending in airstrikes and having the people think its world war three."

Carter squirmed, his cheeks flushing.

"Go ahead and spit it out, Paul. It's obvious you have something to say."

"Sir, I'm sorry, but I have to stress how this is the wrong decision. We need to contain this situation now, not give them more time to spread and grow. Every moment wasted will just make it harder to recover. In my opinion, you need to control this situation or you risk losing the confidence of the public. God knows, they must be wondering what the hell's going on."

"Finished?"

"Yes, sir."

Fitzgerald sat for a moment, letting Carters words sink in. This was the reality of his job. When the big decisions needed to be made, his cabinet and advisors were first to step back from the process so they wouldn't be to blame if the wrong call was made. On the one hand, he was determined to stick to his guns and deal with the situation with as little conflict as possible. On the other, Carter had a point, and the more time they wasted the more the situation was likely to get further out of control. Decision made, he cleared his throat.

"Okay, First things first. Ron, how are we coping down on street level? By that I mean, are we winning?"

"We're containing them. I'm liaising with military leaders from the affected countries and am sharing information. As determined as they are, for the time being they're just too small a force to battle the combined might of the international forces, even as stretched as they are."

"Okay, in that case, I want to proceed as planned. That means solely on the ground. No airstrikes," he looked at Carter as he said it, making sure the vice president understood the command. "I know it's not what you wanted to hear Paul, and I'm sorry about that. But I'm commander in chief, and it's my job to keep the country safe. Causing widespread panic here and internationally won't help anyone, nor will sending in airstrikes that will wipe out countless civilians as well as the targets. You do raise a good point, though, and it's something I should have already addressed with the public by now. Call a press conference. It's time I addressed the nation."

"For the record, I think this is a huge mistake," Carter said, plainly seething at Fitzgerald's decision.

"Be that as it may. If you're right, then maybe you will get to sit in my chair and call the shots sooner than you thought. If you're wrong, then maybe, just maybe you'll learn something valuable. Either way, this is how it's going to go down. If you don't like it, now would be the time to say so."

Fitzgerald waited, holding Carters gaze. The vice president looked like he wanted to leave to the point where it seemed to be taking an extraordinary effort to stay in his seat. Colour flushed into his cheeks and his hands were clenched into fists. Eventually, he exhaled and broke the Presidents gaze. "No sir, I have nothing to say."

"Glad to hear it. Now let's get back to the

business in hand. It's time I told the country what we're dealing with here."

# CHAPTER SIXTEEN

DEPARTMENT OF HOMELAND SECURITY
WASHINGTON DC

MARCUS WATCHED THE FOOTAGE of the Mumbai attacks on the news, their unfiltered images showing in detail the death and the bodies. He knew his wife was there somewhere amid the chaos. He hoped she was alive but feared that she, like the rest, was another victim. The guilt at not trying harder to make her stay raged in him, throbbing like a rotten tooth. He tried to imagine things he should have said that might, just might have made a difference. He stared at the images of the attack on screen, drumming his fingertips on the table top and feeling the glare of his colleagues and advisors, who would never say the thing they all feared.

"Excuse me for a second," Marcus said, snatching up his phone and leaving the room. He was more than aware that he stood in the exact same corridor less than two days earlier and tried to convince Suvari to stay at home. He took his phone and cycled to the number in his phonebook, not sure if he had the guts to make the call until he had already pushed the button and the line was being connected. He waited, grimacing as the agitated Secretary of Defence picked up.

"Mr. Secretary? Marcus Atkinson at Homeland."

"If you're calling to tell me you have more bad news, then I have to tell you we have more than enough to handle."

"No, sir it's not that. It's… My wife was in Mumbai. Dhavari, to be exact, where an attack has just taken place."

"I see," Rose said, not giving anything away.

"I wondered if I could take temporary leave to go out there and find her."

"I hate to say this Atkinson, but how do you know she's even alive? Hell, you more than anyone know what we're dealing with here."

Son of a bitch. Marcus didn't say it, but he was tempted. Instead, he cleared his throat and reminded himself that he needed to play nice. "Sir, I have to hope she's alright. What other option do I have?"

"I understand that Atkinson, but we're in the middle of a major crisis here. We need you to stay where you are."

"Sir, I have to know. She's my wife. I'm not going to be either efficient or productive until I know if she's safe."

"I thought they said you were an emotionless sort, Atkinson. Isn't that why you kept your job after that mess at the school?"

"That's hardly relevant to this situation, sir," Marcus replied, giving his superior the same kind of short tone as he had received.

"Well, I'm sorry, but I can't let you leave. Not until this is over. You have responsibilities. Frankly, I find it unprofessional of you to even ask."

Marcus hesitated, mouth slightly agape as the words sank in.

"Are you still there, Atkinson?"

"Yes, sir."

"And you understand what I'm telling you?"

"Yes, sir."

"Good. Now get back to your desk and keep us filled in about this ongoing situation."

"Yes, sir," He said again, robotic and without emotion. The line went dead in his ear, and he shoved the phone into his pocket. He looked into the briefing room, then the opposite way to the corridor which would take him to the exit. He chose the latter, doing as he always did and trusting his instincts. He knew there was a UN aid team heading out to Mumbai to assist in the relief efforts, and he was determined that one way or another, he would be on board when it left. He walked briskly down the corridor, hoping against hope that his wife was still alive.

# CHAPTER SEVENTEEN

SILOHOME
ADIRONDACK STATE PARK
SANTIC RIVER VALLEY
NEW YORK STATE

JOSHUA SAT IN THE dark, cross-legged on the floor, eyes closed. He was in the bottommost chamber of the silo, the area designated as his own personal quarters. Furniture was minimal. A mattress and sheets, a toilet. Nothing else.

There was something special about knowing he was deep underground, far away from the prying eyes of the world. Soon enough, such luxuries would be a thing of the past, and everyone would know his face. He remembered as a child seeing TV footage of rock stars being mauled by the public as they landed in airports, or crowds of people in Rome desperate to see the pope as he was driven past in his bulletproof glass-roofed vehicle. Before long, it would be him they would flock to. Him they would clamour to see, to touch. The idea made him nervous, and despite his supreme confidence all would go as planned, there were a certain number of variables which could skew things in the worst way. He let out a slow exhale as he looked within himself for the strength he would need, looking for the confidence from his newly changed body to make the next vital step. He was very aware that this next stage was the most vital point of the whole operation. Everything up to that moment could be reversed, abandoned if he chose to. They could break off the attacks, perhaps drift away and go into hiding and live out their lives anonymously. That, however, wasn't what he wanted. It wasn't what his father would have wanted either. Joshua had always been told he would go on to do great things, and yet he never truly believed it. He was sure it was just a case of a parent trying to nurture their offspring in an effort to inspire them to make an effort in life. Never did he anticipate where he would find himself, and to what lengths he would go to free the world from its curse.

Beyond the silence, like a dull rumble, he could hear them chanting his name, the rhythm repeating over and over as they waited for him to make his grand entrance. He knew it was the point of no return. If he went ahead with the next phase of the plan, then he – and his brothers – were in it until either success or death came. He smiled in the dark. He liked the idea. There was something beautiful, almost poetic about it. He could sense them, almost as if they were extensions of himself. Not just the ones with him in the silo, but all of them all over the world. It was an incredibly overwhelming feeling.

A knock on the door roused him from his half trance. "Come," he said as he rose.

Genaro entered the room. "It's done," he said,

his face one of pride.

"Show me."

Genaro approached and held out three vials of faintly luminescent liquid. "As per your instructions, I have modified the virus to give it certain specific characteristics and traits in those who are infected by it. The red vial will increase aggression considerably and reduce feelings of empathy. It will also greatly increase muscular strength. These will be the warriors."

"Why the colour change?" Joshua asked, looking at the faint yellow hue of the veins under his skin.

"Identification. At a glance, you will be able to know what type of virus the user is carrying. Almost like an insignia."

"Very good," Joshua said with a smile. "What about the green one?"

"The green is tailored towards those who you wish to work. Their compulsion and obsessive nature to finish a task is boosted, along with stamina and strength. These will build your new empire from the ashes of the old world."

"And the blue?"

"Breeders. In men their libido and ability to perform are heightened, in women, their virility increased. These will be the blueprints for the first natural births of our kind. They are our future."

"And what a bright future it is. Did you increase the effectiveness of the contagious element?"

"Yes. As requested, these new variants are much more aggressive than the standard formula. A single drop of blood, sweat, or saliva ingested by a target will begin the change, which itself is greatly accelerated. With these tools, you can build your army, Joshua."

"Thank you, Dr. Genaro," Joshua said, placing a hand on the old man's shoulder. "You have excelled yourself. Prepare a list of the men here in the silo of prime candidates per strain of the virus."

"As you wish."

They stood silent for a while, listening to the incessant chants.

"They have been waiting for you for three days

now. Their devotion is remarkable."

"And it will be rewarded," Joshua replied. "As will you. The struggle to reach into the forefront of science which was hampered in the past by a lack of funding or political red tape will soon be a thing of the past. You will have free reign to reach into the unknown, to push the boundaries of science. "

Genaro's lip trembled, and when he spoke, he almost choked on his words. "You would do that for me?"

"Of course. In many respects, you are more my father than the man who gave birth to me. You are to me what I am to them. You have my word, you will stand by my side as the ruler of this new world."

"And how will you announce yourself to them?" Genaro asked.

"As I said to you before, fear is the key. Fear will break the spirit, and so fear is what we shall be."

"We are all with you, Joshua. We all believe you are the one who will finally bring change."

Joshua nodded. "In that case, let us delay no further. Go join the rest of the men Dr. Genaro. Tell them their wait is over. I'll be out to address them shortly."

II

The immense missile launch bay was the only area of the underground compound that had not yet been renovated within the underground silo. The twelve thousand square foot cylindrical space was surrounded by walkways which were originally designed to allow staff to access the perimeter of missiles within the bay awaiting launch. Now, every level was seven deep with men, all chanting Joshua's name. The noise was deafening as the sound rolled from the walls like a natural amphitheatre. Joshua took a deep breath and prepared to walk out in front of his kin. His people. Many of them would perish long before they saw the fruits of their labour, and for that, he was both sad and proud. Taking a second to gather his thoughts, he strode out of the darkness and into the centre of the cavernous space. Upon sighting him, the noise level intensified to the point where it was almost a living thing. Joshua gasped a half breath as the hairs on his arms prickled to attention. The men were in a frenzy as their slender leader walked to the centre of the space and waited, soaking in the adoration of his men, his brothers. He knew he would never experience a feeling like this again no matter what happened. All eyes were on him, and the devotion of his men was illustrated when just by raising a hand, he brought the cavernous void into complete silence. Joshua waited, eyes closed, face turned up towards the silo doors far above him, basking in the calm.

"My brothers," he said, his voice echoing around the chamber. "Today sees the start of a grand vision. A vision which together, we will realise."

He paused for effect, looking out at the

hundreds of eyes which watched him intently.

"The world as we know it is broken. Ruled by secretive, greedy men who claim they know what's best. I, like the rest of you fell for their lies. I, like you, slipped into the daily routine of life. Of being told what I should like, told what I should eat or drink. Told the value of my life was judged by a pay grade. All of you know this. You know about the lies the governments of the world tell us, all to keep their secrets safe and their bank accounts filled with money which they don't need. Yes, my brothers. The world is broken. In fact, it is broken so badly by lies so convincing that many of us don't question them that it will take drastic action to rectify."

He paused again, letting his words roll around the chamber until the echoes faded.

"The truth is, I never expected there would ever be a time when these false leaders would be removed. I never expected any future to be possible where they didn't dominate and control the world and systematically destroy it at the same time. For me, all hope was lost....until something happened, and I was given a great gift. A gift bigger than their lies, bigger than their secrets. A gift which we share. A gift that takes the flawed, broken blueprint of man and changes it for the better. All of you here share this gift. A precious thing no money can buy. That no lies can hide."

He turned in a slow circle, a half smile on his lips as he looked at the army of men above him.

"We are the answer.  A gift was bestowed upon me, and I have bestowed it upon each and every one of you. You are my brothers, my sons. You are the flicker of light in a world long shrouded in the dark. It is a world which demands change, not from me, but from us. I'm just one man. I cannot do it alone. Only with your help, with each and every one of you can we make a difference. As you know, the so-called leaders of the free world attack our own kind overseas and try to stop us. Why? Because they don't understand us. And because they don't understand us, they fear us. And because they fear us, they choose to try and destroy us. I ask you, do we accept this? Do we lie down on our sides and let these liars and cheats and fraudsters kick us into submission?"

The room rocked as the men chanted a deafening 'no' in unison. Joshua went on without breaking his stride.

"Do we let them eliminate us and harvest our unique gift for themselves?"

"No," they chanted as one.

"Or do we do what we were destined to do. Do we take our place as the next evolutionary step for humanity and ensure the survival of a species which is superior in every way to the men we used to be?"

"Yes"

Joshua paused and let the smile melt from his face. "Let me tell you about a vision I had, something shown to me as I was interred in the earth and waiting for my brothers to bring me back to the light. I saw a world of culture. I saw a world of understanding. I saw a world under one rule where everybody had a place. Where things such as money didn't matter. I saw a world of superior humans like us. People like us. Generations built on the foundations of what we are about to do. I saw a world that was better for being free of the self-destructing, mindless people who currently inhabit it. I ask you to answer me now. Do you want change?

"Yes," The men roared.

"Do you want change?"

"Yes"

"Do you want change?"

"Yes"

Joshua waited, again letting the blanket of silence envelop the chamber. "You should know it won't be easy. In order to fix the problems, we have to eradicate the disease. Much like a cancer patient will need to endure surgery to remove a diseased tumour, so we must remove the plague of mindless creatures who inhabit the future home of our children."

"Yes."

"Make no mistake. You will be asked to do things, things which seem despicable in order to make this happen. Blood will be spilled, it is unavoidable. There must be orphans, there must be widows. Some of you will die for our cause. But I say this. Do not fear death, for you will be honoured by us for all of time. You will be tomorrow's heroes, victors on the battlefield who sacrificed all so that we could enjoy the life we deserve. We must cull the plague of lesser humans who currently thrive on our lands and use up all of our resources. We must destroy them much like they destroy our home and each other. Your conscience may see them as women or children. I remind you that they are not. They are an inferior species, a plague which will destroy us if we don't strike first. Some will be turned and join us as masters of the new world. Most won't. "

Again, he waited, letting his words sink in.

"Don't think of them as humans. Think of them as vermin. Think of them as the last relics of a dead race. Destroy them without mercy. Grow our society. Let me lead you to a paradise which you and future generations can enjoy. All who oppose us are our enemies; all who stand against us or look upon us with fear are against us. Believe in me, and I promise you I will give you the world you always dreamed of. The blood of those who oppose us will soak the earth, and from it, our new society will grow. We will strike without mercy, destroy without conscience. Mark today as the final day of the old world. Tomorrow, we give birth to the new!"

He threw his arms into the air as he said it, and all around him the chamber exploded with wild cheers which were even more deafening than before. Adrenaline surged through Joshua's veins, causing him to tremble.

"Now go," he roared. "Go and make our statement. Go and show these people that opposing us is useless. Go now and let us take the world that as the superior species is ours by rights!" he screamed above the din. More cheers erupted as Joshua stood with his arms in the air, watching as the men started to file out of the silo and make their way above ground to the surface. When it was empty, and silence again enveloped the immense chamber, Genaro walked out of the shadows. "Do you think it's possible? Can we change the world?" he whispered.

Joshua half turned towards Genaro. "It's already started. Tonight the world will sleep easy. Tomorrow, they will know their end is near."

"And how do we maintain it? How do we keep control?"

Joshua took a folded piece of paper from his pocket and handed it to Genaro. The scientist unfolded it and read the list of names written on it.

"You know these people," Joshua said, a statement, not a question.

"Yes, or, at least, I've heard of them."

"Good."

"What do you want me to do?"

"Bring them to me."

"For what purpose?" Genaro asked, a flicker of doubt in his eyes.

"Because when the time comes, we will need them."

# CHAPTER EIGHTEEN

## BAGHDAD SEWERS
## IRAQ

TREMBLING AND AFRAID, AKHTAR was just waiting to die. Whoever had grabbed him and his brother whilst they slept had been carrying them for what felt like an age, although he had no real concept of how much time had passed. It could have just as easily been hours or minutes. The stagnant wet stench gave way to a more dry, musty smell which gave him the impression he was somewhere off the main tunnel. He was lowered into a chair, and only then started to fear for his life. The hood was removed from his head, and he squinted at the light which although dull was much brighter than the tunnels.

"Who are you?"

Akhtar blinked, waiting for the man who spoke

to him to come into focus.

"I asked you a question, who are you?"

"I'm nobody," Akhtar mumbled, finally getting a closer look at the soldier who stood in front of him.

He was young, Akhtar guessed no more than early twenties. He had piercing blue eyes and a short buzz cut, and despite looking much too young for active service had an air of authority about him.

"Let me speak to him," another man said in Arabic from behind Akhtar's chair. "It's plain enough he's just a boy."

The owner of the Arabic voice came into view. He was tall and slim, with deep brown eyes and a thin hooked nose. His eyes were brown, his skin the colour of coffee and framed by a long black and grey beard. "What's your name?" The man snapped.

"Please, where is my brother?" Akhtar said.

"He's fine. First answer my questions."

"Hey, easy," the soldier cut in. "We don't do things the same way as you people."

"Us people?" The Arabic man said, glaring at

the soldier. "Remember, this is our country and you are in it. Perhaps our way is better."

The soldier looked like he wanted to respond, then saw Akhtar watching the exchange and decided against it. "My name's Branning, I'm in charge here," He said.

The Arabic man snorted but said nothing.

"What are you doing down here?" Branning asked.

"We had to flee the streets," Akhtar replied, recalling the way those men had killed without mercy.

"Nobody sent you?" The Arabic man snapped.

"Hey, go easy on the kid. Can't you see he's scared?"

"Yes, of course." The Arabic man said irritably and then turned his attention back to Akhtar. "Forgive me. My name is Ali Hamada. You can relax. You and your brother are safe here. Now please, tell us your name."

"Akhtar, Akhtar Mahmood. I was with my brother Youness on the street when those men attacked."

"You were lucky to survive," Hamada said. "Many of our people have been lost."

"Don't tell me you're suddenly growing a conscience." Branning hissed.

Akhtar shuffled in his seat. The tension between the two men was palpable, a very specific and obvious dislike was simmering between them and Akhtar hoped he wasn't around when it finally exploded.

"Where is my brother," he asked again, knowing how Youness would be stressed if he was left by himself with people he didn't know.

"Come on kid, I'll take you to him," Branning said, shoving past Hamada and helping Akhtar to his feet. Branning led him out of the bare-walled room he had been taken to, which to Akhtar's surprise opened up into a large open underground space. Beds were strewn across the floor as well as a small supply of food and weapons. Akhtar counted around a dozen people. A couple were military like Branning, the rest were locals, a mixture of women, children and market traders.

"What is this place?" Akhtar asked.

"For now, it's home," Branning replied as he led Akhtar across the room to another door. "This building was supposed to be an underground pumping station for the new sewage system. It's been empty for a couple of years, so, for now, it's where we are staying."

"Were you on the surface too?"

"He was interrogating me," Hamada said, jogging to catch up with them. "It seems any Muslim man is a terrorist in the eyes of the Americans."

Branning kept his mouth closed, although Akhtar could see him grinding his teeth as the trio crossed the room.

"When the attack happened we were forced to work together to escape. Many lives were lost."

"Was it those men? The ones dressed in black?" Akhtar asked.

"Yeah, it was," Branning said. "Although we don't know why. Communications are all shot to hell. Nobody seems to know anything."

"Who are they?" Akhtar asked.

"Who knows, kid," Branning said as he opened another door leading to a short corridor. "More terrorists most likely trying to push their agenda through fear."

"Is that remark aimed at me?" Hamada said.

Although he was physically inferior to Branning, there was an enigmatic air about Hamada. Akhtar imagined him to be a man used to leading rather than following, and one used even less to being spoken to in the way Branning was addressing him.

"You can take it however you want. Where I come from, we have a thing called freedom of speech. I'm used to calling a spade a spade, scum scum or-"

"A terrorist a terrorist, is that it?" Hamada interrupted.

"If the shoe fits." Branning hissed.

They had stopped walking and Hamada and Branning were nose to nose in the corridor.

"Please, I just want to see my brother," Akhtar said.

The two men stared each other down for a few more seconds, then Hamada averted his gaze and took a step back. "Let the American show you." He spat. "I'm sure he wouldn't want terrorists mixing with the children."

Branning glared at Hamada as he retreated back into the room they had just come from and began to unpack supplies. "Come on kid," he said as he walked down the corridor to the steel door at its end. "Let's go find your brother."

Akhtar did as he was told, conscious of not getting on the bad side of Branning. He had heard horror stories about some of the things the soldiers did to locals or, at least, things they were said to have done. His father told him they were just stories – propaganda designed to make sure the local population didn't trust the soldiers. Despite his friends saying otherwise, Akhtar tended to agree with his father and thought the notion of American and British soldiers murdering civilians for sport was ridiculously far-fetched - especially when they were out here risking their lives to protect civilians like him.

Branning opened the door at the end of the hall and pushed it open. "He was screaming and crying for you, so we had to sedate him," Branning said.

Akhtar peered into the gloom. Youness lay on a rough looking steel framed bed, covers pulled up to his chin. He was sleeping, his nose wheezing slightly as he exhaled.

"Is he alright?" Akhtar asked.

"He'll be fine. In a couple of hours, he'll wake up. It's probably a good idea you're here when he does."

"I will."

"Where are the rest of your family, kid?"

"I...I don’t know." Akhtar replied. "We were trying to get back to our home via the tunnels, but we got lost."

"Where were you trying to get to?"

"We live in an apartment in Thawra."

"Sadr City?" Branning said.

"Yes. Do you know it?"

"Yeah. I was here back in oh-nine when the Muraidi bomb exploded. I helped with the clean-up."

"My uncle was killed in that attack," Akhtar said. "I don’t remember it, but it was one of the only times I have ever seen my father cry."

"I’m sorry," Branning said.

"Are we close? I mean can we get to the surface and go get them? Bring them here?"

A shadow of uncertainty passed over Branning’s face. Not quite a frown but enough of a change for Akhtar to notice.

"What is it?" he asked.

"I didn’t realise. “Branning replied.

"Realise what?"

"How little you knew."

"About what?"

"What's happening out there?"

Akhtar didn’t reply. He simply watched and waited.

"Come with me," Branning said, gently closing

the door and leaving Youness to sleep and returning back the way they had come. Akhtar followed as Branning walked straight past Hamada, the two ignoring each other. Branning led the way to a table in the corner and switched on the television. The picture faded in from black, and when it arrived, Akhtar half wished he had remained ignorant. The footage was grainy and shot from a helicopter high above the city. Smoke and fire billowed from buildings, others still were reduced to rubble. Without the censorship of other countries, the news had no issues showing the violence on the streets and the bullet-ridden bodies which littered it.

"What's happening?" Akhtar whispered.

"Nobody knows for sure. They say it's some kind of uprising or revolution, some shit like that. Either way, going topside isn't an option."

"What about my parents?"

"All you can do now is pray for them."

"But surely you can help, you and the other soldiers," Akhtar said as he stared at the news footage.

"There are no other soldiers or, at least, none we have been able to make contact with. We're on our own."

"But surely, someone will come to help us?"

Branning looked Akhtar in the eye, and the young Iraqi saw something he never expected. He saw fear.

"I don't think so," Branning said. "This isn't just us. This is happening everywhere."

"All over Iraq?"

"All over the world. Whoever these people are and wherever they have come from, they mean business. All we can do now is stay hidden and ride it out until we know what we're dealing with."

"But we need to go, to get out of the city," Akhtar said, fear and desperation making him angry.

"I agree, but we have to be realistic. We have no transport, barely any weapons or food and no idea where these people are who are attacking us or what they want. For now, it's best we stay here."

"But if we stay here they'll find us. It's only a

matter of time." Akhtar said.

"I know. That's why I'll do everything in my power to make sure we're ready. Trust me, if there's one thing the United States Marine Corps teaches us, it's not to give up."

"What about my brother? He's not like us; he needs to be looked after. He won't understand."

"I need you to make him understand. I need you to be ready to go when the time comes."

"What if we don't make it? What if we can't escape?"

"Then we end up like that," Branning said, nodding towards the television screen.

Akhtar looked at the images of the dead littering the streets, unable to comprehend the scale of the loss of life, how many who had been alive just a few hours ago were now extinguished. He wondered if he had seen any of them in life if any of those anonymous faces he had seen passing in the street just before the chaos began were now immortalised on the television screen. Akhtar had decided not to mention what he had seen at the roadblock when he was playing football to anyone, such was the sheer craziness of the situation. However, for better or worse, he trusted Branning, and such information might make the difference between life and death. He wasn't sure it would make things better, especially since the situation already looked bleak without adding how the men in black seemed impervious to pain, even when shot, however, it was still information which might help.

"I know something about these people, the ones who are doing this. I... I've seen them before."

Branning tore his eyes away from the television screen and gave Akhtar his full attention.

"Tell me everything," He said.

Akhtar took a second to compose his thoughts, and then right there in the gloom of the underground pumping station, told Branning all about what happened at the roadblock.

# CHAPTER NINETEEN

VASHI BRIDGE

MUMBAI

INDIA

THE TRUCK SPLUTTERED TO a halt halfway across the Vashi Bridge just outside of Mandala. Suvari had been hoping to get across to mainland Navi Mumbai, and from there out into the dense jungle where they might be able to hide and protect the children from whoever was attacking the city. During the drive, she had seen the devastation and panic and had managed to piece enough together from the radio to know there was a major situation happening with similar attacks all over the world. She sat for a moment, listening to the engine tick as it cooled. The bridge looked incredibly long from where she was. More than that, it was incredibly exposed. The six lanes of the bridge were jammed with traffic as people tried to flee the fire-ravaged city. As she sat, another dull explosion rolled across the water. She had become so accustomed to the noise that she didn't even look back at the fire-ravaged city. Across the bridge, partially shrouded in smog was the industrial suburb of Turbhe, its chimneys spewing acrid smoke into the air. She supposed that there at least might be a place to find shelter and perhaps find more transportation before moving on to the forest area beyond where she would set up some kind of camp where thy could stay in relative safety away from the populated areas of the city. She climbed out of the truck, the acrid air burning her throat as she walked to the back and looked at the frightened children inside.

"Come on, we have to walk," She said.

They didn't move and only stared at her in fear.

"We have to hurry, it will be dark soon."

Still they stared and in a way, she didn't blame them. They were probably as confused as she was. She tried to put herself back to the time when she was living on the streets, at the sheer simplicity and endless struggle of life. They simply didn't understand.

"If we don't go, the bad men will come," She said.

Half a dozen pairs of eyes looked at her from the gloom, and then one by one, they climbed out of the truck.

"Come on, this way," The children followed as she led them towards the maze-like industrial area, hoping she could find somewhere safe for them to hide. As they crossed the bridge, more explosions rocked the city, and as night fell, the sky above Mumbai was alive with the red-orange glow of hundreds of fires as the city was ravaged by its attackers.

# CHAPTER TWENTY

## HARMONY PLACE TRAILER PARK
## WEST VIRGINIA
## USA

DRAVEN HAD REMOVED GENARO'S notes from Herman's wall and spread them out across the table. He was working through them, trying as best he could to get a better understanding of Project Apex. Kate paced the room, looking out of the window as two military jets raced overhead, the sounds of the engines as they shrieked towards the capital deafening.

"Anything useful?" She said, turning towards Draven.

"Plenty, it's just a case of trying to sift through it now and figuring out what we need to do. The research was much further advanced than I ever expected."

"No pressure but we need something soon. As it

is, I'm struggling to get through to Homeland. Things seem to be escalating in ways we never anticipated."

"That can't be good."

"What do you mean?"

"Well," Draven said with a thin smile "If the people who are supposed to be protecting the country stop answering the phone, you know we have big problems."

"Hey, you two might wanna come see this," Herman said.

He was sitting cross-legged on the floor watching the news.

"What is it?" Kate said as she stood behind Herman.

"Looks like your secret is about to break free. The President is about to address the nation."

Draven abandoned the mountain of notes and joined Kate and Herman in front of the television. On the screen was the familiar blue backdrop behind a podium bearing the presidential crest.

"I can't wait for this," Herman said, eyes wide

with excitement.

"This isn't some TV drama." Kate snapped.

"Look, don't get me wrong, I’m as distressed as anyone about what's happening here, but I've listened to your government lie and cover up what's really going on for years. Hell, it even went on before I was born. Remember Roswell? Weather balloon my ass."

"Shh, it's starting," Draven said.

Herman turned away from Kate and turned up the volume on the TV as the President entered the frame. He approached the podium and looked into the camera.

"He looks like hell," Draven said.

"Burden of all those lies, man," Herman replied. "Bound to get to you sooner or later."

"Shhh."

Herman looked at Kate, thought about carrying on then turned back to the television just as the president started to speak.

"I speak to you now, citizens of this great country at a time of crisis." President Fitzgerald said, his gaze unwavering as he looked straight down the camera. "As you have seen via reports from the multitude of news agencies across the world, we are under attack. And when I say we, I don't just mean here in the United States of America. I refer also to our international neighbours, countries whose citizens also face this new threat, this coordinated attack from a group who so far remain anonymous."

The President paused, and referred to his notes in front of him on the podium before going on.

"Make no mistake. Our military forces and those of our neighbours will engage this threat with extreme prejudice, and consider all acts of aggression perpetrated by this new group as terrorism of the highest order. In an unprecedented move, we have decided to unite as one and share information in order to combat this devastating new enemy."

The President remained calm as he referred to his notes, knowing the next passage was the one which would potentially cause chaos. With a show of outward calm which betrayed his true feelings, he went on.

"You will notice I used the word devastating, a word which I wouldn’t use unless there was a specific need to do so. This is one of those times. After consulting with my fellow world leaders and analysing intelligence data, we have reason to believe that our attackers, this as yet unknown group, are infected with a highly potent, highly contagious virus, a virus which if allowed to spread could conceivably lead to the extinction of mankind on a global scale."

He paused, letting the words sink in, knowing that already people would be panicking, others barricading themselves inside their homes or trying to get to relatives.

"At this time, I urge you to remain calm. Plans are in place to control this situation and eliminate this new threat as quickly and efficiently as possible. It is because of such unique circumstances that after deliberating with my cabinet, I have decided to invoke a nationwide state of martial law."

"Jesus," Draven muttered as he stared at the television screen.

"Furthermore, there will be an eight p.m. curfew until further notice. Troops will be patrolling the streets and looking to engage our attackers in small arms combat. You are urged to stay in your homes. Keep doors locked and ensure you are protected. Anyone caught looting, anyone seeing this situation as an excuse to break the law, will be punished. Food banks will be in operation in designated safe zones just as soon as our forces have secured the various communities within our nation. Remember, this is a pre-emptive motion to ensure the security of not just our country, but our world. Many of you will not be affected by this. Those who are will be protected by the brave men and women of the United States military. Forces will initially be located in the following cities."

As the President reeled off the list of cities, Vice President Carter stood at the side of the stage with Chief of Staff Morrison. Carter leaned closer to the chief of staff, wrinkling his nose at the older man's overpowering aftershave.

"This is a mistake," Carter whispered. "All this will do is cause chaos on the streets and make the job even harder."

"It was going to happen eventually," Morrison said. "The public are already getting twitchy. Maybe this is the right call."

"Come on," Carter said with a grin. "You and I both know the old man has lost it. This is just the latest in a long line of bad calls."

Morrison turned to face the vice president. "You should be careful saying things like that. If the President ever found out-"

"Come on Eamon, forget protocol for a second. Man to man, off the record. Do you think we should have gone for a more aggressive strategy?"

Morrison chewed his bottom lip and fidgeted. "Maybe it might have been better to stamp this out before it got out of hand."

"Exactly," Carter said, flicking his eyes to the president as he went on addressing the nation. "I grew up on a farm in Kansas, and my father used to always keep dozens of rat traps in the barn. I mean, he had tons of the things. I always wondered why he had so many. I remember asking him about it one day. He told me he would rather kill the rats before they can breed otherwise they would infest the entire farm."

"What are you saying?" Morrison asked.

"I'm saying even though I'm sure the president thinks he's doing the right thing, all the time wasted on this small arms street-level warfare is giving the rats time to breed. If we're not careful, pretty soon we won't have enough traps to stop them."

Morrison hesitated, choosing his words carefully. "Even if I agreed with you - which for the record, I don't necessarily, - but just say I did. What would you suggest we do? He's the commander in chief. He makes the decisions."

"This isn't about decisions or about who gets to sit in the oval office. This is about the survival of our species. The problem is, as admirable as it is, the president wants to resolve this without any casualties. As much as we all want that, it's unrealistic. My worry is if these people are as contagious as we suspect, then soon enough we won't have the ability to stop them." Carter smiled as he clapped Morrison on the shoulder. "Now I don't know about you, but to me, a few hundred dead civilians is an acceptable loss if it means wiping these freaks out and restoring order."

Morrison frowned, and Carter had to force himself not to smile. He had seen that look before. It was a look of a man who was rethinking his opinion.

"Even so, it doesn't change the fact that we have no power here. We're duty bound."

"Oh, I wouldn't dream of doing anything to jeopardise that. All I'm saying is that in circumstances as extreme as this, it might pay to be prepared."

"What did you have in mind?" Morrison asked.

"I'm about to take a chopper out to the Pentagon to meet with General Shaw. Like me, he's a man who is aware of the huge potential risk of allowing this situation to get out of hand. I want to make sure that if and when the President changes his mind and decides more decisive action is needed, we have it ready to go. Call it a contingency plan."

"Won't the President need you here?"

Carter snorted and stifled a smile. "He doesn't need me or my opinions. Whatever happens from here on in, he'll be making up his own mind about what's best for the country. My job as vice president is to be there with an alternative plan if he fails."

"Look, Paul, I understand what you're trying to do here, I really do, but don't you think you should be cautious? You don't want to be seen as undermining the president."

"Of course not," Carter agreed. "As I said, it's just a contingency plan. God knows, it pays to be prepared."

"Fair enough, I'm not entirely sure why you're telling me anyway."

Carter pulled his wallet out of his pocket and

opened it up, showing Morrison the photograph in the plastic sleeve. "My wife and our two kids, Amy and Aaron. I spoke to her this morning and she's scared. She's relying on me to keep them safe. Do you have kids? A wife?"

"I have a partner, yes. His name is David." Morrison said, holding Carters gaze to see how he would react. Somehow hiding his surprise, Carter went on.

"Exactly. Don't you think David would want you to do what's right to make this country safe? To make him safe?"

"He doesn't know much about this, or, at least, I don't think so. He's on business in New York. I get the point, though."

"All I'm saying is that when it comes to my family, I trust my own instinct when it comes to protecting them, no matter who has the title of commander in chief. As a human being, it's my right to do whatever it takes to protect my family. As I'm sure you would want to do too. Do you see what I'm saying Eamon?"

"I do, I get it," Morrison said with a sigh. "I don't think I can do anything about it, though. Maybe it would have been better if I didn't know how you felt about it."

"As chief of staff, you have a right to know. I'm just making sure people - good people like you and David and everyone else who works here - are aware that I tried to fight for an alternative plan of action prior to the President making his decision."

Morrison nodded. Carter let him think. He could see the chief of staff processing the information. A quote from the Greek poet Aeschylus came to mind.

From a small seed, a mighty trunk may grow.

Under the circumstances, it was quite apt, especially as this seed, the seed of doubt, had been planted well.

"Anyway, I have to go," Carter said with a sigh. "I'm due to meet with Shaw in an hour. Keep me informed of any developments would you?"

"Of course. I'll keep you in the loop." Morrison muttered, still watering and waiting for said seed to blossom.

"Thanks, I appreciate it," Carter said as he took a last look at the president then left the conference room, hoping against hope General Shaw was more inclined to see that the lack of decisive action by the commander in chief could have disastrous repercussions.

Back in Herman’s trailer, the trio watched as a tired-looking President Fitzgerald finished his address and walked out of camera shot.

"This is crazy," Draven said.

"Something must have happened. Things were fairly calm when I came out to find you." Kate replied.

"It’s the contagion." Herman cut in. "My guess is they never figured how easy it was to spread this shit around. Now good old Mr. President is shittin' bricks and looking to resolve this quick so he can stay ahead in the opinion polls."

"Not everything has an ulterior motive you know." Kate snapped.

"For the record I agree with him, or at least, I agree the contagious nature of this being way higher than anticipated has caused panic. Remember, Fitzgerald has only ever known peacetime since he's been in office. This is his first crisis."

"See? He gets it." Herman said. "You should think like a human for once instead of a government stooge."

"Yeah? Well, maybe since I'm such a government stooge, I might have to report you for stealing sensitive government data." She said, glancing towards the reams of paper spread out across the table.

"Hey, that's not fair, I'm trying to help you."

"Please, can everyone just calm down," Draven snapped. "We don't have time to bicker. We need to decide what to do."

"You heard the president," Herman said, flicking his eyes from Draven to the door. "Martial law. Best thing to do is hole up here and see what happens."

"We can't just sit here and hope things get

better," Kate said. "Unlike you, we have responsibilities to try and fix this."

"Don't get me wrong, lady, I'm no coward. But look at the TV screen." He pointed to the images on the screen which were showing looting and rioting in various countries around the world. "That shit won't just be on the box anymore. It will be happening right now out there."

"The President said there would be food banks, he said-"

"Come on," Herman cut in, tossing the remote on the floor in front of him. "Do you really, genuinely believe that people are going to sit at home playing happy families and wait for someone to bring them food? Sorry, but we all know that ain't gonna happen. People are going to go out there and stock up on whatever they can carry, and when the store shelves are empty, that's when they'll turn on each other and start to kill over a box of crackers or a bottle of water. No matter how you try to butter it up and put faith in our so called commander in chief, society is on the verge of breaking down. End of the world, man, end of the fucking world."

"Will you shut up!" Kate snapped. "I'm sick to death of hearing all this conspiracy bullshit. What the hell is wrong with you?"

"Ain't nothing wrong with me lady. It's not my fault if you can't see what's right in front of you."

"This isn't the time." Draven cut in. "Like it or not, the three of us need to work together if only in the short term."

"So what do you suggest we do," Kate said, cheeks flushing in anger. "To say you're our expert, you seem to be taking quite the back seat."

"If by back seat you mean concentrating on solving the task at hand rather than bickering, then yes, I suppose I have. Now like it or not, Herman has a point. Despite the assurances of the President, I don't think it will be too long before people start rioting and looting and whatever the hell else."

"Exactly, which is why we need to stay put." Herman said, giving Kate a smug grin.

"Actually, that's why we need to get out of here," Draven went on.

"What's wrong with here? Is my home not good enough?"

"Actually no, for this situation it isn't," Draven replied.

"What's wrong with it?"

"First off it's too exposed. Second, it's a mobile home so anyone looking for transport if things get crazy might be tempted to take it. Also, there is only one entrance which means there is no escape route if someone decides to attack. It's also no good for defending. The walls to this place wouldn't withstand much if someone came at it with an axe or crowbar. Even worse, if someone decided to open fire on this place, the bullets would go straight through. With nowhere to hide or protect ourselves, we would be sitting ducks."

"You could say that about most of the places around here," Herman mumbled.

"Almost."

They both looked at Kate who was reading a message on her phone.

"Get your stuff together. We're leaving." She

said to Draven.

"Where are we going?"

"Pentagon. The vice president is on his way there. We have been ordered to go and meet him to bring him up to speed."

"I thought we were going directly to the president with this?" Draven said.

"All I know is what I've been told, and that's to meet Vice President Carter at the Pentagon."

"Maybe old man Fitzgerald is feeling the strain of all those skeletons climbing out of the closet, eh?" Herman said, grinning at Kate. "Still, Carter ain't much better. That arrogant son of a bitch needs someone to bring him down a notch or two."

"You can tell him yourself," Kate said as she slotted her phone in her jacket. "You're coming too."

"Me?" Herman said, scrambling to his feet. "No, no I don't think so. I'm busy right now and I have lots of work to do, research, analysis, all that kind of stuff. Good luck to you both, though."

"It's not an option. You have information that

we might need."

"I see what you're saying. I'm still staying here." Herman said, folding his arms.

"No, you're coming."

"As far as I'm aware, you have no reason or right to force me to come along. I read up on this stuff. There's nothing you can do to change my mind." Herman said, shrugging his shoulders and unleashing his best grin.

"Fine," Kate said, then in a fluid motion pulled her pistol from inside her jacket and trained it on Herman.

"Hey hey, easy with the gun, man!" Herman squealed, throwing his arms up and banging his knuckles on the roof.

"What the hell is this?" Draven said.

"He's disobeying a direct order given to me from a military general who has requested his presence. Either he comes along, or I shoot him."

"Isn't that a bit extreme?" Herman said, his voice an octave or three higher than normal. "Come on man help me out here."

"He's a civilian," Kate said, flicking a quick glance in Draven's direction. "He can't help you. You either come of your own free will, or I'll be forced to arrest you and take you in by force."

"Alright, alright, no need to get so twitchy, I'll come with. Just stop pointing that thing at me."

Kate hesitated, enjoying watching Herman squirm, then relaxed and slipped the weapon back into her jacket. "Get a bag and gather the notes, we leave in five."

# CHAPTER TWENTY ONE

## PENNSYLVANIA AVENUE
## WASHINGTON DC

JOSHUA WALKED DOWN PENNSYLVANIA Avenue, and even despite his near immortality and absolute confidence in his plan, nerves were still gnawing at his stomach. Without his own mortality to fear for, he instead worried for his legacy. Society wouldn't easily understand at first why he was going to such extreme lengths. In time, they would, but first he would have to endure being labelled as a murderer, a terrorist of the highest order. He adjusted his bag on his shoulder, comforted by the weight of its contents. Guns. Grenades. Ammo. Plenty of ammo.

Dressed in a crème suit with a white shirt open at the neck, he didn't particularly stand out from the crowd.  Despite the chaos taking place the world over, the arrogance of the American public meant that they always assumed it could never happen to them and that things would be alright as long as it was on the other side of the television screen and someone else had to deal with it. Never did they expect it to happen on their doorstep; never did they think it would come at them on a sunny Thursday afternoon.

As he walked, more of his brothers came. From side streets and cafes, from shops and cars, emerging out from their public hiding places, each man carrying a bag on his shoulder containing enough weaponry to do what needed to be done. Wordlessly they fell in behind him as they walked. He knew the rest of his men were doing the same, the ones on 15th and 17th Street as well as those currently making their way towards Constitution Avenue, all converging on the same place. Joshua knew that in order to be taken seriously, they had to make a statement of intent. One so bold, so brazen, it bordered on the theatrical. One which would let the world know they were a serious force to be reckoned with.

As more men fell in behind Joshua, their presence became more obvious. People looked at them, some curious, others smiling nervously and perhaps sensing something was about to happen. Still they didn't deviate, nor did they slow as the White house came into view, the crowds pressing against the iron railings which surrounded the grounds which provided little in the way of security if someone was determined to breach them. Just another example of the blinkered arrogance of those charged with running the country. To Joshua, those railings made a statement, a statement that said nobody dare cross this barrier because they know the consequences would be dire. It was self-serving arrogance, and because of it, punishment was about to be delivered in the most brutal way possible. Despite having no verbal communication, Joshua and his men all reached the perimeter fences on each side of the property at the same time. As they approached the railings, one of Joshua's men jogged in front, ducked and linked his hands. Joshua threw his bag over the fence, then without breaking stride stepped into the hands of one of his brothers and was boosted over the fence. Gracefully, he grabbed the upper spikes of the railings and vaulted over as the rest of his kin followed suit as they were boosted over onto the grass beyond the fence. People outside pointed and murmured as man after man breached the grounds. Joshua, upon landing crouched and unzipped his bag pulling out the assault rifle. He shrugged the bag back onto his shoulder and led his brothers over the lawn towards the White House as they too drew their weapons.

Behind them, the people started to scream.

II

Immediately after making his address to the nation, President Fitzgerald had returned to the Oval Office and asked everyone to leave. Finally alone and away from the constant chatter of noise and stress of dealing with the ever-evolving situation, Ron Fitzgerald could finally be himself. He sat in his chair and loosened his tie, then resting his elbows on the desk, rubbed his temples.

I'm too old for this.

It wasn't the first time such thoughts had entered his head. He would never admit it, but he was already starting to feel as if the job was getting to be too much for him even before this new situation had reared its head and forced him into action. It was only for the love of his wife he carried on, determined to make her proud, even in death. As the situation escalated, the more work was put on him and the more he could feel his stress levels increasing. He listened inwardly to his body, trying to release some of the tension. He thought back to when he was a child, a simpler time when life was free of decisions which affected the lives of every man and woman in the country. He smiled as the memories came back to him, of sitting outside on the back porch of the family home with his father. The images were clear and crisp, so vivid he could still smell the dry sweetness of freshly cut grass and hear the drone of honey bees. His father had been trying to teach him the guitar on a tired old nylon stringed acoustic which had seen better days. Despite trying his best, he was unable to grasp the coordination to unlock the ability to play with any sort of consistency. He had noticed as he made awkward hand shapes and tried to position his fingers on the frets that the guitar was sounding even more unusual than normal.

"Here, give it to me boy, it's slipped outta' tune." His father had grunted.

The ten-year-old future president did as he was told, and handed his father the guitar, watching as the older man's fingers danced and glided down the fretboard with ease.

"E string's out," He muttered, then began to wind the string using the tuning pegs on the headstock with his left hand as he picked the troublesome string with his right.

Ron never liked that sound as the pitch of the string increased as it was tightened.

"It won't hurt you, son," his father said, seeing his son's discomfort. "These strings will take a lot of winding before they break."

Almost fifty years later, as he sat amid the growing chaos, Ron Fitzgerald found a rare smile at the memory of his father. He felt a lot like that guitar, wondering how much more tension he could withstand before he snapped. He was dragged from his thoughts as the door to his office was opened by a flustered Secret Service agent. Behind him, people were rushing through the red-carpeted corridors.

"What's going on?" Fitzgerald asked.

"Mr. President, we have to move you, right now."

"What’s going on?"

"Mr. President, please. I'm Special Agent Pycroft. We need to move. We're under attack."

Fitzgerald was about to demand more information when he heard it for himself, the dull rattle of machine gun fire.

"They're here in the White House?”

"Not yet sir, but they're getting closer. Let's get you out of here."

Pycroft led the president through the adjoining room to a discreet panel in the wall. He punched a code into the keypad, expecting the wall to slide aside and reveal the entrance which led to the bunker deep below the structure. The console gave an angry buzz, causing Pycroft to flick a nervous glance over his shoulder. He punched in his code again, this time slowly to make sure he didn't make an error. Once again, the panel buzzed at him.

"I'm locked out sir," Pycroft said, listening to the sound of gunfire as it drew closer.

"Let me try my personal code," Fitzgerald said, pushing past Pycroft.

He had only keyed in two digits of his five digit code, when a tremendous explosion rocked the room, showering the president and Pycroft with debris.

Reacting on the instinct honed by his training, Pycroft shoved the president to the ground and shielded him, taking the brunt of the glass shards and debris on the back.

Fire licked around the edges of the room, as somewhere close by, another explosion rattled the building. Pycroft stood, helping the president to his feet. Both of them were covered in pulverised dust, and a large fire licked at the edges of the room, which was shrouded in thick smoke. Pausing to wipe the blood from his eyes due to the laceration on his forehead, Pycroft retrieved his weapon from the ground.

"Try your code again sir," he said to the President, his voice remarkably calm and collected.

With a shaking hand, the president followed Pycroft's instructions, only to be greeted by the familiar tone indicating they were denied access.

"I don't understand," Fitzgerald said.

"They must have locked out the system somehow. Follow me," he said, leading the President through an adjoining door into a room which was so far undamaged. Pycroft slipped on a wireless earpiece and spoke into it as he led the way, gun held in front of him, checking every blind spot.

"This is Agent Pycroft. I have the eagle. Plan A is no go. Proceed with plan B. Repeat, Proceed with plan B."

Fitzgerald jumped as gunfire peppered the wall in the room adjacent to them. He couldn't quite believe what was happening. Shouting. Screaming. The smell of smoke.

"Down, down!" Pycroft said, unceremoniously shoving the president into the gap between the wall and an ornate sideboard filled with expensive plates and silverware. Seconds later, the door at the end of the room opened and one of Joshua's men entered. Pycroft crouched and opened fire, hitting the man in the chest twice before he could take more than a single step into the room.

The man grunted and was thrown against the wall by the impact, and yet didn't go down. Instead, he swung his weapon towards Pycroft and opened fire. Bullets zipped through the air, slamming into the walls and reigning chunks of concrete down on the floor. With his free arm, Pycroft reached up and pulled the dresser over, providing the agent and President with a makeshift barricade. More bullets were fired, wood, glass and concrete showering the agent and president as they pressed against the wall out of range. Showing no panic, the blond haired agent calmly reloaded his weapon.

"Don't you move," he screamed at the president, and then swung into view, peering over the edge of the dresser and getting off three shots. One went wide, shattering the eighteenth-century mirror which hung on the wall. The second and third bullets found their target, one in their attackers forearm, the other in his stomach. Pycroft was sure that would be enough, and yet the injuries only seemed to anger their attacker as he returned fire. Pycroft ducked out of sight, breathing heavily and keeping a close eye on the President.

"He won't go down," The agent shouted. "He took three bullets already and he won't fall!"

"Shoot him in the head," the President shouted, struggling to be heard against the explosions and gunfire which seemed to come from all directions.

"I have a better idea," Pycroft replied, reaching into his jacket. He pulled the pin from the grenade and tossed it over towards the corner of the room, then immediately dived on top of the president. The explosion was deafening, blowing the windows out onto the pristine lawn below. Their makeshift shield was obliterated, as was the door and a section of the wall where their attacker had stood. For a few seconds, even breathing was impossible. Pycroft coughed and stood, pushing splintered wood from his back and legs, and pulling an equally bloody and dusty President Fitzgerald to his feet. The fleshy remains of their attacker were smeared all over the walls and in chunks littering the room.

"Come on sir," Pycroft said, still calm. "We need to get you to a chopper."

III

Over six thousand miles away, underneath the city of Baghdad, Branning, Hamada and the rest of the survivors huddled around the television screen, watching the grainy images of the attack and finding themselves quite unable to fully comprehend what was happening. Grainy helicopter footage of the building with smoke pouring from its windows and pockmarks on its outer walls looked more like something from a movie than real life. Akhtar stood with his brother – who was perhaps the only one amongst them who didn't understand the history-making images on the screen.

"This is insane," Branning said, fists clenched as he watched. "Where the hell is the army? They should be all over this."

"What army?" Hamada said, glaring at Branning. "Your country spreads itself too thin. All your forces are deployed across the world leaving you vulnerable."

"No, we have plenty of troops."

"Reserves perhaps. But the real soldiers, they are here, or helping out the British or French."

"It was a trap wasn't it? Whoever is doing this attacked overseas first to make sure we were unprotected." Branning grunted.

"Of course, they did," Hamada said. "They know how arrogant you Americans are. How much better than everyone else you think you are. It was only a matter of time before somebody decided to try such a bold move."

"Well if you people would stop attacking civilians-"

"Come on," Hamada cut in, shaking his head. "You know why we attack you. You know why my people put Jihad on you."

"You got something to say to me?" Branning said, squaring up to Hamada.

"There you go again," Hamada said, shaking his head. "Always thinking you have the right to be violent and aggressive. Think about where you are. Think about which country you are in."

"We're here to protect the civilians from people like you."

"No, that's only what you have been led to believe. You are here at the orders of some man who hides behind a wall of lies. A man who decides it is acceptable to invade my country and impose his will on my people then has the audacity to call me a terrorist."

"Don't twist this around and give me this shit." Branning spat.

"You were never wanted here. You Americans and British come and try to change us, and then act with aggression when we defend our beliefs."

"You're the one who spills the blood of innocent people. The suicide bombings and random car bomb attacks are on you, not us. The blood of those people is on your hands."

"No, it isn't. Nor is it on yours." Hamada said, remaining calm. "The blood is on his hands."

Hamada pointed to the TV screen which was still showing live footage of the White House. "He's the one who sends men to fight his battles. He's the one who cares nothing of the consequences of his actions because it will never directly affect him."

"What do you mean by that?" Branning snapped.

"After the attacks on your World Trade Centre when the country was in crisis, did your President help those in need? Or did he hide away in his underground bunker until the threat of more attacks had passed? You people blame us for this war, yet it wouldn't have started if your country hadn't involved itself in business that didn't concern it."

Branning was furious, at first at the audacity of Hamada for calling him out in front of everyone, and secondly because a lot of what he had said made sense. As determined as he was not to pay any attention to what he deemed to be propaganda and attempts to undermine him, there was a certain ring of truth to Hamada's words. Branning had often spoken to his squad mates, fellow soldiers thrust into the baking desert heat, and the question would arise as to why they were fighting the wars of other people.

Branning sighed and looked away from Hamada's penetrating gaze, choosing to stare at his own boots instead. "This isn’t the time to get into this. We need to make plans. We won't be able to stay here for long."

"Why not?" Akhtar said, terrified at the idea of going back to the surface.

"Because eventually they will find us, and when they do we're sitting ducks."

"What do you suggest?" Hamada asked, happy

to keep a fragile peace for the time being despite his differences with Branning.

"I don't know yet, but we need to move soon. I think we can both agree those pictures on the TV change things for all of us. It's obvious we're dealing with a group who don't have limits, and whatever they want, it can't be good for any of us."

"I agree," Hamada said. "This is unlike anything I have ever seen before."

The others standing around the television screen gasped. Hamada and Branning only saw the end of the collapse of the west wing of the White House. Fire crackled, smoke billowed and mushroomed into the air from the structure.

"Jesus..." Branning muttered.

On the TV coverage, the reporters were in frenzy, showing a replay of the collapse, the windows filled with a flash of light before the building collapsed in on itself.

"We have to do something," Branning said.

"What can we do?" Hamada replied. "We have no power to affect the outcome of this attack."

“I mean here.”

Hamada looked at Branning, brow furrowed. “What can we do here, Branning?”

"We can fight and take back the city."

"That’s impossible. All you Americans are crazy with your grand ideas."

"You call it crazy, but this is how we do things. Not behind people’s backs or involving civilians in our disputes, but face to face. Man to man."

"Do you not remember how close we came to death before we escaped to the sewers?" Hamada said, shaking his head. "We were fortunate to survive."

"I refuse to sit here and wait for them to find us."

"So what do you say we do? We have nothing." Hamada was clearly frustrated but was holding back from starting another argument.

Branning hesitated, and then looked Hamada in the eye. "We can fight back."

"You and I?"

"All of us."

Hamada frowned, trying to figure out if Branning was serious. "We have nothing to fight with. No weapons. No vehicles" He said cautiously, looking at the frightened faces around the two who were now more interested in his and Branning's conversation rather than events in Washington. "Besides, these people are not soldiers."

"That doesn't matter," Branning countered. "Earlier you said about getting involved in the wars of others. Just look at the news. This isn't just happening here, it's happening all over the world. Whatever this is," he pointed to the television screen for emphasis "Now involves all of us. It's everyone's war."

"These people are civilians, peasants for the most part. It would be like herding sheep to their deaths. That's no fight, Branning. That's slaughter."

"Not if we train them, show them what to do."

Hamada shook his head. "Listen to yourself. Train them? Show them? All we would show them is death and a swift and merciless one it would be. We don't have the time, and even if we did, it would be fruitless. Look at the television, Branning. You think we can battle against a force which is capable of that?"

"At least, I'm trying to do something," Branning snapped, slamming his fist on the desk. "It's better than just staying down here and waiting to starve or be captured."

"You think any of us want to die?" Hamada countered. "Like it or not, these people don't have the training. They're not like us Branning. They don't know what it means to fight and know your life could end at any moment. They don't know the taste of fear or how to overcome it. You would be condemning them to death."

"Okay, so what do you suggest? If you have a better idea I'm sure we'd all love to hear it."

"I do actually have a suggestion," Hamada said, choosing his words carefully.

"Go on."

"As I mentioned, of everyone here only the two of us are soldiers. Sure enough, we fight for a different cause, but we still fight." He paused, waiting to see if Branning would interject. When no objection came, he continued. "Outside of the city in the mountains of the Anbar province, my men wait for me. Good men. More importantly, good soldiers, fighters willing to die for their freedom."

"No," Branning said, shaking his head. "I won't work with terrorists. I won't have them here and jeopardise these people."

"Terrorists? Did you not just say how this is everybody's war now? You choose to label them as terrorists, I choose to see them as men who are fearless, trained and disciplined. They are exactly what we need."

"I won't bring them here. I won't give you the power to take control."

"Come on Branning, you talk as if it's still you against us. You think the fact that you are an American soldier makes any difference? Much the same that my allegiance now matters little. From the second we were forced to flee here to the sewers, we have been engaged in a private war of our own, perhaps stupidly. Now we must work together. If you want to fight, if you want to try and take a stand like you say, then you need my men to do it. There is no other choice."

Branning paced, heart and head screaming different instructions. He turned back towards Hamada. "Assuming I agree, how will you get word to them to come here?"

"We can't get them here, Branning. I have no means of contacting them. We will have to go to them."

"You expect me to go with you into Anbar province? Do you think I'm so stupid? I know what your people would do to me. Prisoner of war, fucking beheadings. I've seen it."

Hamada waited, calm and patient. "If you had suggested such a thing a few days ago, then yes. I would say you were correct. Things have changed Branning." He spoke next in Arabic. " عدو عدوي هو صديقي , it means -"

"The enemy of my enemy is my friend." Branning cut in.

"Your Arabic is quite good," Hamada said with

a small smile.

"You can guarantee my safety when we get there?" Branning replied. "If not for me, for these people?"

"You have my word, Branning. As unlikely as it seems, it would appear an alliance is in all of our best interests. We need each other, Branning. Neither of us may like it, but that is the situation we are facing."

"And what if I refuse?"

"You won't."

"How do you know?"

Hamada raised his eyebrows and held his arms out to his sides. "Look at the alternative? What choice do you have other than to wait here and die in the filth?"

Branning looked at the dozen or so people in the room and knew Hamada was right. There was no alternative. Against every instinct, he made his decision.

"Alright," he said with a sigh. "I'll come with you. When do you want to leave?"

"Tonight. Under cover of darkness."

"If you screw me over Hamada, if you try anything at all or do something I don't like... I won't hesitate to kill you before you get a chance to take me out."

A flicker of a smile passed over Hamada's lips. "Understood. I, in turn, give the same warning to you."

With nothing left to say, both men left the crowd standing around the TV screens to prepare themselves for the mission.

# CHAPTER TWENTY-TWO

## KOPAR KHAIRIANE
## INDIA

SUVARI AND THE CHILDREN hid in the dark, the dilapidated textile factory providing adequate hiding places from the dangers of the streets which had become places where nobody now dared venture. She peered through the grimy glass and looked out over the water to the city. It was lit by an orange glow from fires which still burned freely. She still wasn't sure what was going on, she had no reception to her phone. She was desperate to speak to Marcus, to let him know she was alright. She assumed what was going on was some kind of uprising. She had seen more groups of men seemingly attacking citizens at will as she had fled the city. Others were rounded up and loaded onto trucks headed for a fate she presumed was no better than those left dead and dying in the streets. Her stomach growled, and she glanced at the children cowering in the shadows, their eyes wide and pleading. They were her responsibility now, and it was up to her to keep them safe. None of them had eaten since they crossed the bridge and fled the city, and like an old friend, the once familiar pains of hunger raced through her. She didn't think it was something she would ever have to go through again, especially after all she'd done to make a life for herself, however, the familiarity of an empty stomach returned to her as if it had never left, and in a way was far more frightening than the current situation.

Headlights flashed over the window, and she ducked away out of sight, despite being on the second floor and invisible from her place in the shadows. The flatbed truck rolled towards the factory, kicking up dust in its wake. Suvari felt her stomach somersault as the truck came to a halt, and two men jumped off the back. They were joined by the driver. The two men from the back were armed with weapons, a baseball bat and machete respectively. The driver had a shotgun, which he carried leaning on his shoulder, barrel pointed straight up. All three men had their faces covered. The two from the back were wearing balaclavas, the driver wore a bandana over his mouth and nose and a grubby red baseball cap pulled low over his eyes. She watched as they spoke and gestured at the building, snatches of words making it impossible for her to understand what they were saying.

Please move on, please move on, please move on

She repeated it to herself, mouthing the words silently. Her request went unanswered, however as the three men entered the building.

"Quickly, hide," she whispered in the dark.

The children looked back at her, unmoving, perhaps through fear, maybe through misunderstanding.

"Go now, hurry!" she said, ushering them towards the hulking, rusted machinery which was long dead.

They moved, this time, not in response to Suvari, but the sounds of the men who they could now hear, their voices echoing through the building. Suvari made sure they were all hidden, then closed the door to the machine room. If anyone was to be found, she would make sure it was her and not the children. She moved to an office down the hall, papers and folders strewn across the floor and forgotten, the smell of damp and rot clinging to her throat as fear made her breathe in great ragged gasps. The office was furnished only with a broken desk and an empty filing cabinet, neither of which would stop her from being seen. She turned back, intending to try one of the other rooms, kicking herself for not mapping out the building layout or an escape route, when she heard them coming, heavy boots on steps, hushed chatter. She saw their elongated shadows appear and knew she was trapped. The only option she had was to go back to the machine room, and she wasn't prepared to do that. Left with no choice, she waited for them to come.

She locked eyes with the first of them as he came around the corner. It was one of the ones from the back of the truck, the one with the machete. He seemed surprised to see her. For a second, there was silence, the two locked in eye contact, which was broken when the man spoke.

"What are you doing here? Who are you with?" he barked as he strode towards her.

She couldn't move, and no words came to mind as she stood and stared. He grabbed her by the arm, his grip strong. "Who are you with? Who brought you here?"

She still couldn't answer, and could hear the others coming now, jogging up the steps to join their friend. She tried to squirm away, but the man was too strong, his eyes glaring from the holes in his balaclava. The others had joined their friend, and were surrounding her in the corridor, all barking questions at her at the same time.

Suvari flinched away, fear hot and bitter in the back of her throat. She could smell sweat and alcohol, and beneath that something else. Something coppery. Fear took over then, and she lashed out, scratching at the face of the one holding the machete and contacting only with the fuzzy mask covering his head.

He grunted, and slapped her hard across the face, making white stars dance across her field of vision. She felt them bundle her to the floor, each goading the other on as she kicked and screamed.

"Hold her down," The one she'd scratched said as he set the machete on the floor and started to unfasten his jeans. "I'm going to teach this bitch a lesson in respect."

Suvari thought of her sister, of the haunted look in her eyes which had inspired her to escape the same fate. If she had been alone, she would have fought, but she had the children to think of. They were her responsibility and she had to do right by them. Perhaps if she let them have their way. They would go away and leave her alone. She relaxed her body and stopped struggling.

"Alright, that's better," the one with the gun said. "I want to go second."

"You went second on the last one," Baseball bat said. "It's my turn."

"Alright, whatever. Just get on with it."

Machete pulled his pants down and clambered on top of her, snatching at her jeans. She remained calm, trying to drift away in her mind to a distant place, somewhere away from what was about to happen to her. She thought of the beach, of white sands and cool oceans.

He climbed on top of her and pushed inside

She thought of cool drinks and beautiful foods, perhaps a beach barbecue with her friends and family back in the civilised world.

He was thrusting now, face buried against her neck, hot, foul smelling breath on her skin as he violated her.

She drifted deeper, trying to recall the comforts of her life which seemed so distant, so far away. The comfort of her own bed. Cable TV. Itunes. Fast food. Simple things to anyone else, but proof to her that she had escaped the slums and made something of herself.

His motion was increasing now. Eyes bulging as he thrust against her, increasing in speed as his friends cheered him on.

Fortunately, it didn't take long, and he exploded within her, grabbing a handful of her hair as his body tensed. Tears rolled down her face and into her ears as he stood and pulled up his trousers, making way for the next of his friends, the one with the baseball bat this time. Once again she drifted off to somewhere far away as baseball bat followed his friends lead, only he was much larger and more rough, and she screamed as he raped her, which only seemed to heighten his excitement.

When he was done, he joined his friend, who handed him a cigarette. The two smoked as the last of them took his place, he with the gun and red baseball cap. He clambered onto her, and now no amount of thinking herself away could save her from the horror of what was happening. She might have lay there and let them do as they wanted, knowing when they were done there was a good chance they would kill her.

"Hey, there are kids in here." One of them said, standing at the door to the machine room.

Terror and anger came in quick succession, as did the instinct to protect. She looked up at the leering eyes of her baseball cap clad would be rapist, and something in her snapped.

She reached out and grabbed the discarded machete from the floor beside her, and in one motion, driven by the mixture of emotion surging through her she swung it at her attacker, the blade embedding in his neck.

Blood.

It cascaded, spewing out onto Suvari as her assailant gargled and dropped the gun as he clutched at the blade still hanging from his neck. His friends were too late to realise something was wrong, Baseball Bat only registering Suvari rolling onto her side and firing the weapon a split second before the top half of his head exploded in a shower of blood and bone, his body bouncing off the door frame to the machine room and sliding into a sitting position.

Mr. Machete, realising his weapon was now embedded in his dying friend's neck, held up his hands. She could hear him pleading, yet couldn't make out any words under his balaclava, which suited her fine. She was still angry, furious in fact at what he'd done to her, for potentially putting the children in harm's way. The blood on her was hot, the smell of smoke from the gun strong, the ringing in her ears from its recoil in the confined space making her head throb with dull monotony. Machete took a half step forward, and it was all she needed to justify her actions. She fired. The shot wasn't as accurate as the first, although it still hit her target. She was so close it would have been almost impossible to miss. He took the full force of the round in the stomach, slamming into the machine room door, which buckled open under the impact.

Machete lay half in, half out of the room, trembling and trying to hold his guts inside his body.

Suvari, on the other hand, was surprisingly calm.

She got to her feet, and walked towards her

moaning assailant, sparing a glance at his friends. Red Cap was on his side, eyes open and unblinking, blood pooling around him from the machete wound in his neck. Baseball Bat was a bloody mess, his head a mangled mass of pulpy flesh and bone. Their raping days were over, and now, only one remained. She stood at the door to the machine room at Machete's twitching feet, he was moaning, and she could see a slick coil of entrails which he wasn't quite managing to hold in. He was begging for mercy, and yet the throbbing in her groin told her he deserved none. In fact, she felt nothing at all, only a cold indifference towards him. Without any semblance of remorse, she levelled the gun at him waited, making sure he looked at her, ensuring he knew what was coming. She waited until his eyes grew wide in recognition. She pulled the trigger.

The hammer fell on an empty chamber. Frustrated, she opened the gun, flicking the catch and folding the barrel over.

Empty.

Machete was begging now, begging for mercy,

begging for help, begging for his mother. Suvari ignored all pleas. Instead, she went back to Red Cap and searched his clothes, checking his pockets for extra shells for the gun he'd been carrying before his demise. She couldn't find any, and frustrated she tossed the weapon aside. There was a moment of silence apart, of course from the repeated moans of Machete, who was still trying to hold his innards in the hole in his stomach. She knew he was already dead, and that it was just a matter of time, and yet it didn't quell her rage. Her eyes drifted to the blood spattered baseball bat which had rolled against the wall. Without consciously controlling her actions, she grabbed it and stood, returning to the machine room entrance.

He only grunted once as the first blow came down. She didn't stop until she could no longer lift her arms and the tears had dried up along with her screams of rage. When it was done, Machete's face was unrecognisable, a miss-shaped bloody pulp. She tossed the bat aside, the wood echoing against the concrete floor as it rolled into the shadows.

Suvari looked around, and saw the children looking at her, eyes wide and frightened.

Frightened of her.

She could only imagine how she must look, covered in blood after just murdering three men, three fellow human beings. She told herself they deserved it, yet it didn't make things any easier. Her stomach rolled, and she thought it was a good thing she hadn't eaten anything for so long, or she might have vomited.

"Come on," she said, surprised how steady and even her voice was. "We have to go."

The children followed without question, and she wondered if it was because they still wanted her as their protector or because they were afraid of what she would do if they didn't.

"Don't look, keep your eyes on me," She said, and then paused. "Wait here for a second."

She went back into the corridor and back to Red Cap. She went through his pockets again, this time finding what she was looking for, then returned to the children.

"Ok, come on. Remember, don't look at anything but me."

She led them down the hall, past those she had killed. Despite her orders, she knew the children had looked. She heard them gasp, some started to cry, which cut her deep and caused her more pain than the physical assault she had just endured. She briefly asked herself what might come of it, about what vile diseases these men carried who had raped her. She pushed it aside, telling herself there was nothing she could do about it now either way. She led them downstairs, through the building and to the flatbed truck. She helped the children inside who obeyed wordlessly, the expression on their faces betraying their silence.

They were afraid of her.

Suvari climbed into the cab, and closed the door, seeing herself in the mirror for the first time since the attack. Her face was a mask of blood, but she was still the same Suvari, or at least, for the most part. There was something different in her eyes, she could see that much for herself, and yet couldn't put a finger on what it was. Using the keys she had taken from Red Cap's pocket, she started the van. She had no idea where she was going, and in a way, it didn't matter. All that mattered was the children and keeping them safe. Putting the truck into gear, she pulled away into the night as the city continued to burn at her back.

# CHAPTER TWENTY THREE

## IRAQ FOOTHILLS
## AFGHANISTAN

IT WAS ALREADY HOT. Branning had watched as the sky turned from black to purple then orange and finally blue as the sun crept over the horizon line. Drenched in sweat, he walked alongside Hamada, tense and sharp, ready for anything. Despite their agreement to work together in order to recruit Hamada's men, there was nothing even remotely close to trust. One thing which did amaze Branning was that up in the craggy landscape of rocks, you could almost forget the world was in chaos. It was already well over thirty-eight degrees, and the punishing heat of the day was showing no sign of abating.

"How far?" Branning asked, snatching for breath. He had removed his t- shirt and tied it around his head to keep the sweat from running into his eyes. The pale green material now a few shades darker.

"Not long," Hamada said. "My men should be close."

Branning said nothing. He had long grown used to the icy instinct inside him which told him everything about the current situation was wrong, and yet he wasn't able to do anything to stop it. People were relying on them. Even so, hiding his disdain for Hamada was hard.

"So this is where your kind hide, up here in the rocks."

"We don't hide, Branning. We choose to make camp here because it offers us security. Your people have taken over our cities."

"We came here to liberate this country from people like you." Branning hissed.

"People like us? Citizens of Iraq who are forced to flee like animals because of your countries propaganda."

"Don't give me that shit," Branning said as they

descended down a scrub of rock into a narrow valley. "Nine-eleven wasn't any propaganda. It was real. People watched it on TV all over the world."

"So you think every man of Middle Eastern blood must be punished?"

"We're here to protect, not to punish."

"Come on, Branning. Surely you have seen by now our people don't want you here. Of course, there are a few, but the majority just want you Americans and British to leave us alone."

"People want our help. If you people stopped pushing your agenda, things would be different."

"Our agenda?" Hamada snorted. "Look to your own leaders before you talk about agendas."

Branning was getting angry and had to remind himself how isolated he was and how far away from any help. He squinted up at the sun, and then to Hamada, feeling a pang of envy at how little the heat seemed to be affecting him. They walked without speaking, climbing ever higher and deeper into the hills.

"So," Branning said between breaths. "What do

you think is happening here, with these attacks?"

Hamada didn't answer, at first, waiting until the ground levelled out.

"When I was a boy," he said eventually, "My father told me a story, a legend passed down from my people about when Alexander the Great first came to our lands. Alexander had already conquered most of Arabia, Iraq and Iran, and had set his sights on entering Eastern Persian territory. At the time, it was known as Bactria. Today you know it as Afghanistan."

Branning glanced at the grizzled Middle Eastern man, his face framed against the pale blue sky.

"Alexander spent less than a year conquering most of the known world, yet found himself unable to conquer Bactria for more than ten years. Do you know why?"

"No," Branning said, genuinely interested in Hamada's story.

"Alexander struggled because the people of Bactria did not give up easily. They were warriors, they were proud, they did not like invaders and would do everything in their power to get rid of Alexander and his army. I'm sure this sounds familiar to you, Branning." Hamada said, glancing at the American.

"Alexander was a great warrior, and was used to winning, and so he also refused to give in. He became obsessed with conquering Bactria, so much so that it consumed him completely. Alexander was said to send a gift to his mother, Olympias, from each land he conquered. Olympias sent a letter to ask why his gift from Bactria had not arrived when gifts from other conquered lands had arrived promptly.

Alexander read her letter and then grabbed a bag and filled it with the dirt from the ground of Afghanistan. He sent it back to her with a letter which told Olympias the bag contained the reason for his delay, and that she should scatter the dirt in her chambers and see what happens so that she might better understand his plight. Curious as to the strange reply, Olympias scattered the dirt around her room and waited to see what would happen."

"Go on."

"You're curious, aren't you, Branning?" Hamada said with a thin smile.

“Actually, I am. It’s interesting.”

“Very well, then I shall tell the rest."

Hamada composed his thoughts and continued.

"Later, Olympias had two of her guards come to check on her. Before they entered, one of the guards stood aside to allow his companion to go in first. The second guard returned the offer, insisting the first guard crossed the threshold first. This went on, Branning, back and forth, each growing more and more angered that their offer to allow the other to go first was repeatedly denied. The guards drew swords as Olympias looked on, and they fought until both were lying on the floor dead. Olympias, of course, had seen this unfold, and immediately knew what had happened. She responded to Alexander’s letter, telling him to take his time as she now understood the reason for his delay.

Alexander was said to write back to his mother

to tell her that the dirt of this land is very hostile, even to its own inhabitants, how could it be expected to be kind to invaders. It proved to be true, from that day until this."

Branning glanced at Hamada and then turned his attention back to the trail ahead.

"Do you understand why I tell you this, Branning?"

"Yeah, I think I do. You're telling me your people are willing to fight for what they believe in."

"In part, yes. The main point, in this case, isn't so much about the American occupation, but more about the current situation. We are a small country, Branning, and because of that, we are underestimated. However make no mistake, we will fight for our freedom, and do whatever it takes to defeat this new enemy, as impossible as it seems."

"That's something we agree on at least," Branning said.

"Soon, we will be with my men. Perhaps yet you might change your opinion of my people."

"Maybe. That all depends on what happens

from here on in, doesn't it?"

Hamada gave no response, and the two men walked in silence, deeper into the hostile Afghan terrain.

II

Branning could no longer deny his exhaustion. The intensity of the heat barraging the craggy, inhospitable landscape had become almost too much to bear. He thought he had done a good job of acclimatising to the harsh conditions during the time he had served, however, this was different. This was wilderness survival without the luxury of transport vehicles and fresh water waiting for him at the end of a patrol. They were a million miles away from civilization, so much so that Branning had to remind himself why they were even out there in the first place. As much as it pained him to admit it, he had been forced to respect Hamada's resourcefulness in helping them to survive. It seemed both of their respective cultures had every different methods of living off the land. Hamada found water where there should be none, digging in certain areas in the sandy earth, until the fine ground darkened and moisture was found. He also knew which native plants were good to eat, leaving Branning with little option but to put a little trust in his travelling partner, despite his personal thoughts. Now, at the end of their third day of walking, the sun had finally started to retreat, and hung like a giant, golden eye just above the horizon line, throwing their shadows into long, skinny shapes ahead of them.

Hamada found a cave, a hollow in the rocks large enough to give them a place to shelter and rest. The two had gone through their usual routine, finding wood for a small fire and sharing out the meagre amount of food they had brought with them. They sat now on opposite sides of the flames, soldiers from two different walks of life united together by the most unusual of circumstances. Branning was toying with a branch, dipping the end into the flames and letting it catch, before removing it and watching the orange glow fade away. As was his routine, Hamada had been to pray, which in turn made Branning envious that he couldn't find enough faith in his own god after everything that had happened to want to try and speak to him. They hadn't spoken since Hamada returned, content to enjoy the silence and rest for a while. The sky went from orange to purple, and Branning's twig was slowly burned down to an ember before Hamada spoke.

"You look tired, Branning."

"I'm fine," the American said, locking eyes with Hamada. "I just didn't realise it would take so long to find your men."

"We will find them soon, then we will have the soldiers to fight this war."

"I was actually just thinking about that."

"In what way?"

Branning thought about keeping it to himself, then realised he had nothing to lose by sharing his thoughts with Hamada.

"I was thinking about the people back at the

sewer, the women and the children. They're not ready for what has to be done."

"No, I told you this before we left. Is that not why we are out here in the wilderness?"

"I know that, but my point is, even when we go back, it doesn't change anything. Those people will still be at risk. They still won't be prepared."

"Many of them will die," Hamada said.

"What?"

"Those people, the refugees and children, the frightened women and men. Many of them will die before this conflict is over."

"How can you be so damn cold?" Branning snapped.

"There you go again Branning, thinking the best of everything. All I do is speak the truth. It is not my problem if you do not accept it."

"You say it like you have no faith in them."

"I don't," Hamada said.

"What do you mean by that?"

"I mean, Branning, there are some people made for fighting, and some who are not. Those people we left behind are not. People like you and I are."

"Careful, Hamada, you'll have me believing you don't hate me."

"I don't hate you, Branning. In fact, I don't believe we are very different apart from our respective beliefs."

"You're a terrorist. I'm a soldier." Branning snapped.

"Ah, but reverse the roles and I would say the same. I am a soldier and see you as the terrorist. Point of view makes all the difference."

"Look, that's beside the point. You're saying those people back in the sewers have no chance to survive, is that right?"

"Oh, I'm sure some of them will survive, for a while at least. Some will run and hide, but more will die. This is inevitable."

"Then why are we even bothering to fight at all?"

"Because we are warriors, Branning," Hamada said, the shadows dancing across his face as he smiled. "We know what is required to take a life.

We know how it feels to smell blood and smoke, to know our lives could be extinguished at any given second, and yet we keep fighting. Why?"

"Sorry?" Branning said, not expecting the question.

"Why do we fight? For our country? For our belief? Or because it's in our blood?"

"Are you trying to say it's instinctive? You train to be a soldier, you're not born that way."

"Ah, you see, that's where we disagree. I believe there are certain people who are more suited to a certain way of life. Great poets are born, not created. Great artists have an instinctive gift for transferring their vision to canvas. I believe warriors are the same. People like you and I, Branning, are born with the instinctive will to live the life we have chosen. This is why I say we are more alike than you may think. This is also why I say that, as unfortunate as it is, many lives will be lost before this battle is done."

Branning said nothing, taking a moment to think about Hamada's words. "It's not certain we will even survive this. Whatever is happening, it's global. Who knows how bad it is out there now."

Hamada shifted position, his face hidden in shadow thrown by the light of the fire. "Do you fear death, Branning?"

He thought about it, making sure to give the right answer. "No. I don't suppose I do."

"Exactly. You can't tell me that comes from training? From instruction?"

"Maybe you have a point," Branning muttered.

"See, Branning, you see me only in one way. You look at me, and you see a terrorist. You see a man with an agenda to destroy. However, I am far from this picture painted by the newspapers. I have a wife and family. Like those people in the sewers who we fight for, they are not warriors. When I talk about those who would die, I speak of my own family too. They will not last if this situation continues, which is why I would do anything to stop it. I fight not for myself, for I do not care about my own well-being, but for them. I fight so they can live in peace. If I am to die in the process, then so be it."

"You're no martyr. Nobody will remember you, Hamada. People like us, we will just be another statistic in a war that will kill millions. I think you have too high of an opinion of your worth."

"Perhaps you misunderstand," Hamada said, grinning across the flames. "Anonymity is fine with me as long as it leads to victory. As long as my children and my wife can live as free people, then I will have died a good death."

"In that case," Branning said, tossing Hamada a bottle of water. "I think we are in agreement."

Hamada grinned, and despite himself, Branning found himself smiling too. Hamada stood and stretched. "Get some sleep, Branning. Long day ahead tomorrow. We are close to my people, we should reach them by sundown."

"Best news I've heard all day," Branning said with a sigh as he untied his boots and pulled them off.

"Don't forget to put those above the floor," Hamada said as he unrolled a blanket from his backpack. "Scorpions climb inside and will sting you when you put your feet in tomorrow."

"Thanks," Branning said, setting the boots on a rock before following Hamada's lead and settling down to sleep. For a while, he looked up at the sky, the brilliant and breathtaking blanket of stars making him realise just how insignificant he and everyone else on the planet was. Gradually, he felt his eyes grow heavy as sleep took him to a dreamless darkness.

III

Rough hands yanked him from his dreamless slumber. Snatches of Arabic filtered into his groggy brain as he was dragged roughly to his feet. He squirmed and tried to free himself as a hood was placed over his head and his arm bent up behind his back. He was being dragged, his bootless feet scraping through the dirt. More snatches of Arabic filtered through the heavy, itchy hood, yet there were so many in unison that he couldn't make any sense of it from the little he knew of the language. Any hope of assessing which direction he was moving in was fruitless. He continued to squirm, and this time, the Arabic was easier to understand.

Stop.

Don't struggle.

You won't be harmed.

Branning paid no attention. He knew well enough the consequences for lone American soldiers who were captured out here in the foothills. He could see it coming, him sitting bloody and beaten, tied to a chair as an extremist delivered a sermon to the camera, perhaps warning those who would invade to think twice. Perhaps they would try to get him to denounce the US occupation himself, maybe by promising him freedom which he knew would never come because he knew enough about situations like this to know how it would go. There would be a machete or a sword, and it would be shown to the camera, perhaps shimmering slightly under the low lighting. Those who were taking him would savour the moment, savour the fear which no training would be able to hide. Branning thought the worst part would be the waiting, the anticipation of feeling that cold steel against his neck just seconds before he was beheaded for the world to see.

He squirmed more, desperate to free himself. The Arabic shouts were becoming more desperate and heated just seconds before something struck Branning hard in the head, rendering him unconscious. He didn't feel it as he was bundled into the back of a truck, nor did he see Hamada stroll to the passenger side and climb in as the rest of his men climbed into the other two vehicles and set out deeper into the Iraqi wilderness.

# CHAPTER TWENTY-FOUR

## CHURCH OF HOLY RIGHTEOUSNESS
## DALLAS, TEXAS

MILES FISHER HAD BEEN expecting the apocalypse and was one of the few who were both prepared and unsurprised as the world started to fall apart. The fifty-six-year-old had endured a strict upbringing by his parents in preparation for such an event, who, despite owning only a modest home in San Antonio, had run the Church of Holy Righteousness for three generations. Set in its own five-acre plot of land, the converted ranch house was the base of operations for the church, which had grown from a congregation of a half dozen people back when his great grandfather had first started to preach, to its current number somewhere around the three hundred thousand mark worldwide. Now a multi-million dollar business built on the donations of its supporters, the white ranch had been expanded to include a custom-built glass and steel hall of worship. Every day, Miles would hold his sermons in front of the six hundred strong crowds who wanted to hear his wise words (and could afford the seventy-five dollar entry fee) and perhaps have him harness the power of the Lord to rid them of their sins, before of course being invited to leave a donation. With a congregation which included judges, political figures and even a couple of celebrity country music stars, the donations ranged from very generous to eye wateringly large.

Miles had taken the seeds planted by his grandfather and father and grown them into a juggernaut of a business, a machine which pulled in revenue on everything from merchandise, self-help videos, website subscriptions and of course the ever popular sermons, which were broadcast on local television networks (on a pay per view basis) for those who couldn't get tickets to attend live. Some of Miles' family, particularly his brother, Earl, thought he had lost sight of the point of the church, and that it had become more about money than the message. As a millionaire three times over, Miles could see his brother's point, even if he didn't agree with it. His faith was everything to him, and the money only helped him to spread the word of God. Certainly, his followers believed in him, some to the point of obsession. He certainly cut an imposing figure as he stood at the front of the cavernous hall, his booming voice amplified through the room as he gesticulated and delivered his words with passion. At six feet five inches tall and eyes of piercing blue which stood out brilliantly against his chocolate coloured skin, even for those who entered as non-believers found themselves enthralled by his magnetism and charisma.

He looked out of the window of his bedroom over the fields surrounding the property, some lined with golden corn, others filled with livestock - cows and pigs who were bred and used to sustain the staff of twenty who lived and worked on the ranch. He smiled. For as much as the rest of the world was in chaos, they were in a good position. They were self-sufficient, growing and replenishing their own food. They had a well on the land which gave them access to fresh water, and most importantly, they were secure, the ranch surrounded by a ten-foot barbed wire lined wall.

Miles dressed, putting on his best charcoal suit. After all, even the end of the world was no excuse to be lax about your appearance. He went downstairs to the dining room, the rest of his staff already seated along with his brother. Miles sat in his usual place at the head of the table as one of the girls who worked for him, Nina, poured him a glass of water.

"Good morning," he said as he grabbed a slice of toast and started to butter it. The others looked on, fearful yet respectful, apart from Earl. Earl wore a look of contempt.

"Ain't nothin' good about anythin," Earl said as he took a sip of his coffee. "I hope after sleeping on what you told us last night you're here to give us some good news."

"If you mean about evacuating, I'm afraid not."

"Come on Miles, it's dangerous to stay. You've seen the news, what do we have to gain from staying?"

"Everything," Miles snapped as he took a bite of his toast. He looked around the table, yet nobody but his brother would look him in the eye. "Running away is a bad idea. We have everything we need here."

"We need protection. The authorities can help us."

"No, they can't." Miles said, locking eyes with his older sibling. "Do you think they will have time to help us with the kind of things happening at the White House?"

"People are scared, me included Miles. We're vulnerable here."

"That's where I disagree. In fact, I think this is exactly where we should be. We have food, water, walls to protect us. Fleeing would be foolish."

"None of that will mean anything if those people decide they want what we have. We'll die."

"No, we won't. The lord has spoken to me, and he told me we would be safe." Miles said, offering a reassuring smile to those seated at the table.

"This isn't one of your sermons. I'm your brother. Give me a little more respect."

Miles said nothing, preferring to let his anger cool before he replied. As furious as he was, he smiled. "This is why father put me in charge of the church and not you, Earl. You question your faith too easily."

"And you believe too much in yours."

Miles looked around the table, again somehow managing to hold his temper. "Would you all excuse my brother and I?"

There was no delay. Eager to be as far away from the coming argument they could all sense, the staff filed out of the room, leaving Earl and Miles alone.

Earl poured himself a coffee, the similarities between the two brothers striking. "Poppa wouldn't have wanted this Miles. This isn't why he set the church up. It was supposed to be about worship, not money."

"How can I take you seriously when you say that with a twenty thousand dollar watch on your wrist?" Miles sneered.

"It's just us now, you can drop the act," Earl said as he sipped his coffee, winced at the heat, then set it back on the table. "Regarding the watch, you can have it back if you want. You bought it for me after all, just like you bought all these poor people who work here."

"They are well looked after, you are too. I don't know what else you want from me, I'm doing my best."

"They're scared of you. Hell, they're scared of what's happenin' out there in the world too, they're just too scared to say it to you."

"You don't seem to have a problem expressing yourself," Miles grunted as he poured himself a coffee.

"Come on, you're my brother. You know I love you. You just sometimes need someone to point you in the right direction. Let's get out of here. Find somewhere safe until this whole thing blows over."

"And where would you suggest? I can't think of a safer place than this. We have a natural defence here, a place where we can survive in relative comfort away from the chaos on the streets."

"Only for as long as those people decide they don’t want in, then we're in trouble," Earl said, flashing a smile that was eerily similar to his brothers. "You’ve seen the news. You know what’s happenin’ out there."

"Father believed in me, I wonder why you can’t. I know what I’m doing."

"I do believe in you, Miles. I just don’t think you appreciate how serious this situation is. In truth, I’m worried by how little fear you have."

"I know how serious it is," he snapped, slamming a fist on the table. "This is the beginning of the end. This is what the Bible spoke of. This is when we need our faith the most."

Earl sighed and sipped his drink, suddenly unable to look his brother in the eye.

"What is it?" Miles asked.

"Nothin'."

"Come on Earl, we both know well enough something’s bothering you. Spit it out."

"It's just... I'm not convinced this stuff that's happening in the world has anythin' to do with the Bible. I think it's something else entirely, somethin' that can put us and the people who work here in danger."

"It sounds like you're losing your belief."

"No, it's not that."

"It is, isn't it?" Miles said, leaning closer to his brother, the anger like a physical thing growing inside him. Need I remind you of the word of the good book?"

"No, I-"

"Revelations fourteen-fourteen," Miles said, interrupting his brother. "Then I looked, and behold, a white cloud, and seated on the cloud one like a son of man, with a golden crown on his head, and a sharp sickle in his hand. And another angel came out of the temple, calling with a loud voice to him who sat on the cloud, 'Put in your sickle, and reap, for the hour to reap has come, for the harvest of the earth is fully ripe.' So he who sat on the cloud swung his sickle across the earth, and the earth was reaped. Then another angel came out of the temple in heaven, and he too had a sharp sickle. And another angel came out from the altar, the angel who has authority over the fire, and he called with a loud voice to the one who had the sharp sickle, 'Put in your sickle and gather the clusters from the vine of the earth, for its grapes are ripe.'

"Miles, please-"

"Also, see Isiah, Thirteen-Nine. Behold, the day of the Lord comes, cruel, with wrath and fierce anger, to make the land a desolation and to destroy its sinners from it."

Miles grinned, as he leaned closer, palms flat on the table, fingers splayed wide. "Are you telling me, brother, that this doesn't correlate to our current situation? Are you telling me this Joshua is, just as the Bible said, the one like a son of man, the one seated in his temple who is about to reap the evil from this world?"

Earl stammered, unsure how to respond, because, for as much as he knew it was insane, the way his brother said it with such conviction made it seem plausible.

"Heed the words of Zechariah, Fourteen-One. Do you remember the passage, my brother?"

Earl tried to recall, unable to find the passage within the vault of his brain. Miles saw his confusion, and widened his grin, reciting the passage word for word, showcasing his knowledge to his sibling.

"Behold, a day is coming for the Lord, when the spoil taken from you will be divided in your midst. For I will gather all the nations against Jerusalem to battle, and the city shall be taken and the houses plundered and the women raped. Half of the city shall go out into exile, but the rest of the people shall not be cut off from the city. Then the Lord will go out and fight against those nations as when he fights on a day of battle. On that day, his feet shall stand on the Mount of Olives that lies before Jerusalem on the east, and the Mount of Olives shall be split in two from east to west by a very wide valley so that one-half of the Mount shall move northward, and the other half southward."

Miles sat back in his chair, his grin fixed firmly in place. "This is happening now, my brother. The end is coming, and after, there will be a new world. A world where the good and the righteous will stand by his side as masters of the new earth. There will be many who will be afraid and will come to us seeking shelter that we need to educate, those who we need to show the right way so they might join us."

Finally, the grin melted from his face. "I can't do it alone. I need you, Earl. I need you at my side now more than ever. This is what our father was preparing for, and his father before him. "And what if these people who are burning the world show no mercy even to us? What will we do then?" Earl said quietly, suddenly fearful of his brother.

"You have to have faith that they will. The Lord will save us."

Earl wanted to tell his brother he was crazy, and that faith or no faith, the tidal wave which was sweeping over the world couldn't be contained or stopped, yet couldn't find the words. He knew well enough how stubborn Miles could be, and Earl's protests were only likely to make him dig his heels in even further. He thought this was one of those occasions where he should let his brother win, if only so that he might later reason with him later if things went astray.

"Alright," Earl said. "If father had faith on you to lead this church, then I shall follow you."

Miles grinned and leaned back in his seat. "I knew you would come around to my way of thinking. Do not be afraid, brother. We are standing on the cusp of the new world. We should be thankful the lord has chosen our lifetime for the transition to take place. We are witnessing the dawning of a new world."

"Even so, the staff are worried, scared even. They are afraid to come to you, Miles. You intimidate them."

"I love them like my own family," Miles replied. "They can come to me with anything."

"Regardless, I fear they will take some convincing to stay on the property."

"That's where we disagree," Miles said, flashing his perfectly white teeth at his brother.

"And why would that be?"

"Because when they learn of the chaos which is taking place outside of those walls, they will beg me to let them stay under my protection."

"Some of them are already talking of leaving," Earl grunted.

"Who?" Miles snapped.

"It doesn't matter. Just know that there is talk. If you want to convince them to stay my brother, then you will have to be at your best."

Miles didn't reply. Instead, he placed his elbows on the table and put his palms together. At first, Earl thought his brother was about to pray, and then saw he was simply in thought.

Miles leaned forward and rested his chin on his thumbs as he looked out of the window at the dusty, sun-baked yard. "Call a staff meeting," he said eventually.

"Do you want me to just call them back in?"

"No, not here," Miles replied with a wry smile.

"Do it in the sermon hall."

"Is that wise?" Earl said, wondering what his brother had in mind. "They won't appreciate being preached to."

"That's not why I'm calling the meeting."

"Then why?"

"Because the world has changed, and because of that we need to change too. We need to adapt."

"I don't think I understand," Earl said, not liking the look in his brother's eyes.

"I mean this place. Our message."

"I think our message is good, so did our father and our grandfather." Earl snapped.

"Relax, Earl. This isn't me trying to slur the fantastic work of our family, it's just that as things stand, the message we send as the Church of Holy Righteousness is in some ways redundant. Outdated, especially as we stand on the cusp of such a change."

"What did you have in mind?" Earl asked, unsure if he wanted to know the answer.

"It's obvious the end is coming. We need to

change our policies to reflect that."

"Miles, please. This isn't about balance sheets or running a business. The world is in tatters."

"Haven't you listened to anything I've said?" Miles snapped. For a split second, Earl saw his father. The resemblance was eerie and brought back memories of the strict childhood they endured which at times bordered on cruel.

"Of course, I've been listening," he said with a sigh, "I'm just struggling to make sense of it all."

"And I'm going to explain. It came to me last night as I slept. A revelation, if you will."

He waited for his brother to say something, yet Earl only stared at his sibling and waited.

"I'm changing the direction of the church," Miles said. Earl went to speak, but Miles held up a hand and went on. "Just let me finish before you say anything."

Earl swallowed his words, folded his arms and leaned back in his chair, doing as he was asked. Miles went on.

"It's clear to me that these people have chosen

to take a stand against the corporations of the world. Because he has dared to challenge the established order. Many don't see them as a force of good."

Nor do I Earl wanted to say, yet didn't speak. He knew there was no point in interrupting his brother once he was on a roll. He tuned back into the words spilling from Miles's lips and was increasingly concerned for his state of mind.

"I'm dropping the old name of the church." Miles said around his elastic grin.

"No, you can't do that. You don't have the right." Earl snapped.

"I have every right!" Miles snapped, slamming his palm on the table hard enough to make the cutlery rattle. "The church was entrusted to me. I was given the power to do whatever I feel is best going forward."

"Not this. This is spitting in the face of the work our father did."

"No, it isn't. This is adapting, moving with the times. Do you remember how our church was before I took control? It was festering in the dark ages. Look at it now, it's a thriving congregation."

"Maybe it was better before. Now everything seems to revolve around making money," Earl grunted. "It seems as long as people keep donating and the DVD sales stay strong, the message doesn't matter."

"You don't believe that, not after everything we've been through."

"Will you listen to yourself, Miles?" The world is starting to crumble around us and your first thought isn't to get somewhere safe, but to try and profit from it. What is it, extra subscription? Apocalypse sermons charged at double the normal rate? I don't know if you realise, but the world is dying. Nobody is coming to church, nobody is going to line your pockets. That gravy train is over. All people care about now is survival. You need to see what's happening beyond the walls of this church and wise up fast before it's too late."

"You'll see in time that I was right."

"No, I won't," Earl said. "This is it for me. I'm leaving. I won't stay here and watch this happen."

"You have to stay," Miles said.

"No, I don't. As you keep reminding me, the church was entrusted to you, not me. It's your responsibility."

"If you leave, you will be struck down. The lord is watching us Earl. Through me, he's delivering his message."

Earl shook his head. "No, this is all you. You're not thinking straight. I don't know if its denial or fear, but it ain't normal."

Miles leaned close, and Earl felt the subtle shift from anger to fear. "If you decide you're not with me, then it means you're against me. Against the lord. Against everything, we have been brought up to believe. If I can't trust you to be part of this, then I'll do whatever it takes to make sure you can't stop us."

"And what does that mean?"

"I think you can figure it out," Miles whispered. "You know me, Earl. You know I'll do whatever it takes to win. That's why I was chosen to carry the message of our church."

"And that's the whole point. This ain't our father's message or the message of our church. You're sittin' there talkin' about spreading the word of some group of people who for all we know could just be common terrorists."

"Give me a chance," Miles said. "At least, let me try to show you. If you still feel so strongly about it a few weeks, then I'll go back to the old teachings."

"We might not even have a few weeks, Miles. Not with the way this thing is shaping up, having said that, you haven't done wrong by us yet, so I'll give you the time to convince me."

"That's all I ask."

"Meantime, you need to talk to the staff before they walk out of here and leave the two of us to run this place on our own."

"I will, just as soon as you call that meeting like I asked."

Earl nodded and stood, scraping the chair against the wood floor. "Alright, we'll do it your way. Just don't say I didn't warn you."

Miles nodded and watched as Earl left the room. He turned his attention back to the window, looking beyond the grumpy tan coloured cow which had wandered to the fence of its pen, and to the sky beyond, which was a brilliant and tranquil blue. Miles wondered if yet more chaos had been heaped upon the shoulders of the nations of the world. He certainly hoped so. Fear would win him the day, and fear would be the tool which ushered in a new era. Smiling and incredibly pleased with himself, he poured himself another cup of coffee and began to gather his thoughts ahead of the staff meeting.

# CHAPTER TWENTY-FIVE

THE WHITE HOUSE

WASHINGTON D.C

PYCROFT LED THE PRESIDENT towards the roof. Even though he was trained to ignore everything but the job at hand, even he was horrified by the brutality he had witnessed. He had seen friends - men and women who he knew well, people with families and children who he knew by name lying dead in the halls as those who assaulted the White House mercilessly cut through their defences. Holding the building now was a lost cause, meaning the only option was to flee. So far he had engaged and killed five of the attackers, all of them displaying the same traits of being almost impervious to bullets apart from headshots which seemed to keep them down. Running low on ammunition, Pycroft was desperate to get the President to safety.

"This way sir, keep low," Pycroft said as he cut towards the exit to the roof and the waiting chopper. Another explosion rocked the building, and for a second, Pycroft was certain the entire structure was about to collapse around them. Without thinking, Pycroft tackled the President to the ground and covered him. Dust and smoke lingered in the air, making breathing difficult.

"What the hell was that?" the president grunted from the ground as the rumbling and shaking subsided.

"Could be artillery, possibly explosive charges, who the hell knows that these people have brought with them. Either way, we need to get you out of here sir." Pycroft yelled as he once again helped the President back to his feet.

He paused by the door leading to the roof, checking his weapon was loaded whilst trying to ignore how few bullets he had left, Pycroft took a deep breath and opened the door.

He expected to see the pale white flat roof and the waiting helicopter. Instead, there was nothing.

The entire wing of the white house had collapsed, smoke and fire billowing from the wreckage.

"My god, what have these people done," Fitzgerald muttered.

Pycroft couldn't formulate an answer, and could only think about the loss of life to yet more of his colleagues and friends.

"We need to find another way out sir," Pycroft said, his cool exterior at last betraying him.

"Why would they do this?" Fitzgerald muttered.

"Same reason they locked us out of the bunker. They knew this was the secondary escape plan."

"Where the hell do we go from here, Pycroft?"

For the second time in quick succession, the Secret Service agent had no answer. He would never give up, nor would he tell the President their chances of escape had narrowed significantly. He brought up a mental image of the layout of the White House as he tried to figure out an escape route, yet every one meant putting the President in significant danger. Just when he had given up all hope, his earpiece crackled to life. Through the static, Pycroft heard something which meant they might just have a chance.

"This way sir," he said, leading the President back the way they had come, past the zing of gunfire as it echoed through the building. Pycroft led them through the President's private living quarters and out onto the terrace. The south lawn below was filled with police, fire trucks and soldiers who were working to try and take on the men who had stormed the building. From their vantage point, the devastation was plain to see. Smoke billowed from the collapsed section of the building and muffled explosions could be heard amid the gunfire and screams.

"What are we doing here, it's not safe," the president screamed. Pycroft pushed him to his knees.

"Stay out of sight." Pycroft barked, pushing Fitzgerald to the ground.

He waited, knowing that if any of the men who had stormed the building made it out onto the terrace which ringed the upper floor, there would be no way to defend themselves or escape.

"What the hell are we waiting for, Pycroft?" The president snapped.

He was bloodied and dirty, his suit torn. Somehow it had shattered the illusion of him as a world leader. He was now just a frightened old man.

"Pycroft! We can’t stay here. What the hell are we waiting for?"

Pycroft pointed across the lawn. "That."

The helicopter was coming in low and fast, its nose dipped towards the ground, tail in the air. Painted jet black, Pycroft knew they would only have one chance to board.

"Come on," Pycroft said, dragging Fitzgerald by the arm towards the pickup point which had been relayed to him in his earpiece.

They arrived at the flat section of the roof, skirting around the array of solar panels which covered its surface. The helicopter came in low, hovering at the edge of the roof. The side door slid open, and black-clad men - This time, U.S Special Forces - filtered out, hopping onto the roof. Five of them in all, each clad in protective body armour and armed with automatic weapons. As per protocol, they ignored Pycroft, and instead surrounded the president, ushering him towards the hovering helicopter. Pycroft went to follow, and as he started to walk forward a bullet sliced through the air in front of him, the sound reaching him a split second later. His training took over. He dropped to his knees. Rolled, getting cover behind one of the solar panels. The men who surrounded the president didn't stop to help Pycroft. Their mission was to ensure the president's safety. They bundled him into the helicopter as Joshua's men opened fire from across the terrace. Pycroft returned fire, conscious that he would soon be out of ammo. Joshua's men took cover, and the split second was all he needed. Tossing his weapon on the ground, he turned and sprinted for the chopper, which was already starting to bank away from the edge of the building. Without thinking of the consequences if he missed, Pycroft leapt from the edge of the roof, pushing off with everything he had and aiming for the open door on the side of the helicopter. For a sickening split second, he didn't think he would make it, his forward motion slowing as gravity took over. It was then that his knees hit the edge of the door and he fell unceremoniously into the helicopter. Black gloved hands yanked him inside as the door was slammed shut. The chopper banked up and away from the building, taking its precious cargo away from the chaos. Below them, the building which was once the symbol of America's power had been decimated by Joshua and his men.

II

Riddled with bullets and debris and with air heavy with acrid smoke, the Oval Office sat abandoned. The gunfire was becoming more sporadic as Joshua's men finished off the lingering resistance. Joshua strode into the office, broken glass crunching underfoot. He took in the scene, savouring the smell of fire and death. He walked to the president's desk, running his fingertips lightly over the polished mahogany surface, leaving a trail in the dust which had settled on it from the numerous explosions. He walked around it and lowered himself into the plush chair. It felt good, it felt...right.

He closed his eyes, marvelling at the relative ease of their operation. In the end, it had been as they had expected. Overconfidence had cost the Americans their base of operations. Even though it was just bricks and mortar, the symbolic nature of their act would ensure the world would listen to them. The world was already reeling from their attack; it was time to deliver the final blow.

Genaro walked into the office. "You sent for me?" The scientist said, trying to hide his awe and fear.

"Yes. How close are we to taking full control of the site?

"It's done. The building is secure."

"Good."

"Unfortunately, the president managed to escape. I fear it will only be a matter of time before armed forces retake the building."

Genaro was afraid of how Joshua might react to the news, which made the fact that he smiled somehow more disturbing.

"They won't attack."

"With the president safe, I'm afraid you might be wrong. They won't take this lightly."

"They will scramble around and wait for someone to make that decision. By then it will be too late."

"But the president-"

"-The president doesn't matter," Joshua cut in. "He's just a man, a symbol of the old world which is dying as we speak. When the world hears what I have to say, everything will change."

"Forgive my uncertainty, Joshua, I just don't see how we can maintain our control of this situation."

Joshua smiled and sat back in the chair, enjoying the comfort. "The list I gave you, the list of names. Is it done?"

"Yes."

"They have taken control?"

"Yes, just as you requested."

"Get me access to the controls for the nuclear weapons. I trust they have hacked into the systems without detection?"

"Of course. The people on the list were the absolute best in their field. The government firewalls were no match for their skills once we turned them."

"Good. Make sure they know what to do.

"I'll set them to work Joshua, they will do as you command."

Fantastic work, Dr. Genaro."

"We are still in danger, Joshua. We don't have the men or the firepower to repel an attack. We don't have the time to fortify if a counter attack comes soon."

Joshua smiled again, a gesture which was as creepy as it was confident. "You should have more faith in me, Dr. Genaro. Once I speak to the world, we will have all the time we need."

"How do you intend to do that? How will you

reach them?"

"Technology, Dr. Genaro. I'll use the world's love of technology to my advantage."

III

The chopper sliced through the air racing towards Joint Base Andrews in Maryland. The president had now recovered from the initial shock and was watching through the window as they streaked closer to their destination.

"Mr. President," Pycroft said shouting above the constant thrum of the rotor blades. "We should reach Andrews in the next ten minutes. Air Force One is fuelled up and ready to go."

The president looked the bloodied and bruised Secret Service agent in the eye. "I never got a chance to thank you, Agent Pycroft. You saved my life."

"Just doing my job sir. The rest of the cabinet are already on board and waiting for your arrival."

"What about the White House?"

"Lost sir. The people who attacked now have control."

"Did anyone make it out alive?"

"Initial reports are unclear sir," Pycroft said. "It doesn’t look like there were many survivors."

The president nodded, his brow furrowed. "They really caught us off guard. Sons of bitches have some balls to do this."

"Sir, the public will want assurances about your safety. After seeing the attack on the White House, they'll be fearing the worst."

"As soon as we get in the air I’ll clean myself up and address the nation. Any word from Vice President Carter?"

"He's at the Pentagon sir. He's working on intel. There is so much out there that it’s hard to separate the truth from the speculation."

"I want to speak to him. As soon as we board Air Force One."

"Yes, sir."

The chopper descended as they neared the

waiting aircraft, giving the president an unobstructed view of the streets, where the public were starting to loot and riot through desperation and fear.

II

Air Force One was a customised Boeing 200Bs. From the outside, the white-bodied aircraft with the blue nose and stripe down its side looked to be just like any other of its kind; however its insides were unlike any other aircraft in the world. It was comprised of three floors of offices, medical facilities, and operations rooms, making it akin to a mobile White House. With armour plating strong enough to withstand a ground-based nuclear explosion and electromagnetic shielding across its entire length, it was deemed to be the safest aircraft on the planet. The chopper touched down on the runway beside the idling plane, its crew waiting for the president to board.

Pycroft took his place at the president side as

the sliding helicopter door was opened. President Fitzgerald climbed out, walking across the tarmac with Pycroft at his side. Armed guards waiting by the entrance stairway saluted as the president and Pycroft ascended into the craft.

"Mr. President, sir," said a bloody Chief of Staff Morrison as the door was closed behind them.

"Eamon, good to see you. I'm glad you got out."

"It was luck more than anything. I was on the south lawn when they attacked. I was lucky."

"Any idea what we're dealing with?" the president said as he walked through the plane towards the media room, which boasted an array of computers, telephones and televisions.

"It's a coordinated attack, the bastards drew us in by conducting isolated attacks all over the world just big enough to draw us into sending troops out to help. Because of that, our people are stretched all across the globe and communications are going down at an alarming rate."

"Have you spoken to the vice president?"

"Yes sir, he's at the Pentagon waiting to speak with you."

Fitzgerald paused and stared at the array of television screens, unable to believe how quickly things had gotten out of hand. Almost all of them were showing footage of the White House, which was surrounded by dozens of police and fire trucks.

"Any word from inside?"

"Not yet sir," Morrison said. "Communication networks have all gone to hell. People everywhere are trying to contact friends and families to make sure they're safe. It's causing havoc."

"It's smart," Fitzgerald said. "Without knowing it, the public are helping them to disrupt our operations."

"That's not all sir. We're worried this situation might trigger other terrorist groups into action against us."

Fitzgerald nodded, wondering if they would ever catch a lucky break. "Ground all non-military flights. The last thing we need is another 9/11 on our hands. What about our people who are engaging these bastards?"

"We're losing sir."

"Then send more men."

"It's not that sir, the biters are infecting people at a rate of more than a hundred an hour overall."

"Then kill them damn it!" Fitzgerald spat as he took a seat.

"Sir..." Morrison hesitated, unsure how to proceed. "We have received reports, unconfirmed at the moment but reports all the same which may change things for the worst."

"Spit it out Eamon. This is no time to be holding back."

"Intelligence intercepted three snippets of communications, one from the London, one from Paris, and another in Hamburg. They were all saying a variation of the same thing."

"What were they saying?"

"They were saying the dead were coming back to life, sir."

Fitzgerald nodded, his brow furrowed.

"You don't seem surprised sir," Morrison said.

"Right now I'll believe anything. Try to get confirmation on that. As soon as we're in the air I want to speak to Paul and see if we can get ourselves out of this mess."

"Yes, sir. Shall I give the go-ahead for take-off?"

"Do it."

III

Five minutes later, Air Force One was in the air, climbing with its sixty strong crew of staff and passengers away from the city to cruise at thirty-six thousand feet. The president relocated to his private offices which were located on the top level of the aircraft just behind the cockpit. Morrison was with him as the video call came through from the Pentagon.

"Mr. President," Paul said.

"Glad to see you're okay Paul. I hope you have some good news for me."

"I wish I did. The fact is this is a much worse

situation than we feared. Rather than a series of random attacks by soldiers who went rogue, we believe this is a deliberate and coordinated global attack."

"That's impossible. There isn't an army in the world big enough."

"Sir, this group have already increased their numbers by more than six hundred percent in just a few weeks. We project at their current rate of expansion and infection, they will outnumber our forces three to one within the month."

"Jesus, we need to do something," Fitzgerald said.

"I'm afraid we may have missed our best chance at containing this by not sending out armoured support when we had the chance."

Fitzgerald didn't react to the obvious remark about his earlier lack of action; instead, he cleared his throat and went on. "What about projected death tolls?"

"Globally we are already looking at almost three thousand. That figure is growing by the minute sir. Plus there are those unconfirmed reports about the dead-"

"I know, I'm trying to get some kind of confirmation on that. What about-"

The plane shook, distorting the video link between Fitzgerald and Carter.

"What's happening, sir?"

Fitzgerald didn't answer. The hairs on the back of his arms were standing to attention in the way they had back at the White House.

"Sir?" Carter repeated.

"I'll call you back, Paul." The president said, terminating the call. He walked across his office and looked down the stairwell to the second level. Pycroft poked his head around the corner. "Sir, stay there."

"What's happening?"

"We've been breached." Fitzgerald half descended the steps. The rest of his security team were checking weapons, faces taut as the first sporadic crackle of gunfire rolled down the plane.

"It's one of them isn't it? From the White

House," Fitzgerald said.

"I think so sir. Looks like he stowed away."

"Jesus," Fitzgerald muttered, sitting on the steps.

"Stay upstairs sir, we'll deal with it."

At the rear of the plane, The Apex soldier who had been personally selected by Joshua for this most important of missions had ascended from the level three cargo hold where he had been hiding and opened fire on the security team who were at the rear of the plane, catching them off guard. Knowing Air Force One was fitted with reinforced bulletproof windows, the man rechristened by Joshua as Jacob had no fear of depressurizing the cabin before he could complete his mission. His aim was true, and he sliced through the security team before they could react. Pausing to reload his M16 Assault rifle, he made his way towards the next section of the plane and the panicked screams of those inside.

Pycroft and the presidents six-strong security team moved through the plane. Through the galley kitchen towards the board room. Access was granted only by a narrow corridor, which would give them the best chance of defending the president against the coming attack. Four of the security team moved down the corridor and took up positions at the entrance to the workroom. Pycroft and two other agents hung back.

Pycroft took a deep breath, the seconds stretching into what felt like hours. He was suddenly aware of everything going on around him. The whine of the engines, the light sweat forming on his neck and the crackle of gunfire from further down the plane. It would be a cruel irony now if after escaping the White House they were to fall at this last hurdle. He was broken from his train of thought by the door to the workroom opening. The president's staff, unarmed and frightened, shoved into the room, desperate to flee the gunfire and were cut down, their bodies riddled with bullets as they tried to escape. The president's security team at the end of the hall inched closer, returning fire, although, from his current angle, Pycroft couldn't see their attacker. Fire was returned, peppering the reinforced interior of the plane, the sound absolutely deafening in the claustrophobic confines. Pycroft looked at the man to his right, a bald headed African American who looked absolutely terrified.

"Relax," Pycroft said, trying to force a smile. “We can handle this"

"This is my first week on the job," the man whispered, flinching as more gunfire was exchanged.

Pycroft nodded. “What’s your name?"

"Hamilton. Roy Hamilton."

"Okay Roy, just remember, you trained for this. You knew what the job entailed when you took it."

"I know, I know, I just didn’t think it would be so soon,"

Pycroft ducked as one of the president’s security team were cut down by a trail of bullets, claret spraying from his wounds as he fell.

The remaining members of the security team started to fall back, inching towards the corridor and

Pycroft's position.

"Stay here," Pycroft yelled above the gunfire. "I'm going to go to the president."

Roy nodded and adjusted his position. He wore the look of a man who didn't believe he would survive. Pycroft wondered if he looked the same way.

Without the time to dwell on it, Pycroft turned and sprinted for the stairwell to the president's office. Fitzgerald paced, hair dishevelled, clothes torn and filthy from the White House attack. He looked like a man who was ageing by the second.

"Come on sir," Pycroft said. "I'm moving you."

"Where?"

"Presidential suite. Come on, we need to go now."

Pycroft led Fitzgerald back down the steps and further away from the gunfire.

The presidential suite was located in the nose of the plane. Under normal circumstances, it served as the president's personal living space during flights. It was complete with a living area, bed and private bathroom facilities. It would now serve as the last line of defence against their attackers. Pycroft ushered Fitzgerald into the room, closing the door behind them.

"Help me with this," Pycroft said, moving to the heavy framed double bed.

Together, they moved it, sliding it across the front of the door as a makeshift barricade. It was laughably inadequate, but it was the best they could do.

With nothing else to do but wait, the two men sat on the floor, listening to the chatter of gunfire. Pycroft double checked his weapon was loaded, then stood, pacing the room.

"Do you have any kids' Agent Pycroft?" the president said, then corrected himself. "Hell, I don't even know your first name."

"It's Dale sir. And yes, I have two daughters."

"They would be proud of you, of the things you've done for this country."

"I'm not so sure sir."

"Why's that?"

Pycroft looked at his feet, then back at the president. "Well, I haven't always been a good father. I try my best now, but I feel like I missed so much. I'm the wrong side of forty now, and have already burned too many bridges."

"You're a good man. Whatever happens here today, I want you to know I appreciate it." The president said.

"Well sir, I guarantee I'll do everything I can to keep you safe. We've come too far to give up now."

The president nodded, neither of them mentioning just how bleak the situation was. Dale walked to the door, leaning his ear against it.

There was no noise from the other side of the door. No screams. No gunfire.

"What's happening out there?" the president asked.

"Nothing. It's quiet."

"Do you think they got him?"

"I don't know..." Pycroft whispered. His stomach was tight, and his instincts were screaming at him that something was wrong.

"I think I should-" Pycroft's words were cut off by the plane shaking, dropping out of the sky for a second before climbing erratically. Pycroft was thrown to the ground, his weapon skidding across the ground.

"What's going on?" The president said, eyes bulging.

It was then Pycroft understood what the situation was, and the sick feeling in his stomach told him all hope was lost.

"They never wanted you, sir. You were never the target."

"Then what do they want?"

"They wanted the plane. They wanted control of the plane."

Almost directly above them, with the cockpit breached and the pilot and co-pilot dead, the man christened Jacob took control of the aircraft. With absolute calm, he increased the crafts speed to maximum and pointed the nose towards the ground almost forty thousand feet below, throwing the president and Pycroft against the interior curve of the nose and rendering them helpless.

At the same time, Jacob took control of Air Force One, the man who sent him, Joshua, released a video on social media. It spread quickly, racking up thousands upon thousands of views which rapidly became millions. News agencies played the clip on a repeated loop as the White House attacker relayed a message to the world direct from the bullet ravaged Oval Office. The five-minute video was simple in its composition. Joshua framed in the centre of the shot and seated at the president's desk, hands folded, long hair swept back, piercing gaze staring down the camera. The words were smooth and confident as he relayed his message to the world and ensured things were about to change forever.

"My name is Joshua, and I represent my brothers and sisters who will unite to usher in a new world. For too long you have been deceived, lied to by corrupt governments and greedy, self-serving politicians. It is these people, people including your own president who have lied to you, who have told you there is nothing to fear, who have told you everything will be alright."

He smiled into the camera, a cocky, self-assured expression.

"I'm here to tell you that isn't the case. There is everything to fear. And nothing will be alright. Humanity as a species has spent too long ravaging and overpopulating this planet. We lie, and cheat, and burn our way through our limited resources with the idea it's alright because somebody else will pick up the pieces because it will be someone else's problem. Because of this blinkered world view, Nature and science have combined to find a way to rectify the failure of the humanity experiment. I represent the next step in human evolution. My brothers and I represent a future of humankind without the flaws many of you have. My brothers and I represent the dawning of the new world. Death. Disease. Hunger. Fear. These things will soon become a product of a bygone age. In a single fell swoop, we have taken over control of your infrastructure. Leaders of the world will learn they have neither access nor control of their nuclear arsenal, nor their communication satellites. We control everything. Any attempt to attack us, any move to interfere will be met with swift and violent retribution."

He paused again, allowing his words to sink in.

"Now sadly, because you have been force fed a diet of lies and false promises, I am forced to pre-empt any move to attack us and display the full breadth of our strength. In the next few minutes, a series of nuclear warheads will be launched at randomly selected targets through the world. These cannot be stopped, nor are they about terrorism or pushing a political agenda. It is meant as a warning, a show of our ultimate strength. Like Noah's flood, it's time to wipe the slate clean. This time, we are the flood waters, we are the force of nature which will consume the earth and leave behind only the good. This is the future, this is unavoidable. This is how it must be. Today is the beginning of the new world. Today is the start of the era of Joshua."

At precisely the same time Joshua's video

address finished, two things happened.

Firstly, Air Force One, piloted by Jacob, ploughed into the ground at almost six hundred miles per hour, decimating a huge section of the city of Washington as it disintegrated on impact, instantly killing the President of the United States.

At the same time, nuclear weapons launched remotely at Joshua's command from the US, Britain and Russia impacted sites in Tokyo, Berlin and Paris, killing millions of people. In the Oval Office, Joshua walked to the window, watching as those who were gathered on the lawn abandoned their posts, fleeing to families in the hope of surviving. Joshua smiled. The devastation of what had already happened was just the start, a small taste of what was to come. He looked at the lawn as the dead bodies riddled with bullets or maimed by explosions started to rise, dragging themselves to their feet as the Apex virus replaced the function of the dead brain with its own unique form of life, its will to survive at all costs and spread its seed making them valuable weapons, the bitten who would die and be reborn in order to further spread their virus. It was a complete circle of life.

Genaro walked into the office, standing beside Joshua.

"It's done. We control all communications."

"Good."

They watched as the dead shambled aimlessly in search of hosts to infect.

"Our gift really is special. I didn't think you could pull it off, but I stand corrected."

Joshua smiled as he watched the reborn dead go out into the world. He felt like a proud father watching the first tentative steps of a child.

"This is just the start. They think they know fear only because they haven't yet seen what is to come."

"Everything is in place."

"Good. Begin phase two. This is the birth of the new world we always wanted."

"They can't stop us now, can they?"

Joshua turned to the older man and smiled. "Nothing can stop us. Nothing at all."

www.ingramcontent.com/pod-product-compliance
Lightning Source LLC
La Vergne TN
LVHW011926070526
838202LV00054B/4510
* 9 7 8 5 1 9 8 9 4 2 0 3 5 *